I0822357

THE GINHOUSE HOLLOW

THE GINHOUSE HOLLOW

a novel inspired by a true story

KOREN FREEL

ISBN 979-8-9886938-0-2 (ebook)
ISBN 979-8-9886938-1-9 (paperback)
ISBN 979-8-9886938-2-6 (hardcover)

Publisher's Cataloging-in-Publication data

Names: Freel, Koren, author.
Title: The ginhouse hollow / Koren Freel.
Description: Camas, WA: Koren Freel, 2023.
Identifiers: LCCN: 2023914047 | ISBN: 979-8-9886938-2-6 (hardcover) | 979-8-9886938-1-9 (paperback) | 979-8-9886938-0-2 (ebook)
Subjects: LCSH Family--Fiction. | Secrets--Fiction. | Murder--Juvenile fiction. | Mental illness--Fiction. | Disability--Fiction. | Historical fiction. | Mystery fiction. | BISAC FICTION / Women | FICTION / Historical / Mystery & Detective | FICTION / Family Saga | FICTION / Psychological
Classification: LCC PS3606 .R44 G56 2023 | DDC 813.6--dc23

Printed in the United States of America
First published in 2023 by Koren Freel
KorenFreel.com

Cover and interior design by Danna Mathias Steele
Editing by Alison Imbriaco

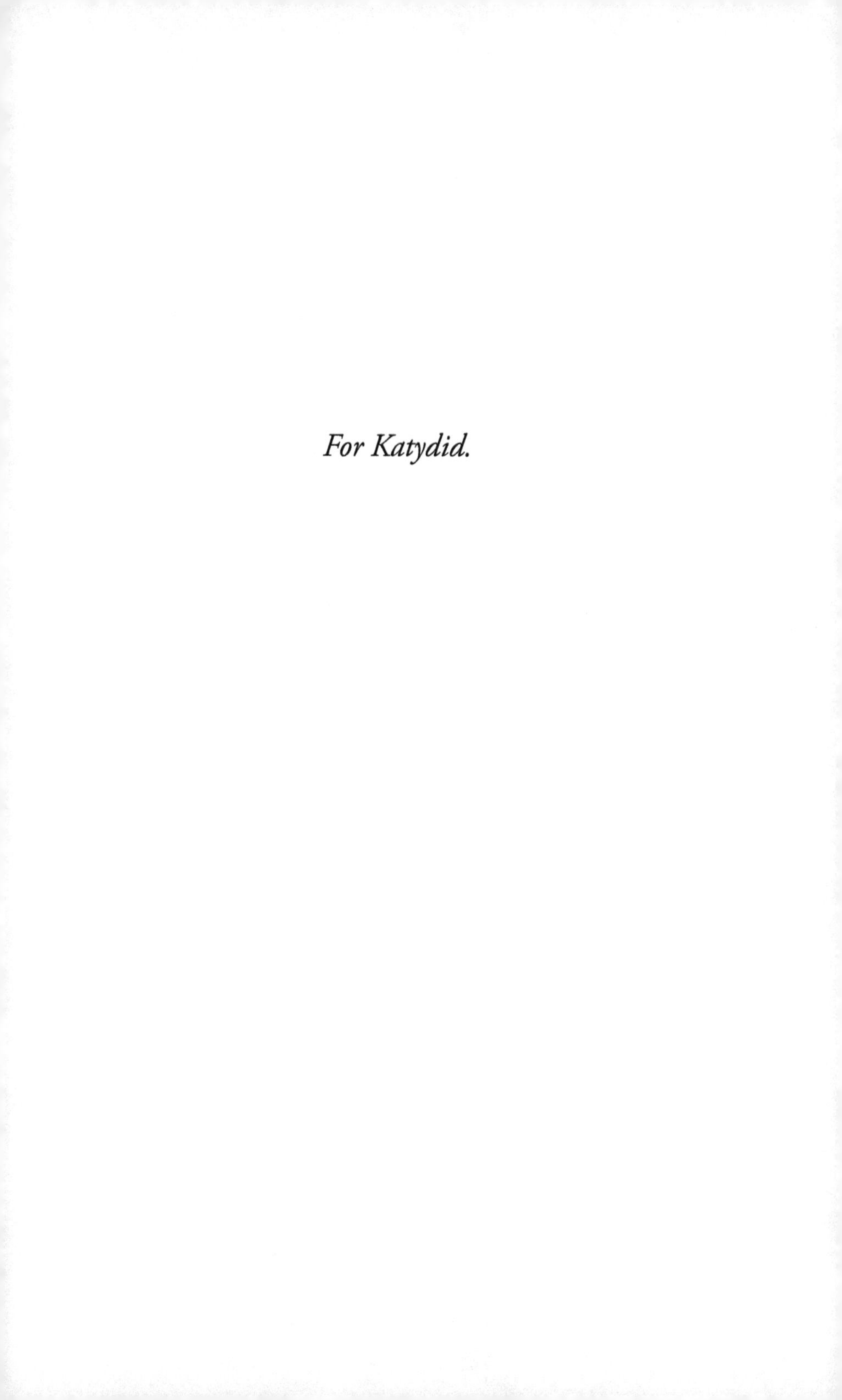

For Katydid.

A Promise Made

RYNN, 1989
TEXAS

MY MOTHER IS A NATURAL-BORN storyteller. She can spin an adventure so outlandish you'll wonder if any of it's true, then turn around and weave a woeful tale with a life lesson. Her best stories, like this one, do both while revealing the beauty of Riverton, Alabama. A haven blessed by the southern hospitality of the Bible Belt, and a place where proximity to a mountain hollow defines where you live. By day Dark Hollow's leaves shaded my mother's woodland playground, and by night they held the orchestra of clicking katydids surrounding her childhood home in song. And inside that home lived the family she cherished. Whose love and nurture shaped the compassionate person my mother became. The person whose stories painted the illusion of an idyllic upbringing, where nothing tragic occurred on the back porch steps.

She hid her secrets well.

I uncovered one on a Friday evening in 1989. Kickoff was fast approaching, and the only thing standing between me and an explosion of school spirit was freshman English. Specifically, the family history report I'd barely started and didn't have the luxury of finishing over the weekend. My parents instituted a "homework-first" rule when they realized I'd become more interested in extracurriculars than my grade-point average. The enforcement was stifling but warranted. Otherwise, Monday would roll around and another red zero would loom next to my name.

English was my second favorite subject behind Art. My pen was as mighty as my paintbrush, cranking out creative essays in mere minutes. But I found my latest assignment daunting as it leaned more heavily on research. Still, the instructions were simple:

Part 1: Draw your family tree going back four generations.

Part 2: Choose one relative, no longer living, and write a one-page report about their life.

Part 3: Present your report during class.

I had precisely two hours to finish my assignment before my best friend's mom would pull into my driveway, horn honking. If I wasn't outside within thirty seconds, she'd back out and leave. More than once she'd kept driving as I chased after her car, her eyes fierce in her rearview mirror. She wouldn't care if it was the biggest game of the season. Or that my ulterior motive for wanting to witness every single second of it had more to do with ogling number twenty-two than with a district title. So I skipped my after-school ritual of diet Coke and Cheetos in front of the TV and got to work the second I arrived home.

The family tree was up to me to draw. It had to, of course, be in the shape of a tree and have spaces along branches for family names and their birth and death dates. I had sketched mine in class earlier that day as my teacher played a continuation of *Romeo and Juliet*—an escape tactic she used when she'd had enough of her students' lip by Friday.

My muse was the majestic magnolia embellishing my front yard. Its branches tickled my bedroom window like the slow creep of a spider across the nape of a neck. If I sat still inside, the songbirds and squirrels, hopping from limb to limb, didn't mind me watching them. And the knothole near the top, too high to stick my curious hand into. I was sure something called it home.

I did my best to do my magnolia justice, curling the veining on the leaves ever so slightly, and drawing the glorious white blooms that fill its canopy each warm season with pressure as delicate as their milky petals. I even added a hovering hummingbird near the place my father's name would sit. His favorite to admire.

With my masterpiece nearly complete, all that was missing was names. My ignorance of them was jarring. Some came easily. Others only partially. And one name didn't come to me at all. The second hand on my Swatch ticked in unison as I jiggled a pencil between my fingers, staining the space reserved for my maternal grandfather with a cloud of gray freckles. Had it not been for this assignment, how long would it have taken me to realize his presence was missing? Not only from my family tree but from my entire life.

He died before I was born. That was all the information my mother had offered. And until that moment, I'd never wondered *why* that was all she'd told me. Naturally, I locked in on him as the subject of my report. Because not only did I have a knack for procrastination, but making a simple task overly complicated during a time crunch was my superpower.

We'd visited my mother's hometown of Riverton three summers before. My grandmother, Grace, still lived in my mother's childhood home. But I couldn't recall a single instance of anyone mentioning my grandfather. No toast to honor him or trip down memory lane with photo albums spread out across the living room floor. No old war stories or "remember that time when" laughter over something inane he'd done.

Hidden in plain sight was a single wedding portrait at the secluded end of my grandmother's hallway. Past a row of faces, I knew only the current versions of. He stood tall behind my seated grandmother with his hand resting on her shoulder. My resemblance to him was haunting. My steely blue eyes stared back at me as if wondering who *I* was.

It was the only proof he'd ever existed, that he'd walked down that hallway in his pajamas. Bounced the infant who would become my mother on his knee as he read his morning paper. Or sat at the kitchen table after a long workday, eating the supper my grandmother spent the bulk of her afternoon cooking.

With each tap of my pencil, my curiosity grew. Why had my mother omitted him from her stories? What could he possibly have done to warrant complete silence? Faster, I tapped, begging for answers that would never come to me, no matter how hard I drummed that pencil. And in one agitated blow, I snapped the dulled tip clean off its yellow spire.

I could have chosen any of my dead relatives as the subject of my report. I might have written a lovely homage to my aunt Faith, describing how she was a loving mother of four. Or an eerie piece about an uncle on my father's side who owned a duck hunting lodge and the hundreds of stuffed fowl that adorned every surface of that musty place. No. I had to pick someone I knew absolutely nothing about. Someone I wouldn't know shared my same curly locks if it weren't for that hallway portrait. But I just couldn't shake the mystery of it all, luring me to reveal the ghost of my grandfather.

I flicked the pencil from my hand, spinning it across my drawing with the vigor of a helicopter blade, then sprang from my chair and flew down the hallway toward my parents' bedroom. Having little to go on, I wasn't sure what to look for. But I knew the one place that may hold clues.

I tossed up one corner of the perfectly spread comforter and crouched next to the trove hidden under my parents' bed. Reaching past the stacks of patterns my mother had yet to sew, I slid her well-traveled powder-blue train case to the side, shifted a few wrapped presents she likely forgot were there, and saw what I was searching for, stranded dead center.

I lay on my side, extending my arm toward it. With the cold metal bed frame cutting into my collarbone, I squeezed the last inch out of my stretch. My middle finger brushed it, nudging it farther away. *Ugh, seriously?*

I glanced around for a long object I could use to scoot it closer. The walking cane my mother used when her arthritis flared. Or the old Louisville Slugger my father relied upon for home protection. Both were always leaning against the corner near the doorway—except when I needed one. There was absolutely nothing among the items that made up their midcentury modern decor that could reach my target.

I held my breath as I shimmied the top half of my lanky frame through the field of dust bunnies, grabbed hold of the tattered hatbox, then inchwormed my way back out. I hadn't seen the box in quite some time. Judging by its position under her bed, it wasn't something my mother looked at often. I traced my finger through the dust coating the monogrammed *S* for her name, Sloane, and hoped she wouldn't notice my intrusion.

A waft of nostalgia enveloped me as I unlatched the lid and propped it open. Lifting the stacks inside to take inventory, I discovered a rhinestone hair barrette at the bottom. I pulled it out to get a better look, never having seen her wear it. Its brilliance shimmered in the beams of the setting sun pouring in through the bedroom window.

I pulled my cuff over the heel of my hand and wiped the haze from the hatbox's tiny lid mirror, then clipped the barrette into my teased spirals. It glittered with each tilt of my head, and I wondered who'd gifted it to her. What sentiment did it hold for my mother?

As the sun warmed my auburn highlights, I held up an old photo of my mother from college to compare our features. Had her hair not turned bottle blond, we could have been the same image reflecting in that mirror, with those same steely blue eyes I saw watching over the secluded end of my grandmother's hallway.

"Rynn?" my father called out from down the hall.

I froze midmovement, as if encased in plaster, and held my breath to keep it from escaping through my parents' open bedroom door. My stomach sank, much the same as it did each time he caught me sneaking in after curfew. How was I going to explain the mess scattered in front of me if he walked in?

Blood drained from my lifted arm, still holding the photo of my mother next to my flushed face. With each passing second, gravity tugged at its feathery weight with the force of a thousand elephants. My hereditary comparison from moments before had quickly gone south. My mother's face now stared back at me in disapproving judgment, as if somehow knowing I was touching her precious moments.

There was no noise from the hallway. I imagined my father standing outside the doorway, deciding how best to punish me for invading my mother's privacy. At the very least, I'd lose any chance to cheer for my unwitting paramour as he ran past me with a football.

My ears rang as hypnotizing stars danced through my vision. Just as I was about to pass out, the hall bathroom toilet flushed, and footsteps retreated down the hallway. My arm dropped to the floor as I gasped for air, and the cold rush of blood flooded into my sleepy hand. *Jesus, that was close. I should get out of here before I get caught.*

Or…

I replaced the hair barrette where I'd found it, then untied a blue ribbon from a stack of letters. The return name and address on the top envelope belonged to my uncle Osee in Alabama. I unfolded the stationery tucked inside and read his letter, but it divulged nothing noteworthy. Just a status update, of sorts, and a photo of his house.

The remaining envelopes revealed more of the same. Letters between my mother and her sister, Faith. None of which included references to my grandfather. Then there were the letters between my parents. I hadn't realized they'd spent time apart, and those felt too private to read. I may have been snoopy, but I wasn't a heathen. Plus, what teenager willingly subjects themselves to the mushy sides of their parents? Not this one.

Rounding out the rest of my mother's hatbox memories were a few more photos, but none were of her as a child; a stack of baseball cards with a rubber band looped twice around it; a single fake gold coin, twice the size of a silver dollar; animal figurines that had the same molding style and plastic stands of green army men; and an incomplete sheet of S&H Green Stamps stuck precariously to the back of a saver book. The wavy, spit-dried pages crinkled as I pulled them apart. It looked as if she'd given up halfway to her next reward. Too bad. We could have had the matching water pitcher to go with the olive-green prism tumblers we still drank from.

One peculiar thing in the box stood out, however. Postcards with no stamps, all addressed to my great-uncle, Bishop. His relationship had always confused me, and it took a second to recall that he was my grandmother Grace's brother and the only uncle my mother, Sloane, and her siblings, Faith and Osee, had. I remembered that none of them addressed him as Uncle. Everyone just called him Bishop. And he lived with my grandmother in the same house where my mother grew up. Money was tight, and he was…different. Enough that trusting him to live on his own didn't seem possible. So their atypical living arrangement made sense.

The postcards were mainly from vacation destinations on the Gulf and East Coast, but their notes read more like phone messages than travel breadcrumbs.

"Weatherman says a cold snap is coming. Best cover your tomatoes, Bishop!"

"Tell Grace congratulations! Her peach pie was the clear winner."

I reckoned Bishop knew who the unsigned sender was. But why did my mother have them?

After nearly an hour of sifting through grainy photographs and handwritten letters that captured a moment in time, I was no closer to the answers I sought. The realization that the roots of my family tree were an enigma was not what I'd expected to find when I opened that box. Sure, I recognized a few faces in the photos. But I had no notion who they truly were. I'd met them only a handful of times, when paying attention was my most underdeveloped trait. And of all the memories my mother saved in her old hatbox, not one of them helped fill the space hovering above her tree branch on my family tree. The one reserved for my grandfather, now mired with the graphite scars of my tapping pencil.

Defeated, I hurried to tidy the mess I'd made of my mother's memorabilia while conjuring an alias to take my grandfather's place. Perhaps he could pass as an airline pilot who died in a plane crash. Or a police sergeant who died the day after he retired. Anything plausible to finish my report and set out for an evening of teen spirit. As I slid my mother's memory box back under the bed, it caught the corner of another. A box I had never seen.

I dove back under the bed and came out with a Bankers Box labeled "UA." It stank of a damp root cellar and had a sallow patina only decades of life can produce. I carefully lifted the top, fearing torque may crumble it to bits, then thumbed through the folders inside and randomly selected one. A page of handwritten notes dated December 15, 1956, slid from the folder and floated into my lap.

> Summary of ECT: His nurse recorded he experienced no pain during the sessions. He was given sedation before beginning, and he had no recollection of the treatment. His medications were adjusted (increased) after session 15. By session 22, his memory loss and

> hallucinations had worsened. Doctors disagreed over his progress and continuation of treatment, which ended after session 27, when he fell into a coma after an experimental increase in electrical dose.

The note was concerning but intriguing just the same. And the rush from finding something likely not meant for my eyes was impossible to ignore. I riffled through more pages, desperate for something conclusive to fall out. It was obvious I was reading snippets of medical records, but it wasn't obvious to whom they belonged. The only page with a possible name had fallen victim to what looked like spilled coffee. The letterhead at the top, however, was telling: "Alabama State Psychiatric Hospital, Tuscaloosa."

I reviewed what I knew:

One. The medical notes were about a male patient who fell into a coma.

Two. This occurred at a hospital in Tuscaloosa, Alabama, in 1956.

Three. Per an old Rand McNally map I found in the UA box, Riverton, the town in Alabama where my mother grew up, wasn't unreasonably far from Tuscaloosa.

And four. No one talked about my grandfather, who died before I was born in 1974.

Although I'd at first relegated my grandfather's death to natural causes, I began wondering if he'd been dealt a more sinister destiny. What if these hidden records were about him?

What if the reason no one talked about him was that he was a lunatic? A criminally insane lunatic, who was the subject of experimentation at a state mental institution. He wouldn't have been the first. Mental institutions had a long history of dancing around ethical boundaries, according to my social studies teacher. And if he fell abruptly into a coma, as the note suggested, did that imply whatever happened was an accident? And what the hell was ECT?

An hour ago, all I cared about was pining over a high school football player who didn't know I existed. Now, I was hot on the trail of my grandfather's demise, with my love of television mysteries and cheesy horror films guiding my investigation. But this plot wasn't cozy enough for *Murder, She Wrote*. I sensed it was more graphic. Improbable, perhaps.

Just as I was picturing *Young Frankenstein's* monster coming to life with a zap of lightning, the phone on the bedside table, right next to my ear, rang as loud as my scream.

I wrapped my hand around the cradled receiver and prepared myself for the wardrobe crisis happening on the other end of the line. Every Friday, without fail, my best friend called from atop a pile of clothes, near tears, begging me to be honest about which outfit she should wear. I'd already decided I'd pick option one because that's what she'd end up wearing anyway. And I had no time to waste discussing which shade of acid-washed jeans made her butt look perky.

I picked up midring.

"Hello! How would you like to own—"

"Stop calling this number!"

The spiel of time-share sales was unmistakable. The same man had called every night that week, undeterred by my idle threats and choice words. With zero remorse, I slammed down the receiver, releasing unmitigated fury across every cilium of that telemarketer's eardrum.

I unclenched my teeth, took a deep breath, then let it out slowly as I counted backward from five—a technique I'd read about in *Seventeen* magazine for controlling teen angst, which I had no shortage of.

The clock on my parents' wall showed I had less than an hour to finish my assignment or miss my ride to the game, and all I'd found were unsettling notes that may have nothing to do with my grandfather's death. Perhaps my imagination was running wild, as it tended to do, and his comatose ending wasn't at the hand of a crazed doctor. Or even his ending at all. What clue was I missing? I had to refocus, but I'd exhausted every lead I knew to follow.

Except one.

It would take years for me to learn the fastest way to find an answer is to ask someone the question.

After brief consideration, I ruled against asking my mother. She would have told me if she felt open to discussing her father's manner of death, so her silence spoke loud and clear. Plus, she wasn't due home from her evening commute for another half hour. My older sister, Leigh, was a phone call away at college, but it wasn't late enough to avoid the pricey long-distance rates I'd been warned not to incur. And there was no guarantee she knew any more than I did. That left me with one person to ask, and I found him in the garage, sanding his latest birdhouse creation. The same person who almost caught me snooping mere minutes before.

As I explained my assignment to my father, he confirmed the names I'd written on the branches of my family tree, then helped me fill in their birth and death dates. When he reached the eraser-worn space hovering above my mother's tree branch, his face turned sullen as he spoke. "Hardy Morgan, death 1954."

At last, I had a name. But it wasn't enough. I had to know if those medical records were his and if he was my family's proverbial black sheep. But according to what my father had just said, he'd died before the date on the note about the psychiatric patient, so the records couldn't have been about him.

Or could they?

The note was a summary and seemed to have been written by someone other than a nurse or doctor. So plausibly someone wrote the note after his death. That was my hope, anyway. A nice little medical murder would really make my family history report pop.

I pressed my father for more, grilling him with a barrage of questions like an inquisitive preschooler. "I looked through Mom's memory box. Why are there no pictures of Hardy? And why doesn't she tell stories about him? Is it because he did something criminal? And what's with all the weird medical notes she has stashed under y'all's bed? Were they his? Was he insane?" *Dammit. I just outed myself for snooping under my parents' bed. Just keep talking. Maybe he didn't notice.* "And *how* exactly did he die? If those notes are about him, they said he fell into a coma. Did he never wake up from it?"

My father lowered his voice tersely. "Rynn, your mother was standing beside Hardy when her uncle Bishop shot and killed him, and she was the only witness. She's the only one who knows what happened. Okay?"

His gaze locked onto my dilating pupils. In his rush to quench my thirst for answers, he'd done the exact opposite.

"And those notes are just old college papers. Nothing more," he added, hoping to squash my interest in them.

My voice caught in my throat. The only other time I'd felt the sensation was when my tree swing broke, dropping me flat on my back, gasping for air like a carnival-prize goldfish as the broken board floated back and forth between me and the sky. At that moment, the reason no one spoke of my grandfather came into focus.

Then a tornado of confusion set in, scattering disjointed thoughts like splinters of a destroyed Kansas farmhouse.

Was my mother shot too?

Did Bishop go to jail?

Wait...why did Bishop live with my grandmother—his sister—if he shot and killed her husband? It must have been an accident, right?

Before I could open my mouth for a second round of interrogation, my father banged his sanding blocks together and broke my trance. Through the cedar mist, he swore me to secrecy over what he'd divulged and made me promise to never ask my mother about it, fearing it would send her straight back to the horrific memories of that traumatizing night. Not wanting to defy him or cause my mother pain, I agreed.

I never made it to the football game that evening. Not that number twenty-two would have noticed. After quietly inhaling my suppcr and avoiding eye contact with my mother, I sat at my bedroom desk and penned a completely fabricated report about my grandfather Hardy's life. I went with the police-sergeant storyline; his ultimate demise: diabetes. I'd recently learned about the disease in health class, and according to my teacher, eating sugary foods like donuts was a contributing factor. Donuts…cops…it didn't take much for me to make that leap.

Hardy's actual cause of death was much more intriguing, but high school is disastrous enough. Mention a crazy great-uncle and murdered grandfather and I might as well claim a seat at the outcasts' lunch table. So when I stood in front of my class that following Monday and delivered my grade-A performance, instead of embarrassed, I felt honored. The grandfather I described had been an upstanding officer of the law with an impeccable career, who died the day after he retired. His fake life had tropes of a hero's journey and seizing the day, for you never know what sick irony tomorrow may bring. My English teacher, who doubled as the drama teacher, ate it up. Even applauded when I finished. Now *that* was embarrassing.

I had no choice but to will myself into believing the falsehood I'd created about my grandfather's life. It was easier than admitting I desperately yearned to know the truth. Those medical notes were never his. For all I knew, they weren't for an actual patient. And after all the questioning my English assignment inspired, I'm not sure I was better off. Is it worse to have an insane grandfather or a murdered one? Or no knowledge about your grandfather at all?

My mother loved the drawing of my family tree so much, she framed it and hung it in the hallway right outside my bedroom door—a daily reminder of the knothole near Hardy's name I'd promised never to reach into. Over time, my curiosity about the mystery of his demise faded. But as happens with every family's skeleton, something unexpected will coax the brittle bones from the shadows in which they hide if you wait long enough. I had to wait thirty-one years for that something to happen.

A Promise Broken

RYNN, 2020
WASHINGTON

I WAS A FEW MILES away when my mother called to ask what type of cheese I wanted on my sandwich. We had a standing monthly lunch to catch up on each other's busy lives. My parents' house sits on a bluff overlooking the Columbia River, and when it's not raining, you can see the ships. But it always rains in late October. It had rained that morning, just as it would every morning until June.

She called me from her backyard, annoyed over how many bird feeders my father had put in the yard. While he recovered from knee surgery, it was her task to fill them, although I told her I'd do it when I got there. But admitting she needs help is not something my mother excels at. So between the rain-slick rocks below the bird feeders and my mother's aging sense of balance, the scream before the phone line went dead was painfully predictable. If you've ever wondered if a minivan can drift around a corner at fifty miles per hour, it can.

I found my mother on the damp embankment below a swarm of hungry yellow finches, slumped next to a bloody boulder and the remnants of her shattered eyeglasses. As I pulled the phone from her hand, she awoke and turned toward the noon sky, revealing the puffy purple swelling swallowing her right eye. Heartbroken, my tears fell to the gravel as I guided her up the path toward the driveway. A walk that was becoming all too familiar.

It was her second fall that year. The first was the fault of a wobbly stepladder and resulted in a fractured wrist, for which she was still wearing a brace. I knew her loss of independence was nearing. She did too. The year before, she'd climbed the Spanish Steps of Rome. Now she was heading to the emergency room, poised for another long, painful recovery.

As the swelling around my mother's eye ballooned, I worried what damage may lurk behind it. I hugged the center line, flattening the back-road curves. Praying the local cop had something better to do that day than wielding his radar gun. And praying the cross hanging from my mother's neck was the protection she believed it to be.

"Mom, do you remember what you were doing when you fell?" I asked.

"I was following the yellow brick road with the Tin Man," she said.

Her reply was too confident, and for a moment, I feared a concussion.

"Hard to fool a retired nurse, Rynn." She shook a loose pill from her coat pocket and swallowed it dry. "I know it looks bad, but I assure you, I'm fine. Just localized pain."

"What did you just take?"

"Not sure. Hopefully, an Oxy."

"Mom! Shouldn't you wait for the hospital to give you pain meds?"

"It's going to be hours before they give me something. So no. And relax, it was just a Tylenol."

While it had knocked her down a few notches, no amount of pain could tame my mother's wit. Grocery lines. Social events. Funerals. It didn't matter. If there was an audience, she was entertaining it. And she always had a comeback locked and loaded.

The hospital was a solid twenty minutes from my parents' house. Factoring in a few traffic violations, I estimated I could beat an ambulance there. As she cupped her hand over her eye, shielding it from the blinding sunlight, her body tensed with every imperfection of the asphalt. In hindsight, faster medical attention inside an ambulance would have been the wiser choice. But that scream before she fell—the urgency of it—told me to get her to the ER as fast as possible.

"Hang in there, Mom. We're almost there," I said. If she'd noticed, she didn't care that I'd blown through an empty intersection.

St. John's was full of an ER's usual suspects. I'd been in them enough, usually sitting beside my accident-prone husband, to know the same cast of characters typically fills its waiting room. A manic thirty-something woman in pajamas who keeps switching seats. Someone in the back corner attempting to sleep across four chairs with a jacket balled under their head. A plump, unkempt man bobbing his knee at the admissions staff. They had likely been next in line for hours, but because of my mother's age and worsening condition, she rolled straight past their scowling faces to the front of the line.

As the nurse checked my mother's vitals, she asked what landed her in such a state.

"Boxing match," my mother said.

The nurse looked at me for clarity, confused by her deadpan reply. I'd learned long ago it was best to go along with my mother's charades. So I gave a wry smile, shrugged, and said, "Yep, she just won't retire from fighting."

I snickered, signaling the nurse she was also clear to laugh. And that she did. Too hard, as if she'd desperately needed the release.

The nurse inserted an IV port into my mother's hand and started her on hydration. Next came the long lull between the nurse leaving the exam room and a doctor entering it. In the sterile silence, save for the steady beeping of the heart-rate monitor, my mother's mortality seemed to weigh on her. She reminded me she'd never forgive me if I put her in a nursing home.

"I'm not kidding, Rynn. Roll my old bones down to the Columbia and push. I've worked in enough nursing homes to know that's not how I want to live out my days," she said.

"Jesus, Mom. I'm not doing that. I'll take care of you."

"Oh, great. Mac and cheese for supper every night."

"Hey, at least it'll be soft food," I said.

"Oh, yeah? Just be glad my fall didn't end me up like Bishop. Then you'd *really* have your hands full."

My poor posture snapped into perfect alignment. Her muddled grammar told me that was *not* a Tylenol she'd popped on the car ride, but did she just say what I think she said? Outside of an introduction, it was the first time I'd heard my mother say Bishop's name aloud, let alone refer to his condition. I had to keep the conversation going. *Please, please don't let the doctor walk in now.*

As I surveyed my nearly seventy-nine-year-old mother lying on the gurney across the room, eye swollen shut and face scraped to beat hell, I knew time was not on my side. I may never get another chance like this, imperfect as it was. I had to muster the guts to say something—anything—before the opportunity faded.

I drew in a deep breath. Before my mother could move on to the next topic, I exhaled the request I'd been waiting three decades to make. "Mom, I've wanted to ask you about Bishop for a long time. I don't want to upset you, and you can say no if you need to, but would you be willing to tell me what happened to him and why he shot your father?"

Her hand clenched so tightly that the tape securing her IV hydration port lifted. My face flushed instantly in regret. I'd caught her off guard and in intense pain—perhaps not the best time to ask someone to relive the most traumatizing moments of their life.

Then her hand relaxed, and the beeping of her heart rate stabilized. "Okay, I guess I can do that," she said with a few small nods. "But not now. There's not enough time to tell the story before the doctor comes in. At least I hope there's not. I wanna go home. Honestly, I thought you already knew what happened. But now that I think about it—hmm—how would you?"

We agreed that two weeks from then, on November seventh, she'd tell me the story. And for two weeks, I mentally rehearsed what I'd say. This was arguably the most personal conversation I was going to have with my mother, and I wanted my words to convey the empathy she deserved.

I also wanted to ensure no interruptions. So, before I left my house on November seventh, I called my sister, Leigh, to fill her in and asked her not to call or stop by our parents' house. She lived closer to them than I did, and it wasn't out of the ordinary for her to pop in unannounced.

Leigh let out a nervous laugh when I told her. "You're kidding. You actually asked her that? While she was lying there in the ER?"

"It's not like I planned it. She made an offhand comment about Bishop, and I just blurted it out."

Leigh scoffed. "I asked her about it once, and she chastised me. Told me how inappropriate it was for me to ask about something so painful. I felt shame over that moment for years. I wonder what changed her mind?"

"I don't know. Maybe she's finally ready to tell us. You probably just asked her too soon."

"Or maybe it was the drugs talking."

I laughed. "Yeah. Thank God for coat-pocket meds. I can't believe she broke her damn face."

"Call me the second you can. I want to know everything," Leigh said.

Like me, Leigh had spent most of her life wondering what caused our great-uncle Bishop to shoot our grandfather. We'd talked about it a few times, but neither of us had learned anything more than what my father told me in 1989. After thirty-one years, the mystery overshadowing our family was going to be revealed. We were finally going to reach inside that knothole scarring our family tree and find out what lived inside.

AS I DROVE THE OLD Pacific Highway to my parents' house, I thought back to that exchange with my father. And the school assignment that first prompted me to ask about my grandfather's death. It had been years since my father swore me to secrecy, but in his eyes, there was no statute of limitations on a promise. My mouth soured with guilt, but there was no turning back.

I took a swig of my lukewarm latte and embraced the surrounding nature to calm my nerves. As the rain clouds broke, the sun pulsed through the passing trees like the flicker from my childhood stop-motion books, transporting me back to 1986. Back to my first visit to Riverton, when I showed Leigh my latest creation on the banks of the Tennessee River.

"It's you dancing in your pointe shoes, Leigh." I fanned the stapled pages to bring the tiny dancer to life.

Leigh held her hand to her forehead, shielding her eyes from the blazing sun.

"The ribbons are too long," she said, deflating my attempt to make nice after a squabble over the beach towel we were sharing.

Riverton was an isolated nook where the only road into town ushered you into a world of generations-old farmhouses leaning beneath the shimmering constellations of a pitch-black sky. Apart from the familiar twinkle of lightning bugs hanging in the air, it was a far cry from my city life in Dallas.

There was only one choice for haircuts and hardware. But when it came to food, that's where the competition flared. Three adjacent diners, all displaying declarations of the best grits in town and what looked to be an ongoing price war, flanked one side of the downtown drag. It was hometown Americana at its finest, and it was dull as all get-out. But something was soothing about its tree-lined streets named after the ones that shaded them. And the lack of heavy traffic was a welcome change.

Shortly after we arrived, my mother sent Leigh into town for groceries. The extra mouths were quickly depleting our grandmother's meagerly stocked kitchen, and it lacked the assortment of junk food we had at home in Dallas. I tagged along with Leigh since there wasn't much else to do. Deprived of teenage creature comforts, my grandmother's house had no boom box for recording the weekly "Top 40" countdown. No television connected to Nintendo. Hell, no television period. Just jigsaw puzzles of patchwork quilts and an out-of-tune piano.

The mile or so jaunt ran alongside a rushing creek. We stopped briefly to skip stones, which we both failed at, as we marveled at the rainbow of flora popping against the simplicity of the riverbank canvas. Birds soared through the water's cooling mist, and tadpoles trapped in the craggy pools were sprouting legs. I could have played there for hours, but Leigh's interest waned. So we trekked on to the Riverton Market, the only grocery in town.

Inside were six aisles of shelves, short enough to see over. Leigh grabbed a wobbly cart and navigated through the pantry staples, while I wandered off to explore. I wasn't expecting to find much, but a pleasant surprise awaited me in the back corner—a pinball machine.

It had a stream of quarters butted against the side edge of its glass top, and a group of boys huddled around, eagerly awaiting their turn. They hadn't noticed me before I tried to add my quarter to the wait list. The boy playing flicked it off the edge, sending it rolling across the freshly mopped linoleum. As I chased after it, the boys roared with demeaning laughter and booed at my stomping foot, which saved the quarter just shy of the dusty black hole underneath the canned goods shelf. At least their disappointment was brief as they returned to the entrancing blinking bulbs as if I'd never been there.

Leigh had seen what happened from aisle five. I annoyed her as well, but she wouldn't stand for anyone giving me a hard time but her. She grabbed a few items from the chest cooler, paid the cashier as he bagged the small sack of groceries, then walked over and handed me an ice cream sandwich, making sure the boys saw I had one and they didn't. Turning to leave, she *accidentally* unplugged the pinball machine with her foot as she grabbed my hand and bolted out the front door. We came to a giggling stop around the corner, then made our way back to our grandmother's house before the boys could find us, enjoying the sweet reward of our melting ice cream sandwiches.

The girls in town were as unwelcoming as their brothers. My trendy ensembles were straight off the pages of the newest ESPRIT catalog, and their snooty looks weren't fooling anyone. Especially their mommas. They could smell an outsider the second they set foot on Main Street, and no daughter of theirs was going to be influenced by some big-city girl's high-falutin ideals. With each yank of a daughter's arm, they made it clear I would not be sipping sweet tea in front of the beauty shop anytime soon.

With no one to play with, I found myself stuck in superficial conversations with the family I barely knew. Some I'd met when they visited us in Dallas, but my memory of them was spotty. The oddness of that dawned on me. Most kids grow up knowing their kin. But there I was, twelve years old, visiting my mother's hometown for the first time.

I longed for the relationships my friends in Dallas had with their grandparents and extended family. Where cousins were built-in playmates, and aunts and uncles served as stand-in parents. But I was too young to understand what Leigh was chatting about with our older cousins and too old to enjoy the company of their crawling counterparts. I was the singular middle cousin, which made for a boring summer vacation. Still, I did my best to converse and enjoy exploring the unfamiliar landscape.

I wasn't the only one struggling to fit in, however. My parents' jovial spirits had turned placid as morning dew on a patch of crabgrass. They were choosing their words wisely. As if avoiding something—or someone. It was nothing like the Norman Rockwell painting I'd envisioned, with a close-knit family sitting around a long, bountiful supper table, laughing and sharing memories from a bygone time. Instead, we ate in awkward silence, filled only by my mother's desperate attempts to promote discussion and limited by the obvious elephant in the room—Bishop.

Rather than channeling Norman Rockwell, Bishop bore an uncanny resemblance to Norman Bates. I repeatedly told myself his name was Bishop, not Norman, so I wouldn't accidentally call him that. I feared he might become unhinged at such a suggestion. But then again, I wasn't sure he knew who Norman Bates was since there was no TV in the house.

Bishop rarely talked, but when he did, his words dribbled out like a thick pour of molasses. Half the time, I couldn't make out what he was saying. The other half I understood the words, but they still made no sense. On the day we arrived, and every day after that, Bishop warned me and Leigh to stay out of Dark Hollow, the thick blanket of trees stretching behind our grandmother's house. He said there were deadly painters roaming around inside. It took three days for me to realize he was saying *panthers*, not *painters*. Then I freaked out over actual panthers lurking behind the house where I slept. Still, I never saw a watchful yellow glow from the brush and wondered if Bishop was just trying to scare us.

He greeted everyone with an offer of Wrigley's Doublemint gum. It didn't matter if he had already seen you that day or not. Others politely declined, but his mannerisms intrigued me, and I took a piece every time. In a slow, shaky maneuver, he'd pull the pack from his front pants pocket and use his thumb to slide the top stick out just enough from the others below, making it easy to pluck from the package. And as I did, the stick would droop from being warmed inside his pocket.

Bishop would watch eagerly as I unwrapped my stick and gave it a quick brush with my finger to whisk away any clinging lint. As I popped it into my mouth, he'd make chewing movements in unison with mine. Only he didn't have any gum in his mouth. I'd smile and nod as I chewed and make *mmm* noises . Then he'd nod back and walk away, usually retreating to his creaky rocker on the screened-in front porch.

Once I was sure Bishop was gone, I'd spit the gum back into the wrapper and hide it in my pocket, then throw it away when he wasn't looking. I must have chewed five packs of droopy gum that visit. To this day, anytime I'm standing in a store checkout line, I'm reminded of Doublemint's tongue-chilling sensation when I spot the highlighter-green package glowing within the rack of candies and gum.

I never learned why Bishop was the way he was, but by the end of that trip, I understood that his differences afforded him freedoms most could never possess. He was unencumbered by the corporate ladders that preoccupied my parents and the perfection my sister chased on and off the dance floor. His knowledge of the world stopped at the county line, and he didn't seemed as bothered by that as I would have been. He went along to get along and was oblivious to others' judgment, both hidden and overt. And he projected a unique serenity in a world I found increasingly complicated. I wished everyone were more like him.

The last time I saw Bishop, he gave me and Leigh a warm Coke as we were leaving to return to Texas. He stood motionless in the dirt-rut driveway as we drove away, looking satisfied as I gulped down the simmering bubbles. As much as he initially creeped me out when we arrived, I instantly missed his quirkiness and regretted not spending more time with him. Sadly, I never got the chance to enjoy Bishop's company again.

MY REMINISCENCE FADED AS MY minivan crawled to a stop in my parents' driveway. A curling wave of apprehension crashed in my stomach, dampening the southern comfort I had been feeling moments before. I twisted my hands around the notches of my steering wheel, then checked my paling reflection for any ounce of lingering confidence.

Would retelling the detailed story of her father's murder send my mother into a flood of sobs? Possibly. She was such a strong, sure woman. Rarely did she cry in front of others, but this was deeply personal. I hoped whatever was about to happen wouldn't tarnish the loving bond we had. I paused outside the front door and whispered a brief prayer before letting myself in. To whom, I didn't know. But if someone divine was listening, this was the moment I needed them to hear me.

To my relief, my mother was smiling and eager to get down to business, despite her still bruised and swollen face. She and my father were sitting side by side in their recliners. As usual, he had not been told of the day's events. If my mother divulged plans too far in advance, he'd fuss if he didn't agree. So she typically gave him information on an as-needed basis.

For once, I was glad that was their repertoire. It gave me the chance to explain I'd kept my promise to him for thirty-one years, then apologize for breaking it.

My mother interrupted the disapproval wrinkling my father's face. "It's okay, hon. I've held this in long enough. I don't know what promise the two of you made, but I think it's time she knows the truth."

"Then I guess I get to hear the whole story too," he said.

Wow. Even he doesn't know. I sank further into the couch, pulled into the cushions by the gravity of what was about to unfold.

Usually, my mother's stories flowed with the eloquence of cowboy folklore. This time she started right in the middle of the action, with no elaborate introduction or detailed scene setting. As if wanting to hurry and say it out loud before she changed her mind.

"I looked up and Bishop was on the top step. I thought it was a coincidence, him coming out of the house as we were heading in. I paused at the bottom step, so he could come down first. But he just stood there. I heard the panic in Daddy's voice as he shouted at Bishop, asking him what he was doing. And in the next moment, I heard the ringing in my ears. I watched Bishop slowly lower the gun to his side and—"

Her voice quivered through the word *gun*. "Mom, are you sure you're okay telling me this?"

She chipped at the red polish on her fingernails. "I am. I've had sixty-six years to make peace with what happened, and I've lived a lifetime since then. And let's face it. Time is not on our side. I'm the only one left who can tell you what happened, Rynn. So, if you want to know, we best not wait."

"Okay, Mom, if you're sure," I said, "and thank you for this. It's been a mystery to me my whole life, but I could never bring myself to ask. That's what I promised Dad—that I wouldn't ask."

"Oh, I see. What did he tell you?"

"Enough to fuel a lifetime of wondering. When I was fifteen, he told me you were standing next to Hardy when Bishop shot him and that only you knew the full story of why Bishop did it. He asked me to never speak of it again, knowing the pain it would cause you. Since then, I've wondered what happened that night and why. And how you forgave your uncle Bishop. At least I think you forgave him because I met him before he died. And I don't think you would've introduced me to him otherwise."

"Well, first off, Bishop wasn't the only one I had to forgive. And if you wanna know all that, I have to tell the story from the beginning for it to make sense."

I folded my legs under me and covered them with the plush throw blanket adorning my parents' worn leather couch, then placed my cell phone on the armrest. "Do you mind if I record this? Leigh wants to hear the story too."

"Oh, good idea," she said. "You need to record it because I'm only going to say it once."

She sat back in her chair as if to settle in for a spell, took a sip from her three o'clock medicinal scotch and soda, then set it on the side table between her and my father. A bead of condensation trickled down the beveled glass to the glazed coaster as she adjusted the bandage over her fractured orbital bone. And when she nodded, I pressed Record.

New Orleans

SLOANE, 1948
LOUISIANA

RYNN, THE STORY YOU'VE SPENT a lifetime wanting to know has taken *me* a lifetime to understand. I was standing beside my father when my uncle Bishop shot him. That much is true. While the reasons he did it were all around me, years would go by before I learned them all. For each person present the night my father died, a separate storyline played out. I promise by the time I'm done telling you *my* story, you will understand how I know *their* stories. And to do that, I have to start at what I know to be the beginning.

I was seven years old, and we lived in New Orleans, where I was born. My sister Faith was four years older than me, and my mother, Grace, was pregnant with my brother, Osee. We lived in an upstairs two-bedroom apartment on Prytania Street, close to the train yard where my father, Hardy, worked as a locomotive operator.

Daddy was fourteen years older than Momma. They were both from Riverton and had known each other their whole lives before they married. But they spent almost their entire history separated by circumstance.

Before he drove trains, Daddy was a minor-league ballplayer. He was rather good, too, and his team's picture once hung in a baseball exhibit at the Atlanta airport. I saw it while on a layover, and he looked just like I remember him, with his chiseled jawline and piercing blue eyes. When I was growing up, we didn't have a camera. So there weren't a lot of photos of him. I wish now I'd taken a picture of the one at the airport.

I'm not sure when he stopped playing baseball, but at some point he hung up his cleats, so to speak. He got on with the railroad through a teammate who'd also realized his allure as an aging ballplayer was fading. They'd had a good run but knew they'd never be called up to the majors.

From then on, railroad tracks lined the distance separating Momma and Daddy. He'd be gone five to ten days, with a few days at home in between. His job afforded them the lifestyle he wanted for Momma, and before too long they were married and resettled in New Orleans.

Faith was already born, and their dreams of growing a family were coming true. But for all their good fortune, the most devastating, unimaginable thing that can happen to a parent happened to them. Their second daughter, Lila, died from colitis a few days before turning three. Born between me and Faith, she was the quintessential pretty child everyone adored. Her curly locks bounced and bright green eyes sparkled with every beat of her infectious giggle.

Faith talked about her all the time. When Lila died, Faith was approaching the age when little girls play with baby dolls, and to her Lila was her real-life baby doll. Faith helped dress and feed her, and she adored her role as Lila's big sister. So I suppose when Lila died, Momma and Faith both felt like they'd lost a baby.

Momma kept Lila's memory alive, and every year on her birthday, she served angel-food strawberry shortcakes in her honor. The family would share what few memories God gave with her, and while Faith would smile as they reminisced, she'd be distant for a few days after. She never quite got over losing Lila, and I think that played a big part in why Faith later became a pediatric nurse. I also think she experienced loss way too soon in life, which caused her to cling to every relationship she had, good and bad.

Everyone was excited when Momma was pregnant with Osee, but nobody more so than Daddy. He was positive Momma was having a boy and couldn't wait to walk the train yard with his son and take him along on engine rides. He tried to show me and Faith once, but we were more interested in the tailored dresses the ladies boarding the train were wearing. When Osee was born, Daddy's dream of having a son came true.

By the time I was seven, Daddy was one of the top locomotive drivers. His route was from New Orleans to Mobile, and he was gone only a few days at a time. A much better fit for raising a family. Momma did her best to keep tabs on me and Faith, but as her delivery date drew closer, she was happy to let Daddy track us down when we were late for supper.

Prytania Street wasn't far from the French Quarter, and that last year we lived in New Orleans, Momma talked Daddy into watching the Mardi Gras parade, since he happened to be home when the festivities were in full swing. We spent the whole day weaving our way through the French Market and stopping to watch the street performers as we snacked on beignets from the Café du Monde. Oh, how I loved their beignets! Their powdery sugar coating was messier than a pig in a rain shower, which made eating them even more delightful.

I remember standing at the edge of the street curb, eager for the parade to start. Faith had told me the masked people on the floats tossed candies and trinkets to the crowd, so I was bursting with anticipation over what treasures would land at my feet. When a gold coin glittered among them, you'd think I'd discovered a pirate's booty by how frantically I bounced up and down, holding it in the air for all to see. Faith quickly rained on my celebration by telling me it was just a useless tin doubloon and I couldn't buy anything with it. But to me, that coin was priceless. It came to me on a perfect day.

I don't remember which krewe we watched, but their purple and gold floats, coupled with the roaring fanfare blasting down Canal Street, were magical. I got to experience Mardi Gras only that one time, and it's one of the most vivid memories I have of my life in New Orleans.

The city was full of mystique, with lush private gardens and unassuming alleyways leading to exclusive speakeasies.

But what fascinated me most was an old cemetery a few blocks from our apartment. The famous Lafayette Cemetery No. 1 was a favorite place for kids to ride bikes because of the paved pathways running throughout it. Mini roads, barely wide enough for a hearse. You could ride all day without the worry of typical street traffic.

To get to the cemetery, I had to cross a busy intersection. Momma insisted that Faith help me across, but she never did. She and her friends would head out on their bikes, and I'd follow them on my trike, but they would never wait for me. Instead, Faith would speed up whenever she noticed I'd caught up with them. She deemed my reluctance to retire my tricycle embarrassing and didn't want her little sister cramping her style.

It's a wonder I ever made it across that intersection by myself, but I did. One particular day, I followed Faith and her friends over, and as usual they sped off as soon as they saw me approaching. Faith did always wait at the cemetery gates to make sure I'd at least gotten that far. But after that, I was on my own again.

Two giant live oaks flanked the front entrance, their branches fanning over the iron trellis bridging the open gates. As I rode under them, I'd plan my route. Half the fun for me was finding Faith and her friends and annoying them because I'd done so.

I knew every nook and cranny of that cemetery. The vaults lining the perimeter were like white castle walls guarding the family tombs and graves inside. Some displayed names so deeply chiseled you could read them from two paths over. On others the names were barely legible, with the once crisp edges of the letters eroded and stained black.

Their facades, adorned with crosses and cherubs or angels with broken wings, cast gothic shadows during the lingering light of day. Statues of weeping women and crumbling columns littered the cramped plots, some with broken closure tablets still resting where they fell. They all served as my location markers as I pedaled down the hallowed paths.

The graves sit above ground in New Orleans, which gave me the heebie-jeebies when I realized bodies were decomposing on top of the surface instead of six feet below it. But the dead don't seem so macabre after you pedal past their graves day after day. I fabricated backstories for each family and waved as I passed, asking about their day, which also embarrassed Faith to no end, but I didn't care. I reckoned if I was a resident of the Lafayette Cemetery, I'd be bored lying there all day and I'd want someone to at least say hi to me.

Later in life, I realized how iconic Lafayette was. Still is, I mean. It's home to the bones of historical figures and stories that have intrigued people for generations. My favorite is the secret garden, where four childhood friends made sure they'd get to play together in the afterlife. They each have an identical tomb in the only quiet corner of the cemetery, and it's said they were part of a secret society called the Quarto Club and performed anonymous acts of kindness for the people of New Orleans. It's one of those stories you keep waiting for someone to make a movie about. Then go see it twice, because it's that good.

But I'll never forget the most notorious story to come out of Lafayette No. 1. Well, to me, anyway. I'd found Faith and her gang abnormally quiet, straddling their bikes just shy of the Earhart family's massive tomb.

I snuck behind them, careful not to let my shadow stretch beyond theirs. "What y'all doin'?" I said.

They spun around to shush me, flapping their hands like they were dribbling a basketball, then turned their attention back to the tomb. So I inched my trike ahead of their bikes to get a better listen.

Voices were coming from inside. "This is for me, this is for you… One for me, one for you…"

I thrust my trike backward, tripping over the pedal when a wheel hung up on Faith's left sneaker. As I scrambled to stop my fall, I grabbed the hem of her T-shirt.

"Dammit, Sloane!" Faith tugged the fabric from my clenched hand and pulled me upright by my arm.

"I'm gettin' out of here! The dead people's talkin'!" I said as I regained my balance and finished rolling over Faith's foot.

"Shush, shush, shush!" Faith pleaded as she grabbed my handlebar to stop me.

The air fell silent. Then we heard rustling inside the tomb. The dead Earharts had heard us! I flipped my trike around, and the bikes were gone. Gone! They had a good five-grave head start on me, and I was on that stupid tricycle trying to catch up to them. I pumped those pedals so fast my feet couldn't keep pace. With each rotation, my knees jammed into the handlebar, dinging the bell with the impact.

I knew my way out. But I was so terrified the Earharts were coming for me, I made a wrong turn at the weeping-lady statue and ended up right back where I'd started. Faster I pedaled, and as I looped back around, I corrected my wrong turn and kept going without looking behind me.

As soon as I crossed under the entry trellis, I shot out my feet, digging my sandals into the sidewalk to stop. I peered cautiously over my shoulder, keeping my body facing forward in case the rest of me needed to pedal again. I was fairly sure the Earharts couldn't cross a cemetery border and I was safe. But this was New Orleans, and its dead people were obviously playing by their own set of rules.

Later when I busted through our front door, I found Faith sprawled across the couch, reading a magazine. She pompously tipped it toward herself. "What took you so long? Maybe if you'd learn how to ride a bike, you could keep up with me."

I don't recall if I did this or not, but I'm guessing seven-year-old me stuck my tongue out at her.

Over supper, I told Momma all about the dead Earhart's talking. Of course, she didn't believe me. "Sloane, you best not be making up such stories," she said.

Faith's smug smile hit me from across the table, roughly translated as, "You dummy. That's what you get for talkin'."

I had the last laugh, though. That Sunday, plastered across the front page of the *Times-Picayune*, was confirmation my story about dead people talking was true. Well, it wasn't *actually* dead people, but I still felt vindicated after being accused of telling tall tales. Turns out, thieves were using the cemetery tombs to hide and divvy up the loot they had stolen in a string of store robberies across three parishes. That's why they were saying, "One for me, one for you."

The newspaper headline, in what was probably a desperate attempt to grab sales, read "Grave Robbers Captured!" From that day on, we called the thieves grave robbers, because the newspaper was right. Their headline was more sensational than "Store Robbers Captured." Momma clipped out the article, and every so often, she'd open her scrapbook and read it to me, laughing at the thought of my little feet pedaling my trike as fast as it would go because we truly believed the living dead were coming for us.

In all actuality, the robbers were hiding *between* the tombs, not inside them. But it sure sounded like their voices were coming from inside. The newspaper journalist missed one fun bit of irony, however. The Earhart tomb just happens to be the resting place of the honorable Judge John Howard Ferguson. He died in 1915, and I'm not exactly a fan, seeing as how he was pro-segregation and all, but Momma loved how those bandits chose the tomb of a judge to hide behind and wound up getting caught.

AFTER THAT ADVENTURE, I WAS ready to retire my beloved tricycle. No way was I getting left behind again the next time something shady went down in that cemetery. So I asked Momma if we could trade in my tricycle for a bike. She took me and Faith down to the department store the next day, and before I got the chance to pick one out, Faith stole my new bike out from under me, complaining hers was too small for her and it was unfair that she wasn't getting a new bike too. Then, in a move I had not calculated, Momma bought *Faith* the new bike and gave me her janky old one. I guess that's how it works, though. The oldest gets the newest.

A few days later, Daddy taught me how to ride Faith's old bike. My growth spurt was taking its sweet time showing up, so Daddy lowered the seat as far as it would go. My tippy toes barely reached the pavement. Learning wasn't as hard as I'd expected, but I still preferred the stability of my trike. Riding is much more enjoyable when toppling over isn't a concern. Knowing how to ride a bike had upped the game of annoying Faith, though, since I could now keep up with her and her gang. And that alone made my *new* bike priceless.

The next evening when we came home from riding bikes, Faith was already inventing fresh examples of how I was still an embarrassment. Momma was having none of it when she called us to supper, her lips pursed and her hand clenching a letter while she tried to referee our escalating elbow nudges. Her eyes were red and swollen, but not from chopping pungent yellow onions, which was usually the cause.

Momma sat at the table and explained that the letter was from my grandfather Tom. We called him Papa T because it was more fun to say than Grandfather Tom. He was asking Momma to travel home to Alabama and help with our grandmother Louellen, who everyone affectionately called LeLe. She'd found a lump in her chest a year prior and had fought valiantly, but her battle was nearing an end.

Momma and Daddy discussed options and landed on the one that took us all to Riverton with an open-ended return. Momma was worried we wouldn't make it in time if we took the bus, which didn't leave for a few days. So Daddy bought his boss's old green Hudson. Where we lived, everything was close by, and we didn't need a car. But Daddy had been saving for one so we could take trips outside the city, and coincidentally, his boss had been telling him he wanted to buy a newer model.

The morning after Momma received the letter, Daddy asked his boss if he'd be willing to sell his old car for cheap. He explained the situation and asked for a couple of weeks off, and luckily his boss agreed. He even gave Daddy a great deal on the car—two hundred dollars.

It thrilled Daddy to own a car again. He had sold his previous one to pay for the furniture in the apartment. It also gave him peace of mind. If Momma needed to stay longer than two weeks, he could drive back and forth from New Orleans to Riverton to see us. As it turned out, he was right about that.

I couldn't wait to visit my grandparents. I was too young to remember the last time I'd seen them, but Faith wasn't. As we packed that evening, she reminded me that Riverton was in the middle of nowhere and its name explained the only fun thing about it.

"It's called *River*-ton for a reason," she said. As if my pea-size brain couldn't figure out there was an actual river there.

"Can you swim in it?" I asked. The Mississippi was too dangerous to swim in, so a safe place to cool off on a hot day was a selling point to me.

"Well, yeah, but you don't get it, Sloane. Once we get there, we'll be stuck. And I'll have no one to hang out with but you. There's nothing to do there! I'm gonna miss the start of summer, and me and my friends had big plans."

"What plans?" I asked.

"Just... plans!" she said, dumping her sock drawer upside down into her suitcase.

"Well, I don't want to hang out with you either, Faith!" I said, then stormed off. A total lie, but she cast the first stone.

I believed only half of what Faith said, anyway, and was certain Riverton had more to offer. I hoped she'd just suck it up and make the best of it for Momma's sake, seeing how her momma was dying and all. But of course, that's not what happened.

As we left the next morning, Faith displayed an impressive attitude. She dropped her suitcase on the ground at Daddy's feet, right as he reached out to take it from her. Then strutted like a peacock and flopped onto the back seat with her arms crossed, stomping her feet together on the floorboard.

I gleefully jumped in on the opposite side with my satchel of toys, humming "Buttons and Bows." Faith flicked away the strap of my satchel as it landed on her bare knee, but I was impervious to the daggers she was glaring. I was eager to look out my window to watch for farm animals as we drove along and eat the picnic lunch Momma had packed for us.

Riverton was a leisurely day's drive, but Momma herself had never driven it. She'd never learned to drive and preferred to walk anywhere she needed to be. Occasionally, she took the bus home to Riverton for a visit, so she knew all the best places along the way to stop and rest when Daddy needed to stretch his back.

The first hour was mesmerizing as the cityscape morphed into plantation country. A few homes were visible from the road, and I marveled at their majestic columns and expansive grounds. I was too young to understand their history then. All I knew was they looked like the elaborate dollhouses I'd seen in storefront windows. I'd desperately wanted one and imagined my dolls lazing the day away on the fern-filled veranda, nibbling on cookies and sipping mint juleps. Then descending its staircase as they were introduced at their nightly gala.

As I fluffed the tulle of my favorite doll's dress, my eyes grew heavy, and I was lulled by the rhythm of the tires and the hot car. My head bobbed as I tried to keep it upright, and I noticed Faith had already fallen asleep. I knew better than to mess with her, but I couldn't help myself. I took a second doll from my satchel and held it an inch from Faith's sleeping face, then tickled her knee so she'd wake up. Well, she sure did. And the first thing she saw was Lucille, adorned with haphazard marker makeup and a God-awful asymmetrical hairstyle.

"Sloane!" Faith snatched Lucille, rolled down her window, and promptly threw the doll out. I climbed on top of her, trying to save Lucille, but I was too late. Daddy skidded to a stop on the highway shoulder, yelling at us to get out.

Faith squeezed in an idle threat before Daddy was close enough to hear her. "You've gone and done it this time, Sloane. You're gonna pay!"

"Girls, I know you're both tired of being in the car, but you can't be pulling these tricks while I'm driving. You'll make us wreck!" Daddy said. "Now Faith, walk back there and pick up whatever it is you threw out this time."

"But, Daddy!" Faith pleaded as she pointed her finger at me.

"I don't care what the prank was, Faith. You can't keep throwing things out the damn window!"

I giggled when he said that. The week before, she had thrown all my pillows out our apartment window when I tried to instigate a pillow fight while she was practicing applying eyeliner.

Daddy turned his attention toward me. "And you're not off the hook either, Katydid."

That was my father's nickname for me since my middle name is Kay. Like the Katydids that chirp incessantly during the hot summer nights. And because I was usually to blame for something. Katy-did…it.

"I don't know what you did this time to scare your sister, but you best be apologizing the second she gets back here."

I hung my little head to hide my chagrin. Faith came stomping back, dust pluming from her sandals, and held Lucille straight out at me. "Here's your ugly doll back."

Daddy glared at her. "Watch it, Faith, or you'll be riding up front next to me."

I grabbed Lucille and shook the dust out of her hair. "Thanks for getting my *ugly* doll back, Faith. I'm sorry she scared you."

Daddy hurried us back into the car. "Everything okay?" Momma asked.

"It's fine. But why do they keep throwing things out the damn windows?"

Momma pursed her grinning lips as she glanced back at us with her "Girls, please stop annoying your father" face.

Momma knew she better reset the tone, or it was going to be a *long* road trip. She set down her yarn and needles and asked me if I liked black or brown horses better. I told her black, of course, because *Black Beauty* was one of my favorite stories. Then she promised me that for every black horse I counted on the way to Riverton, she would match me in dollars toward a new dress. She was familiar with the sights along the highway and knew the horses preferred grazing away from the speeding cars. It was a decent distraction from messing with Faith, but I wasn't going to amass a fortune from counting black horses.

With the mood in the car improving, Daddy whispered something to Momma. She turned around and said she wanted to remind us what our family in Riverton looked like, in case we'd forgotten. Which I had but didn't realize I had until she said that. She described Papa T as looking the same as every other grandfather with gray hair, but he looked more like a farm grandpa than a city grandpa. He worked at a cotton mill and always wore overalls and work boots, and his favorite hobby was bank fishing.

LeLe had thick blond hair before losing most of it to chemotherapy, a new cancer treatment. She'd been part of a medical trial for the experimental medicine and considered it her last contribution to helping others. She was a lover of fashion and wore silk headscarves to liven her ill reflection, so Momma and I had made her three new ones, using my head as a mannequin.

Last, Momma described her younger brother—my uncle Bishop. He still lived at home with Papa T and LeLe. Momma said he talked only when the need arose but somewhere inside was sarcastic humor that would leave you in stitches. He was tall and thin like Daddy, and as a kid, he loved to run. He could beat every kid on the playground in a foot race and aspired to be a track and field star, but something happened that changed his course.

She explained it wasn't just LeLe that Papa T needed help caring for; it was Bishop too. That he was "not correct."

"What do you mean, 'not correct'? Is he always wrong or somethin'?" I asked.

Momma smiled at my innocence and adjusted herself to get comfortable, hand hugging the back of the front seat to hold her position toward me and Faith. Then she told us a story that would set the stage for everything that happened after we arrived in Riverton.

The Golden Bicycle

GRACE, 1939
ALABAMA

GIRLS, YOU'LL SEE WHEN WE get there, but the Tennessee River surrounds Riverton in every direction but south. Think of it like this: Hold up your left hand, palm toward you. Riverton is the tip of your index finger, and all the space around your thumb and other fingers is the big Tennessee River. And all the lines on your palm are river branches and hollows scattered about. Bishop and his best friend, Jack Jr., who almost everyone called Junior, were fourteen in the summer of 1939. They spent their days plinking cans and hunting rabbits, but their favorite pastime was exploring all those branches and hollows.

I was twenty-four, and Faith, you were two years old. Sloane, you weren't born yet. Your father and I were married, but I was living back at home with Papa T and LeLe while your father trained in New Orleans for his new job with the railroad, so we could save for our apartment.

One day, Bishop and Junior set out to the Ginhouse Hollow to check if anything new had taken shape. It usually hadn't, but the anticipation of finding something fresh in a town that always stayed the same lent them hours of free entertainment. The hollow is on a steep bank overlooking the big river. The easiest entrance was down a long dirt road on the opposite side of town, past the last house on the right, which belonged to Mr. Davies. Once you stepped beyond the curtain of longleaf pines, you may see a skunk or two teetering away as you approached. Hopefully, not a snake, but they lived there too. And if you were really lucky, you caught a glimpse of the White Thang—a sort of hairy, albino bigfoot that likes to roam the hollows of Alabama.

The hollow backs to a cotton plantation and its namesake gin house. Bishop and Junior knew once they saw the glare from the metal roof and heard the shrill of the cotton gin inside, they needed to turn back. The summer before, they'd been caught plucking cotton bolls off their leggy stems and knew better than to test a man holding a shotgun.

Well, the boys didn't find White Thang that day. But they did discover a fallen tree, which wasn't there the last time they'd checked that hollow. They walked its perimeter, looking for a hornets' nest to poke and branches for makeshift swords. When they got to its treetop, they saw something peeking from beneath the umbrella of leaves. A bicycle. It had been at the base of an adjacent tree the whole time but wasn't visible until the fallen tree's branches tore through a blanket of kudzu vines, exposing the bike in all its golden, rusted glory.

They untangled the remaining vines, picked up the bike, and gave it a push. The wheels and frame were in straight order, but it looked like an old rusted-out hubcap hanging on the outside wall of a highway gas station.

"Well, I saw it first," said Junior.

"No, I did," said Bishop.

They couldn't agree who claimed it first, and sharing the bike was an unlikely option, so they did the only logical thing their teenage-boy brains could think of. They wrestled for it. Neither had a bike of his own. And neither had any money to fix one up. But someone was going to go home the winner of a not-so-shiny rusted-out bicycle that day.

Junior's dad, Jack Senior, was a high school wrestling legend, and while Junior had never wrestled on a team, he presumed his genetics made him a shoo-in for the win. Feeling confident, Junior told Bishop they needed a flat spot away from all the vines and downed tree branches to have their wrestling match.

Bishop spotted a clearing in the distance. "There! I'm going to pin you over there!"

They laid some ground rules as they weaved their way to the open spot. First, no hitting faces, because their mommas would be teed off. Second, no biting, because that's how girls fought. They crouched and slapped hands in a low five to start their match. Waves of laughter echoed through the hollow as they fabricated moves and a point system to determine the winner. Sweat trickled down their bony spines as they called time-outs, propping themselves against their knees to catch their breath under the hot summer sun.

With each maneuver more ridiculous than the last, their friendly match took a hostile turn when Bishop's sneak attack swept Junior's feet out from under him. Junior landed flat on his back, and Bishop, being about a foot taller and twenty pounds heavier, sat on his chest and didn't get off until Junior tapped out.

"I'm the Ginhouse Champion!" Bishop proclaimed as he leaped around with raised fists.

Ire flooded Junior. His desire to win was almost more than his fear of admitting failure to his wrestling-champ father, whose trophies beamed in his face as soon as he walked through the front doors of his school. A man who woke up every day and did push-ups before the sun rose and didn't filter his disappointment in his son, who wasn't doing the same. And try as Junior might—no matter how well he wrestled or how fast he ran during recess, no matter how high he jumped—Bishop's height advantage always gave him the winning edge.

Junior sprang from the ground and jolted Bishop with both hands to the chest. Thinking Junior was still playing, Bishop hardly pushed back, laughing as he brushed past Junior to go claim his prize.

But the laughter wasn't returned. Junior's eyes squinted and his clamped jaw dimpled as he blocked Bishop with his outstretched, stiffened arm. The playful push Bishop had given Junior ignited his fiery testosterone. He tightened his fist. He tried to restrain his rage. But the threat of his father's embarrassment won out. With the full force of his runtish frame, Junior landed a deafening haymaker on Bishop's right ear.

Bishop stumbled forward as his slick-bottomed sneakers, worn to no tread, slipped on the loose, pebbly earth. He tried to regain his balance, swirling his arms like a wild windmill, then overcompensated and stumbled backward, his feet barely keeping him upright.

Regret consumed Junior as he watched Bishop's confusion. Scared he'd just ruined his best friendship, he reached out for Bishop's arm to help steady him. That's when he noticed. The clearing they'd been wrestling on wasn't just a flat rock. It was a cliff. And Bishop was veering dangerously close to its edge.

Junior launched himself toward Bishop's leg and caught the hem of his jeans as the rest of his friend went over the side. Bishop's weight dragged Junior across the scorching cliff top as he struggled to hold his position. Hanging upside down from Junior's grasp, Bishop struggled to reach for a nearby muscadine vine, twisting and kicking, pinching Junior's hand against the serrated ledge.

Junior wailed at the rip of his skin as his hand reflexively let go.

Junior lay still, covered with dust, with an elbow skinned from being raked across the very pebbles on which Bishop had slipped. Fear took hold as he realized what he'd just done. He stretched out his arms and grabbed the edge of the cliff with both hands, then slid his body up to meet them and slowly peered over.

Bishop came into focus. Foot…legs…torso…head. Splayed on his back, he lay on a second cliff below. His right leg was bent at the knee, with his foot tucked under his left leg, in a number-four position. The drop was at least one story by Junior's calculations. And below the cliff where Bishop lay, the Tennessee river lapped at its muddy bank.

Junior curled his knees under his chest. "Bishop…Bishop? Bishop!"

He scurried to one side of the cliff and met a thicket of blackberry thorns. He ran to the opposite side, sliding as if he were sliding into home plate. He felt the sting of dirt grinding into a fresh wound as he ripped the knee from his hand-me-down jeans. No thorns, but a straight drop. No switchbacks or rocks to use as steps. There was no safe path down to Bishop.

Junior frantically paced, then took off running. He felt the sting of his skinned knee opening and closing with each bend. His mouth was dry, coated from the dust kicked into the air when he slid. He gave zero consideration to the dangers he'd face as he ran back through the hollow alone. But he had to forge a plan to help Bishop. Suppertime was approaching, and everyone would be home cooking. So Junior ran to the first house he saw. The last one down the dirt lane and the first one outside the hollow.

Junior slapped on the front-screen door with his flattened-out palm. "Mr. Davies? Please, please come help!"

A tall, burly black man slowly approached the door with a baseball bat running parallel to his right leg. "What's the issue? That you, Junior?" Mr. Davies called out.

"Please, Mr. Davies! Bishop fell off a cliff, and he's not moving. I can't climb down it to help him."

Mr. Davies looked at Junior and took stock. His clothes were dustier than usual, and a scraped knee was peeking through a hole in his left pant leg. A smeared streak of dried blood ran from his elbow to the tip of his pinky finger. "Son, I don't have a car. I got a bicycle, though. You can use it to fetch help if you promise to bring it back."

"Yes, sir. I promise, sir. Thank you!" Junior said.

"All right, come on," Mr. Davies said, then led him through a path of wispy grass. He opened the door to a dilapidated shed and wheeled out his bike, which was too tall for Junior. He hopped on and jerked the handlebars side to side while his feet flittered before finally landing on the twirling pedals.

As he rode away, Junior yelled back to Mr. Davies. "I promise!"

Junior stood up and pumped the bike as fast as he could go, leaving a cloud of dust trailing behind him. As he passed the cemetery and rounded the corner into town, it occurred to him he'd hit Bishop over a bike neither of them owned. And there he was, riding a different bike he didn't own, in a race to save Bishop's life because of what he'd done.

He cut through the alley between the five-and-dime and post office, passed his own house, and went straight to Bishop's instead, two houses down. When he hit the front-yard grass, he backpedaled so hard the wheels sliced through it, leaving a smooth streak in the clay. In one swift motion, he laid the bike on its side and skipped up the front porch steps two at a time. He stopped for a moment at the top to catch his breath, then flung open the screen door and ran straight through the front room, past Papa T sitting in his reading chair, and into the kitchen where LeLe and I were prepping supper.

LeLe stood at the sudden intrusion. "You okay, Junior?"

"Yes, ma'am, but Bishop fell, and he's not movin'."

LeLe dropped the knife she was using to chop carrots, and we hurried to the living room, where Papa T had overheard the entire exchange. He chastised Junior for not going straight to the sheriff. Then he looked at me. "Grace, you stay here. No tellin' how long we'll be, and someone should stay back at the house."

LeLe grabbed her purse and followed Junior out the back door to Papa T's sedan. It was a short drive to the station, where they caught Sheriff Dossie as he was leaving for the evening.

Without pausing for breath, Junior told a thirty-second rendition of what happened and where Bishop was. And with every word, Papa T's anger grew.

"Tom, take Junior and LeLe over to Mr. Davies's house. I'll call for Doctor Waddell and meet y'all there," Sheriff Dossie said.

Papa T nodded. "LeLe, you get in the back. I want Junior in front with me."

LeLe rolled down her window as she shut the door. "Sheriff, please tell the doc to hurry. It'll be gettin' dark soon."

"Yes, ma'am, I will." He tipped his hat as Papa T hit the gas.

Papa T turned his attention to Junior as he drove away toward Mr. Davies's house. LeLe slid across the bench seat to the middle so she could hear the conversation in front.

"What the hell were you two thinking, wrestling out on a bluff? You best be sure I'll be talkin' to your daddy 'bout this. I've half a mind to fetch him right now. And what were y'all fightin' over, anyway? Well? Damn it, Junior. Answer me!"

Junior's eyes welled as he realized the whooping he was in for. He might as well skin a tree switch now and save his daddy the effort. He recounted the entire story again, apologizing repeatedly for what he'd done. LeLe sat helpless in the back, certain Bishop was dead out on a cliff. Or had rolled over and fallen into the river below and drowned. Papa T drove faster, now understanding the urgency of the situation. Time and nightfall would be their worst enemies.

Sheriff Dossie arrived at Mr. Davies's house a few minutes behind Papa T. He retrieved a flashlight and climbing rope from the trunk of his squad car. "Let me grab my snake charmer. Then Junior, you're gonna lead me, Tom, and Mr. Davies to Bishop."

As he returned, loading shells into his shotgun—his "snake charmer"—Dossie continued, "LeLe, you stay here and wait for Doctor Waddell. When we get to Bishop, I'll send Junior back here to you. Junior, you guide the doc back to Bishop. Y'all got that?"

LeLe swooped her arm behind and down her legs to flatten out her dress as she sat on Mr. Davies's top porch step, then placed her purse in her lap.

Junior led the way back to Bishop. It was about a ten-minute walk, five if you run it, and the sun was quickly fading. Sheriff Dossie turned on his flashlight and gave it to Junior, then handed his shotgun to Tom and told him to keep a lookout. Getting struck by a rattlesnake or copperhead would massively complicate the dire circumstances, and that hollow was chock-full of 'em.

Dossie prepared a rope harness for rappelling as they wound their way through the hollow. No one spoke other than to affirm Sheriff Dossie's instructions when he gave them. As they approached the cliff where Bishop fell, Junior paused and pointed. The thought of seeing Bishop scared him, but he had to know if he was okay. He summoned the courage to walk to the edge and peer over, shining the light down on the half-shaded cliff. Bishop was still there, in that same number-four position.

Sheriff Dossie took the flashlight from Junior and scanned the area, looking for the best path down the cliff. As the light panned, Junior saw something he hadn't seen before; a glistening on the rock next to Bishop. "Jesus, there's blood on that rock!"

Sheriff Dossie traced the angle of Junior's outstretched arm. He focused the beam of dim light onto the rock below, hoping whatever Junior was seeing was anything but blood. A setting sun can cast illusions in the haziness of dusk, but the muddy sheen coating the top of that rock was unmistakable.

Papa T leaned against Mr. Davies to stop his buckling knees. Declaring it the better option than through the brambles, Dossie set the flashlight on the ground, aimed toward the trees alongside the sharp drop-off.

"Mr. Davies, Tom, you take the end of this rope and don't let go," Dossie said as he wrapped it around the biggest tree he could safely reach. "We'll use this trunk as leverage as you lower me. Got it?"

"Yes, sir," said Mr. Davies, as Papa T nodded and gripped the rope.

Dossie placed the knotted harness he'd made around his waist, secured it to the lowering rope, then stepped out to the edge of the cliff to mark his landing below. The river's breeze fanned his back as he turned to face the men.

As Junior handed Dossie the flashlight, he saw a smidge of unsteadiness. "You ever done this before, sir?"

"No," said Dossie, as he tilted his head and peered into the shadows below.

The Rescue

GRACE, 1939
ALABAMA

BY DOSSIE'S CALCULATIONS, DR. WADDELL would arrive at Mr. Davies's house soon. "Junior, go wait for the doc with LeLe. Then bring him back here with my deputy, who should be there by now," Dossie said.

"Yes, sir," Junior said as he took off running into the darkening snake-filled woods.

"Okay, on three start lowering me. One…two…three."

Inch by inch, Papa T and Mr. Davies lowered Sheriff Dossie down the side of the cliff until they heard him holler, "That's good!"

Mr. Davies tied the end of the rope they were holding to a smaller tree so it wouldn't fall, then stepped to the edge of the cliff to verify Dossie was safely down. The sheriff was on bended knee with his fingers on Bishop's neck, checking his pulse.

"He's alive!" Sheriff Dossie shouted.

Mr. Davies put his hand on Papa T's shoulder and gently shook it. "He's gonna be okay."

Sheriff Dossie knew Bishop's neck might be broken and he shouldn't try to move him. But he needed to check where the blood was coming from. He gingerly ran his fingers through Bishop's jet-black hair, then wiped the tacky proof onto his pant leg. The swelling from head trauma may mean life or death. Plus, he had to get Bishop out of there before the local wildlife caught wind of a wounded animal.

Right about then, Junior was approaching Mr. Davies's house. LeLe was still sitting on the top porch step, purse in her lap, waiting for Dr. Waddell to arrive. Deputy Hayes was prepping for the rescue at the back of his police car when Junior burst through the trees.

"What's the update?" Hayes called out. LeLe jumped from the steps, shadowing Junior as he made his way across the yard.

"The sheriff's rappelling the cliff to Bishop. He told me to come back here and wait for the doc, then take y'all to the cliff."

"How long does it take to get there?" Deputy Hayes asked.

"About ten walkin' minutes, sir," Junior said.

"Okay, hold tight. The doc should get here soon. Junior, tell me what happened while we wait."

LeLe handed Junior a cup of water she'd retrieved from Mr. Davies's well. He chugged the water without pause, then retold the entire saga, feeling even more shame than he had the first time he'd admitted what he'd done.

Deputy Hayes believed Junior's story, even if there was more he wasn't telling. But in that moment, the only thing that mattered was rescuing Bishop and getting him to the hospital. "It's gonna be okay, son. We'll talk more about this later and sort everything out. Now, let's have a look at your scrapes."

Out on the cliff, Papa T could barely see Mr. Davies as the sun switched places with the moon. They had known each other for a long time, and though segregation ran rampant in Alabama, Papa T treated Mr. Davies the same as he did everybody else. That's just the kind of man he was.

Down below, Dossie held Bishop's hand and gave it a light squeeze. Bishop didn't squeeze back. He took a blade of grass from the patchy cliff wall and feathered it across Bishop's cheek. His nose didn't squinch. All Dossie could do was sit beside Bishop in the darkness and wait helplessly. He had watched Bishop grow up and had a son his same age, and he couldn't help but think how he'd feel if this situation was reversed. If it was him, not Tom, scared of losing his only son.

Like a beacon of light beckoning a storm-battered ship, the slow glow of headlights intensified as Dr. Waddell's Pontiac station wagon approached Mr. Davies's house. LeLe stood and waved her arms back and forth overhead, running across the yard to greet him as he stepped out with his medical bag. Hayes explained the situation, with Junior standing close to his rib. Then the men hurried to gather medical supplies and a papoose board from the back of Dr. Waddell's wagon.

"Okay, son," said Dr. Waddell, "lead the way."

LeLe watched as Bishop's rescuers disappeared, once again, into the trees, leaving her alone on the front steps. By this time, though, word had gotten out something was happening, and people started showing up. With each arriving neighbor, LeLe was both grateful for the company and anguished by the multiple times she had to retell the unfolding story. It was her only son lying motionless in a dangerous hollow, after all.

This was Junior's third trek out to the bluff. His body felt worn out. Mentally exhausted and hungry from missing supper, he kept going without complaint. He had to be strong for Bishop.

Papa T and Mr. Davies showed the doctor how they had lowered Dossie down the cliff. "Okay, do the same thing, but lower the papoose board first. Then I'll go down," said Dr. Waddell.

Papa T and Mr. Davies lowered the papoose board until Dossie once again yelled, "That's good!" Dossie untied and positioned the board next to Bishop and waited for Dr. Waddell to join him.

Once he reached the bottom, Dr. Waddell assessed Bishop for broken bones and checked his head wound. He and Dossie carefully slid the papoose board under Bishop and secured his body to it. When they were ready, they positioned the board so as soon as the men from above started pulling, the board would lift vertically, with Bishop facing outward away from the cliff, and his head toward the night sky.

Sheriff Dossie called to the moonlit faces watching pensively from above, "Okay, say a prayer!"

Mr. Davies unwrapped the rope from the tree trunk and repositioned it over the cliff's ledge. Hand over hand, he and Papa T pulled up Bishop's dead weight. Their palms burned against the taut rope, which was fraying as it raked across the rocky ledge, until the top of the papoose board peeked at the cliff's edge. "Okay, hold the rope there, and I'll guide the board the rest of the way by hand," Deputy Hayes said.

Hayes grabbed onto the papoose board as the rope snapped and fell, nearly pulling both him and Bishop over the ledge with it. He dropped to his knees and strained with all his might. Papa T and Mr. Davies rushed to help him, and with one last burst of strength, the men laid Bishop safely on the ground.

"We got him!" Hayes shouted.

"Good, get ready to pull us up! And hurry!" Dossie said. He tried to ignore the rustling from the flanking bushes. Something was out there, and he wasn't waiting for it to make an appearance.

Junior stayed by Bishop's side while the men threw down a new rope and retrieved Dossie and Dr. Waddell. Then they used it to prepare the board for transport back to Mr. Davies's house. They fashioned five shoulder loops and attached them evenly around the papoose board to distribute the load, then hoisted it into the air for the return trip. Junior didn't let go of the board at Bishop's feet the entire way back.

The bouncing light from inside the hollow signaled LeLe they'd returned. She whimpered at Bishop's stillness and the gauze wrapped around his matted hair. She knew Jesus heard her prayers because Bishop was still alive, but he needed to get to the hospital to keep it that way.

The men loaded Bishop into Dr. Waddell's station wagon and watched as it drove away. Papa T followed behind in his car with LeLe. Deputy Hayes repacked his gear and left to go back home. Just another day in his book, but one he wouldn't soon forget.

Sheriff Dossie assured the crowd of neighbors who had assembled in Mr. Davies's front yard that Bishop was going to be okay. He shook Mr. Davies's hand and thanked him for his help, then walked over to Junior, sitting defeated on the ground next to his squad car. The back of the boy's head rested against the passenger door, and a dirty forearm balanced on his scabbing knee.

"Get in, Junior, I'll take you home."

"Sheriff Dossie?"

"Yes, Junior?"

"Can you take me to Bishop's house instead of mine? There's something I gotta do."

"What?" asked Dossie.

"I gotta take Mr. Davies's bike back to him. That's where I left it. At Bishop's."

"In the morning," Dossie said. "First, you gotta explain to your momma why you're so late for supper."

When they arrived at Junior's house, Jack Senior was on the porch. They had heard the chatter about what was happening out at Mr. Davies's house and were headed that way. I know, because I'm the one that did the chattering. Papa T had told me not to leave the house, but I figured Junior's momma would want to know why he wasn't home yet. A part of me also wanted to tattle on Junior for what he'd done to my brother.

"Junior, wait in the car for a sec while I talk to your daddy." Dossie walked the path to the house. He explained how badly Junior had messed up but said that, like a real man, Junior had taken ownership of what he'd done to make it right. Jack cocked his head to the side and jerked it at Junior, signaling him to get out of the car.

Junior walked slowly, trying to delay facing his father for as long as possible. As they crossed paths, Sheriff Dossie gave him a reassuring wink.

Dossie had one more stop to make that night. I was still at the house taking care of the evening chores when he came in and collapsed into a chair at the kitchen table. I poured him a jar of sweet tea and fixed him a supper plate, then he told me that entire story. Well, the parts I didn't witness, anyway. He wanted me to know Papa T and LeLe had gone to the hospital with Bishop and likely wouldn't be back home until the next day.

After Dossie left, I put Faith to bed and cleaned the kitchen, then retreated to the front room couch. I tried to fall asleep, but my mind raced with images of Bishop lying out on that cliff, half-draped over the edge and near falling into the river below. I pictured copperheads surrounding him and Sheriff Dossie shooting them away as he rappelled down the hillside to save him. Eventually, I fell asleep and woke the next morning to the sound of two car doors shutting. Two, not three.

IT WAS A COUPLE OF months before Bishop came home from the hospital. For the first two weeks, he was in a coma. He was so still, a part of me feared he may never come out of it. Then one day, he just sat up and opened his eyes. That's what his nurse said.

I visited him with Papa T and LeLe every week. His speech had slowed, so I helped him practice saying common words. But he struggled to turn them into sentences. His mind was… different.

The day Bishop came home, everyone was at the house, eagerly waiting to greet him. No one more so than Junior. The doctors hadn't allowed him to visit Bishop while he was in the hospital, fearing it would cause Bishop distress or bring back memories he said were missing from that day. But there was no keeping Junior from being there when Bishop came home. And when Bishop came through the front door and saw Junior standing there, his grin said what his voice couldn't. There was no distress. No memory trigger. Just a kid who missed his best friend.

It took a couple of weeks to adjust to Bishop being home. Everyone fussed over him for a few days, but soon we realized Bishop was still Bishop, just with some new quirks. His gait was different and no longer included the usual chaos surrounding a teenage boy's steps. He was easily confused and sometimes repeated himself. And he took long pauses, as if mentally flipping through the pages of a dictionary to find the right word.

As much as I wanted to start my life with Hardy in New Orleans, I delayed moving a few months longer so I could help LeLe with Bishop. During that time, Bishop and I became close. Returning to school was not an option for him, so LeLe and I became his teachers. We didn't bother with complicated subjects like algebra, because he would never remember it correctly, anyway. Instead, we focused on regaining his independence.

Repetition was key. If I showed him the way to the post office and back every day in a row, by the eighth or ninth time, it would stick. I followed covertly behind a few times to make sure he arrived safely. Since then, Bishop has been in charge of mail. He's also in charge of fetching water from the well and kindling for the cooking fire.

Before long, Bishop was becoming a new man. One who could survive the hand he'd been dealt, albeit with help. There was one new thing, however, that posed a tremendous threat to him. Bishop never sleepwalked before his fall, but he had quite the affinity for it after. It happened so frequently, Papa T installed brass bells over both the front and back porch doors. The type you hear chime as you enter and exit an antique bookstore. Bishop never tried escaping through his bedroom window, but if he had, the thorns of the holly bush below it would have surely woken him.

Before Papa T attached bells to the doors, our neighbors had some unexpected visits from Bishop. In the wee hours of dawn was when he wandered, and it's a wonder he didn't get shot. Our next-door neighbor, Harts Barnett, found him sitting in his car once and rocking on his front porch another time. And Junior's momma found Bishop sitting at her kitchen table one morning, finishing the last piece of pie she'd saved for herself.

He was never too destructive, but one morning we woke to Mrs. Barnett banging on our front door. Bishop was next door in her flower garden, sweeping the blooms off her prized tulips. He was doing a good job of it, too, launching them into the air like he was swinging for the back nine. Papa T had to splash him with water from Mrs. Barnett's watering can to wake him up. Bishop felt so horrible he offered to glue all her flowers back together with his airplane-modeling glue. I swear she almost took him up on it, just to teach him a lesson.

But the worst sleepwalking episode he had, and the one that resulted in the addition of the bells to signal a door being opened, nearly got him killed. Behind the house, there's a small spring that flows out from the hillside. Nothing beats the refreshment of its crystal clear water trickling into your cupped hands. Bishop and I stopped at it all the time for a drink, so it made sense that he would visit the spring during a sleepwalk. But guess what also visited during the summer? Snakes.

They burrow during the winter, but during the warmth of summer, you have to be vigilant as you wander. And one of the deadliest of all snakes lives by water. Thankfully, Bishop woke up the second his bare feet sank into the small stream that the spring feeds. Because if the cool water hadn't woken him, the cottonmouth stalking him would have.

He entered the back kitchen door with muddy feet and startled Papa T, who was making his morning coffee. Bishop explained where he'd woken up and how he was moments from being struck, and the bells appeared over the doors later that night. I rather liked them too. They set my mind at ease that Bishop was safe, and we all subconsciously became attuned to them.

Bishop was distraught when I finally left for New Orleans, and I harbored guilt over doing so. But Hardy and I needed to restart our married lives together. I visited Riverton as often as I could, and Bishop has made as good a recovery as anyone could expect. His speech has improved in the ten or so years since his fall, but you—Faith, Sloane—you girls need to understand he may say things funny or get a word wrong here or there, and that's okay. And he might be uneasy with us all in the house when we first arrive, but don't worry. He'll adjust. Try to treat him like you would anybody else.

Riverton

SLOANE, 1948
ALABAMA

RYNN, YOU LOOK AS STUNNED as Faith and I were after Momma finished telling us that story. Given the era, it's hard to believe all that happened and Bishop still survived. But he did. Momma believed in miracles, and she said the fact that his name was Bishop must have placed him at the front of the line when God was handing them out that day.

Still, Momma's description of Bishop made me uneasy. Faith whispered that she remembered him from her last visit to Riverton and that he made weird faces and stared a lot. I wasn't sure if she was trying to scare me and get me back for my Lucille prank or if she was telling the truth. At any rate, my excitement for our arrival had waned, but I continued my hunt for black horses as Daddy drove on. I was currently at five.

We stopped for lunch halfway at a town called, ironically, Meridian, and Faith and I jumped out the second Daddy stopped the car. We waited impatiently for Momma to gather our picnic, scanning the area to see where we were. I spotted a pond at the end of a path through magnolia trees. Some were in bloom, and their sweet musk lured me their way.

"Well, go on. We'll meet you there," Daddy said, knowing I was about to wander off.

Faith looked at me with a wicked smile. "Let's race!"

I knew that meant I had five seconds before she started running, so I shot down that path faster than a jackrabbit. And just as I approached the grass surrounding the pond, Faith's scrawny legs whizzed past me so fast she had to stop herself on the back of a duck-feeding bench to keep from running into the water.

I never won our foot races, but I didn't care to anyhow. I just wanted Faith to play with me. We had a glorious time mimicking the bathing ducks and trying to get them to quack back at us. Then Faith pulled down a magnolia branch as we stood on a picnic table. We each picked a new bloom, tucked it between our fingers, and displayed our elaborate rings with the limpest of regal wrists.

Suddenly, in unison, Faith and I looked at each other as if to say, "Do you hear that?" The faintest tones of carnival music floated in the breeze. Momma and Daddy had caught up and were watching us from the path, waiting for us to notice the music.

"Is there a carnival here?" Faith asked.

"No, but if you go through that door, you'll see where the music is comin' from," Momma said, pointing to a courtyard across the pond.

Faith grabbed my hand as we jumped off the picnic table and took off running. The music grew louder as we approached, and the smell of cotton candy mixed with popcorn wafted through the courtyard. I thought for sure Momma was wrong and a clown-led marching band would be on the other side of that door.

Faith pulled open the door, and a menagerie of painted animals and blinking amber lights flew by. An usher in a pin-striped uniform welcomed us, proclaiming the best time in town. We both stood still, in awe of the most exquisite carousel we'd ever seen.

Still holding my hand, Faith skipped us to a red velvet rope strung between shiny brass posts, and we took our place in line behind a dozen other kids staring at the wondrous twirling zoo. Daddy stopped at the ticket counter to pay for our ride, then picked me up and set me on his shoulders so I could see above the crowd.

Faith and I had our animals picked out by the time we got to the front of the line. I'd called one of the two giraffes, and she wanted the tiger. When it was our turn, we both bolted for our animals. Faith easily jumped up on her tiger, but the giraffe was too tall for me to reach. I bounced beside it, claiming it from the other kids until Daddy lifted me onto its patchwork back.

My imagination ran as wild as the majestic animals on the carousel. I was high in the air, bounding through the grasslands of the Serengeti. Nibbling on leaves only the long, yellow necks of a giraffe can reach. Faith was hunting the antelope in front of her, gaining on him with each revolution. The chariot ahead of me holding Momma and Daddy served as a safari jeep, barely dodging the deadly lion that was chasing them.

They looked back at me a few times, no doubt to make sure I hadn't fallen off my giraffe. I remember the sleeves on Momma's polka-dot dress waving gracefully through the air like a flag on a high pole, and her flipped shoulder-length brown hair shielded by the gallons of hairspray she set her style with. My hair had blown back out of my face for a refreshing change.

As the carousel slowed, Daddy helped me off my giraffe. Faith ran over, and as we stepped off the platform, it felt like we were still going in circles. We walked diagonally toward the door, giggling at our dizzy feet. It had been the best surprise, and I prayed I would dream about the carousel that night so I could ride it as much as I wanted, each time on a different animal.

We strolled back to the grass by the pond, and Faith and I compared notes about who had the best ride. Momma spread out a blanket, and we all lay down to rest before digging into our picnic. I'd almost forgotten what Momma had told us about Bishop when Faith asked, "Do you think Bishop would have liked the carousel?"

"I believe he would," she said, realizing his story was still weighing on our minds. So she redirected our thoughts by telling us all about the town of Riverton and how it was actually a replica of itself.

The Tennessee Valley Authority flooded the original town in 1938, the year before Bishop's fall. They built the Pickwick Dam and a series of new locks to supply power to the region and provide boats safe passage through the treacherous shoals of the Tennessee River. I had no clue what a lock or shoal was, but they sounded dangerous.

She said it was as if the TVA erased Riverton's map dot and drew it back one inch to the right. The original town was still out there, though—as an underwater ghost town. There was an inn, a doctor's office, two general stores, and a millinery shop out there under the water. And before the TVA built the new ones, smaller locks were used to control the waterway. They were still out there, too, and in the heat of the summer when the water level fell, the tops of those old locks would pop up out of the water. I perked up at the thought of ghosts swimming around in an abandoned inn and trying on fancy hats at the millinery shop.

Before the TVA flooded the town, they moved its two churches to the top of the hill next to the cemetery. Which was already there because of the high water table. Otherwise, like in New Orleans, the dead don't stay buried for long. I remember thinking Jesus must have reached down from the sky with both hands to help because how in the world do you move an entire church, let alone two?

But the part of what Momma told us about Riverton I liked best was its one-coach train called the Doodlebug. It connected Riverton to the larger, nearby city of Sheffield, which had everything Riverton didn't. She promised us day trips to the library, malts at the diner next door, and occasional trips to the department stores for new clothes. By then I'd counted seven black horses and was well on my way to a new dress.

I loved to read, and while Riverton had a small library, I couldn't wait to visit the bigger one in Sheffield. My excitement for our adventure had returned! Faith was still unconvinced, but I saw a half smile when Momma mentioned malts.

We packed up our blanket and half-eaten peanut butter sandwiches and headed back out on the road for the second leg of our trip. The scenery wasn't much different, but I was eager to swim with ghosts and take the Doodlebug train. I was no longer worried about Bishop, so I suppose Momma's story did the trick.

FAITH AND I FELL ASLEEP, and as we approached Riverton, Momma reached back and shook our legs to wake us up. It was exactly how she'd described it. The enormous river was off to the left, and we turned right at the cemetery to head toward town. Daddy drove down Main Street and pointed out the places Faith and I might want to go. The five-and-dime for candies, the post office so Faith could mail letters to her friends back in New Orleans, the little library that would suffice, and the beauty shop filled with ladies drinking lemonade, giving us all a long glance as we drove by.

We pulled into Papa T and LeLe's house on Blankenship Lane, and as I got out of the car, I heard the trickle of water nearby and took note. The house was a weathered blue in desperate need of a fresh coat of paint. A tall set of wood steps led to a screened-in porch, which covered the right front half of the house. On the opposite side was a large picture window that took up the other half.

Mosquitos were coming out for their evening feed, so I rushed up the steps to dodge them. I opened the screen door to find a man sitting in one of two wooden rocking chairs, watching us get out of the car and walk up to the house. He didn't stand, but I could tell he was tall because his knees stuck out from the rocker seat. I knew right away it must be Bishop. I smiled and said hi as I waved a little wave. He hesitated before lifting a finger from the arm of the rocker.

Between the two rockers was a table made from stacked milk crates, holding a half-drunk jar of tea and an opened pack of chewing gum. Filling the space at the end of the porch was a bed-sized couch covered in needlepoint pillows. They were all shapes and sizes, with patterns in every color of the rainbow. It looked like a delightful spot to take a nap.

I wasn't sure what to do, but I saw the front door leading into the house was open, so I went on in. I looked up as I passed through the doorway and saw one of the brass bells Momma had told us about. If I could have reached it, I'd have given it a push.

LeLe was asleep in the front room in a makeshift hospital bed. The legs of a wooden dining chair poked out from under a sheet above her head. Confused, I leaned in to take a closer look. Someone had flipped the chair upside down, so the back spindles, padded with blankets and pillows, made a ramp to elevate her shoulders and head. I thought it was an ingenious improvisation to prop her up.

The bed sat at an angle in front of the picture window. I don't think she had seen us pull up, though. Her eyes were closed. I suddenly worried she might already be dead, so I stood still, blocking the way for everyone coming in, not knowing where to go.

Momma nudged me with her knee, then led me over to LeLe. "Sloane, you remember your grandmother LeLe?"

I didn't. "Hi, LeLe."

She opened her eyes, and as soon as they refocused on Momma's face, she reached out for her. "I'm so happy you made it home in time, Grace. And that can't be Sloane. Oh, look at that pretty dress!"

Faith walked in and stepped up next to me. She said hi to LeLe and asked how she was feeling, hesitant to get too close.

"Oh, I'm okay, Faith, dear," LeLe said. "My old body just gave up sooner rather than later. But you needn't fear; come closer."

Papa T poked in his head from the kitchen. "Oh! I didn't hear you all come in. Grace, come help me finish supper, then we'll all catch up."

Daddy took Momma's place in the chair sitting next to LeLe's bed, and Faith and I told her all about New Orleans and the grave robbers, our picnic halfway to her house after the carousel, and how many black horses I had counted along the way. It was nine, by the way. Faith had helped me keep a tally but only because Momma promised her an equal payout if she did.

LeLe wanted to know every detail of our stories. She reached out to feel my hair and ran her finger across the row of embroidered flowers on Faith's dress as she reminisced about how she used to wear flowers in her hair. I was so intent on telling LeLe our stories that I didn't notice Bishop had snuck in and sat behind us. It wasn't until Momma called us to supper that I noticed him. He still hadn't said a word, and he stared at me and Faith as we walked toward the kitchen table.

"See, I told you," Faith whispered in my ear as we sat down.

Bishop sauntered into the kitchen so quietly you'd have thought he was floating.

"There you are, Bishop!" Momma said as she reached out to hug him. His face lit up as he hugged her back. A little too hard. Momma's face looked like she was choking on a pecan.

Not knowing if Bishop remembered us or not, Momma introduced him to me and Faith. He gently shook each of our hands. "Nice to of met you," he said.

I remembered what Momma had said about him sometimes saying things wrong. "Nice to of met you too," I said.

Momma smiled and nodded at me in approval. Bishop said little else that entire night. Only an occasional interruption to tell Momma how happy he was. It was obvious he'd missed his sister.

After dinner, Momma had a surprise for us. An upright piano sat against the wall of the front room. The one she had learned to play on. It was a richly stained oak, but the scrolls and inlays weren't as fancy as other pianos I'd seen.

We didn't have a piano in our apartment in New Orleans. Momma was our church pianist, so she practiced there, although she didn't really need to. She played beautifully, and

I loved to sing along. She pulled the small bench out from underneath the piano, lifted the top, and chose a music book from inside. Then she sat down and folded the piano's hinged key cover up and out of the way.

We spent the rest of the evening singing along to our favorite hymns. Momma even threw in a Christmas song to mix up the playlist and make us laugh. She promised to give me lessons once we settled in at Papa T and LeLe's, and I held her to that.

The house was large, with enough bedrooms for everyone, but they needed a sprucing. So, that first night, Faith slept in the front room with LeLe. I started there, too, but then remembered the porch bed covered in colorful pillows. I took my sheet out to the porch and got comfy, and it didn't take long before the trickle of the stream nearby lulled me fast asleep.

THE NEXT MORNING, FAITH TRIED to convince me to switch sleeping spots with her. She told me the couch next to LeLe was the most comfortable couch she'd ever slept on and that she had dreamed about the carousel all night. But I'd been conned by Faith more times than I could count and wasn't giving up my porch bed so easily.

That day, Daddy and Papa T got our temporary bedrooms set up for us. Faith came clean and said LeLe woke up every few hours, and Papa T would be right there to fetch her whatever it was she needed. He knew precisely when she was going to wake up, and every time, the muffled ruckus woke Faith up. That's why she wanted to switch beds.

Breakfast was a real eye-opener. I hadn't noticed the night before, but the kitchen had only a small stove with a burner big enough for a tea kettle. They did most of the cooking outside over a fire, which was in the side yard off the back kitchen door. That's how Momma had learned to cook, although I'm sure she preferred the full-size stove our apartment in New Orleans had. Bishop kept that cooking fire going most of the day, stoking it morning, noon, and night. The smoke kept bugs at bay, so it was the place to be if you could stand the extra heat.

Then there was the bathroom, which I found to be more of a situation than accommodation. There was one inside the house that everyone shared. Not a big change from our apartment in New Orleans, other than more people to share with. But there was also an outhouse if we couldn't wait our turn inside. I tried to use it once, but Faith all but ruined my ability to use an outhouse for the rest of my life.

She told me it was full of ten-eyed spiders and that a troll lived under the toilet seat. I wasn't falling for it, but the rustic little shack scared me just the same. Well, one day, she was using the inside bathroom and wouldn't let me in. I pounded on the locked door, promising her my share of dessert if she would hurry. All that did was incentivize her to drag out whatever she was doing in there.

"If you gotta go so bad, use the outside potty. But watch out for the troll!" she said.

"Fine, I will!" I huffed, then stormed off to prove my bravado.

I cracked open the wood-planked door, hoping no spiders would wrap their fuzzy legs around the frame and pull me in so they could suck me dry of all my blood. Nothing with ten eyes stared back at me as I poked my head in and checked the corners. It reeked, but understandably so, and a roll of paper hung from a stick chained to the wall. I was sure that since Faith had lied about the spiders, the troll was a lie too. So I went on in, gathered up my dress, and sat down. Right as I started peeing, a terrifying, low-pitched moan came echoing up from behind me.

"You! Get off my seat, little girl!"

I jumped off that seat so fast I hit the wall and knocked the toilet paper stick down the hole, then flew out the door. Pee streamed down my legs as I ran across the yard with my underwear around my ankles. Momma came running out to see what had happened. I ran straight into her arms and told her I'd sat on the toilet-seat troll's head.

"Now, Sloane, what'd I tell you about tellin' these tales?" She didn't even try to hold back her laughter.

Well, of course, it was Faith back behind the outhouse. She waited at the kitchen door for me to go inside it, then snuck outside and made that horrible troll moan as I sat down. I never used that outhouse again. Never.

But back to breakfast. After we ate, Momma said we were underfoot, so she shooed me and Faith outside to play. It was the perfect time to find the source of the running water I'd heard when we arrived. I knew I'd have maybe an hour before

Faith got sick of me, so I quickly convinced (begged) her to follow the sound of the water with me to see where it led.

It didn't take long to find out. One of the river branches Momma had told us about was just around the bend. It was a good size, too, about one train car's width. The water wasn't rushing hard. More of a gentle float. And the rocks littering the riverbed looked like a sunken field of orange and yellow marigolds. Faith and I took off our sandals to check the temperature. Cooler than the air, but not by much.

We splashed around and plunked rocks as Faith driveled on about how much her friends in New Orleans must miss her. She was adamant that their summer sucked without her there, as if she was their sole source of entertainment. She was doing a good job of convincing herself of that, anyway.

There was plenty of shade from the surrounding trees, and wildflowers bloomed all around us. It differed vastly from the Lafayette Cemetery and Mardi Gras parade, and I was quickly falling in love with it all. But with every unfamiliar landscape comes a new set of dangers. I was about to get my first lesson on why I had to be incredibly careful while playing in Alabama waters.

Upstream, a stick floated toward me. I figured I could catch it if the water kept flowing the way it was. But as it got closer, the stick slowly wriggled side to side. Like a spaghetti noodle in boiling water. I thought this must be some unique stick and reached out to grab it.

It was almost in my hand when I felt myself being pulled out of the water. Someone had a hold of me from behind, and large hands dug into my armpits. As my feet cleared the waterline, that stick morphed into a snake's hissing mouth, inches away from the water dripping off my toes.

I hit the sandy riverbank, and as I turned around, I saw Bishop throwing rocks at the snake and Faith lying on the ground next to him.

Bishop looked at me and shook his pointing finger at the snake darting away from the riverbank. "Moccasin!"

It befuddled me why he called it a shoe, but I figured his brain somehow confused it for the word *snake*. He shot me and Faith an odd stare that seemed to last an ungodly long time, then he turned and loped off toward the house.

The birds had stopped singing. The trees had stopped swaying. Like they all stopped what they were doing to watch the show below. But the water still trickled. I looked at Faith, wanting her to confirm what had just happened. She started to cry as she stood up and brushed the sand from her dress.

"Are you okay?" I asked. "Did he push you down?"

"If you hadn't talked me into comin' here, none of this would have happened!" she said as she stomped through the rocky bank to the road.

That stung. Minutes before, we were forging a bond. Laughing and exploring a new world together. It's funny how a mood can change in a flash. Then it dawned on me as I was walking back to the house alone. Any uneasiness I felt over Bishop was gone. He had saved me and Faith from that hideous water snake, even if he did push her. Which I was still unsure of. I'll never forget the pearly white of its mouth as it tried to sink its sharp fangs into my big toe, thus beginning my lifelong hatred of snakes.

NONE OF US TOLD WHAT happened at the river, but Momma and Daddy were suspicious since we all kept quiet at supper. Not abnormal for Bishop, but Faith and I usually bickered over something dumb, like whose feet were invading the other's space under the table.

Momma and Daddy gave each other that parental intuition look. You know, the one that implies they know something's up. But instead of questioning us, they sat back and enjoyed a rare uneventful and quiet supper.

As I lay in my bed that night, all I could think about was that snake. I'd close my eyes, and he'd be on the backs of my eyelids, slithering closer with every twitch of my eyeballs. I'd open them, and he'd be up on my ceiling, hissing. Waiting for the right moment to strike his fangs into my bare feet.

I thought maybe he wouldn't be in Faith's room, so I tiptoed across mine and slowly opened my half-closed door. The snake wasn't in the hallway, so I continued the six paces to Faith's door and gently tapped on it with my stubby fingernail.

"Faith?" I whispered in my not-so-quiet whispering voice.

"Go back to bed, Sloane," she whisper-yelled back.

"I can't. The snake's in my room."

There was a long pause, during which I assume she was deciding if she wanted to be a good big sister or if she was still mad at me from earlier. "Fine."

I slowly turned her doorknob and opened the door. She looked annoyed but flung back her sheet. I quietly closed her door, then leaped over to her bed, jumping in as she covered me up.

"Snakes can't get you if you're under the covers," she said.

The Doodlebug

SLOANE, 1948
ALABAMA

FOR THE NEXT FEW DAYS, I stayed close to the house and at Momma's side. Bishop did too. He watched as she took care of LeLe and helped Papa T with chores. And when she took a break, she'd sit with Bishop and tell him stories about New Orleans. The yearning in her voice told how much she missed it, but she knew she was where she needed to be.

I had more or less settled into my new living arrangement and asked Momma for chores. They were everyone's focus for the better part of the day, and I wanted to do my part. There was never a shortage of things to be done, and even though times were simpler back then, in a lot of ways, they were harder. There were no shortcuts like there are today. No high-end drawer microwaves or hidden paneled dishwashers to do the cooking and cleaning for us. Or stacked front-load washers and dryers to do our laundry. We eventually got a modern refrigerator, but for the longest time, our house only had an icebox.

Momma gave me two jobs. First, I dried and put away the supper dishes for whoever was washing them. Now, this may seem like a simple task, but remember, I was a short seven. I stood on a wooden stool to receive the wet dishes and towel away their streaks before stepping off the stool and set the dish on the table. Over and over, step after cautious step, until all the dishes were dry. Then I positioned my stool at the dish cupboard, and one by one took them from the table and stacked them in place. It was tiring. Probably why Momma gave me that chore, so I'd fall asleep the instant my head hit my pillow.

My second job wasn't as labor intensive. I held the clothespin basket for Momma and handed them to her as she hung our clothes on the line to dry. I enjoyed that time with her and the clean scent of the wet linens. They were my cool cotton maze on a hot day, with the sun's heavenly glow through the white threads lighting my way. Round and round I'd go, jumping out from behind the sheets to scare Faith if she wandered past.

Daddy's list of chores was more demanding. A diseased apple tree needed to come down before it spread its destruction to others, a new cedar-shake roof Papa T hadn't gotten around to needed to be installed on the outhouse, and Daddy's "new" used car needed some maintenance. He took me along to the service station to buy some motor oil, then let me help change it. And by help, I mean I got to hold the copper funnel until he needed it. But not before I dropped it in the dirt several times while sailing it through the air, spurring the *dammit, Katydid* face I frequently got from Daddy.

Faith wasn't content to finish her chores in a leisurely way like the rest of us, however. She'd knock them out right after breakfast, then head to town after lunch and not come back until supper. She had met a group of kids her age and was trying to get in good with them. I was happy she'd found them, thinking she wouldn't be so pissy over missing her friends in New Orleans.

She wasn't the only one who left right after lunch, though. As Faith made her way to town, Bishop stalked her and hid behind bushes any time she looked back at him. Except he did it on delay, so she knew exactly where he was the whole time. It annoyed Faith, but because of what had happened with the water snake, she didn't try to stop him. She knew other dangers may lurk and she might need Bishop to be her savior again. She just didn't like him treading on her independence.

I, of course, found it entertaining. It gave Bishop something new to do, and I was grateful for the help in goading my big sister, intentional or not. But the flip side was I had to listen to Faith complain about it every evening when she returned home.

Two weeks after we'd arrived in Riverton, Momma and Daddy called me and Faith out to the porch and told us Daddy had to go back to New Orleans the next morning. The time off his boss had given him had expired, and he needed to get back to work. Faith was ecstatic, thinking that meant we were going back with him. That's not at all what it meant.

They had decided only Daddy would return and that he would visit us in Riverton when he could. The idea of not seeing my father every week devastated me. But Faith? She was just plain pissed. She stormed off to her room to sulk and refused to speak to anyone for the rest of the night.

The next morning, Momma cried as Daddy drove away. Faith barely said bye to him. Bishop watched from behind the woodshed instead of in the driveway with us. And as I looked at Momma's growing belly, I knew it wouldn't be long before I saw Daddy again. I patted her tummy to let Osee know he would be okay.

We'd gone back inside and holed up in our rooms, wanting to be alone. Faith was singing Judy Garland songs, no doubt in front of her mirror. Poorly, too, I might add. She was so loud I couldn't hear my dolls talk. I banged on the shared wall between our bedrooms to let her know I was not at all happy about it. Momma heard the ruckus and came flying into my room. She told me to grab my nine black-horse dollars and meet her outside, then told Faith to do the same.

Wait. Did that mean we were finally going on the Doodlebug train? I strapped on my sandals and ran outside. It did! Papa T was waiting in the car to take us all to the Doodlebug for our first trip to Sheffield. Even Bishop seemed excited, although I was sure he'd taken the trip before.

We pulled up to the train station, and Papa T parked the car. I had imagined it looking like the pictures I'd seen of Grand Central Station, with businessmen in sharply pressed suits and ladies in colorful high heels bustling about. In reality, the Riverton Station was a single-track depot at the edge of town. There was no bustling. And the only suit around belonged to the train conductor. Just a bunch of normal-looking people, in sensible everyday shoes, sitting on benches waiting patiently for the train to arrive.

Papa T bought our tickets, and the countdown started. My anticipation was almost too much for me to bear…or anyone else. Would the train look like an actual doodlebug? I'd hoped not because they were a boring, dull gray. And all those creepy little feet under their bug-sized armadillo shells reminded me of the overgrown hairs poking out from Papa T's nostrils. My face contorted in disgust as I imagined that. Faith thought I'd made the face at her, so she moved to the next bench over. If I'd known sooner that a twisted face was all it took to make her move away from me, we'd have had a lot fewer fights.

The train pulled in and clanked to a stop. Black, with crimson accent stripes above its streak of open windows, it looked more like a ladybug than a doodlebug. It was an adorable, baby version of the engine Daddy drove. The conductor took our tickets as we climbed aboard, exchanging mine and Faith's with a Tootsie Roll.

The inside was much like the buses in New Orleans, with rows of bench seats separated by an aisle down the middle. I claimed a seat in front. Faith tried to sit in the back, but Momma called her over to sit next to her, behind me and Papa T.

I turned around to smirk at her. She curled her upper lip, then turned her attention out the window, gnawing on her Tootsie Roll, as the train began pulling away from the station.

I was excited to venture outside of Riverton and hoped Sheffield had as many lavish buildings as the French Quarter.

That ended up being a letdown, as I didn't understand how unique New Orleans is. There truly is no place like it. And while the sights along the way to Sheffield were a showy display of nature in full bloom, nothing stood out. The road running parallel to the train rails was the only connection to the small, isolated town of Riverton. Just as Faith had described.

We got off the train smack-dab in the middle of the action. The library was across the street from the station and would be our last stop before heading home, since books were the heaviest to carry. So our first stop was the department store for our new dresses. We passed by lively storefront windows displaying the latest fashions and fads, stopping at each one to marvel at the creative ways they displayed their merchandise. My favorite was a camera shop that depicted a mannequin father taking a photo of his mannequin children with a fancy new camera. I wish I had more photos from my childhood. Over time, details fade, and we forget the little things that give places and people their personalities.

The department store had four floors full of everything someone might need. Momma stopped to fantasize in the model kitchen, and Papa T took Bishop to the sporting goods section to get new fishing bobbers. Faith and I ran up the steps to the second floor, where I immediately found the perfect dress. It was goldfinch yellow and had a navy blue ruffle running across the bottom hemline. Sleeveless and flowy, it was simply perfect for a summer day. But it was ten dollars, and I had only nine.

Momma told me it was okay, that she'd make up the rest. When I was older, I realized the genius of her dollar-a-horse parenting maneuver. She had that dress purchase planned well before we left New Orleans. But why not leverage it into occupying her antsy child at the same time?

Faith was taking her sweet time picking out a dress. She'd go into the changing room with a fresh stack of options, then come out twirling, waiting for us to say it was even prettier than the last dress she'd modeled. She was only eleven, but it was obvious she'd been graced with all the good genes. Her stick-straight black hair played perfectly off every hue of fabric she chose with a brilliance every girl in school envied. And when Faith ended up needing glasses, instead of being embarrassed like most kids, she made a fashion statement out of it and ignited a frenzy with her cat-eye frames. The girls back in New Orleans clamored to buy glasses, even if they didn't need them, just so they could look like Faith.

Bishop was getting pacey, and my interest in helping Faith was waning. Momma hung back with her while she decided which dress to buy, and Papa T took me and Bishop over to the Southland Diner. Chrome and red accents with a black-and-white checkered floor gave it a sleek, modern look, and an elevated row of white vinyl counter stools lined the shotgun dining room. Papa T and Bishop sat down at an open booth by the door. I hopped onto a stool and spun around until a pretty waitress came toward me. Her apron matched the crisp white walls, and as she passed the boy working alongside her, she flirtatiously snatched his soda-jerk hat and rested it atop her perfectly curled blond hair.

Her cherry lips glistened as she asked for my order. "A chocolate malt and french fries, please," I said.

Papa T overheard my order and chuckled over his menu. My daddy always said fries tasted better dipped into a malt instead of ketchup, and boy, was he right. It was the ultimate salty-sweet pairing. Bishop looked at me as if I was the weirdo and not him. I didn't care. They were the ones missing out. And if I ate what my daddy would have chosen, I could feel like he was there with us.

Momma and Faith finally joined us, and we all enjoyed lunch together, me at the counter picturing myself wearing the waitress's hat, and the others in the booth by the door. They watched the cars drive by and the people shuffling along the sidewalk, while I watched the waitress bop along with the jukebox and tend to her customers. She made it look so fun; I thought one day I'd like to work in a hip diner and blend milkshakes too.

We had an hour left before boarding the Doodlebug, and it was time to move on to the library. It was the part of our trip I'd been waiting for all day. As Papa T opened the glass entrance door, the blue ruffle on my new dress fluttered in the rush of bought air. I had insisted on wearing it out of the department store, claiming the dress I had on had a hole in it (it didn't).

As I stepped inside the library, the woody scent of knowledge welcomed me. I made a beeline to the librarian's desk to ask where the middle-grade books were, and without looking up from her work, she pointed to her left. I whisper-yelled,

"Thank you!" as I ran off, never to be seen again until I emerged with a stack of books so high I couldn't see over them.

I followed the sound of Papa T's laughter, trying my best to keep the top book from sliding off. Faith rolled her eyes and shook her head. Momma tried to get me to put a few back, but she knew that was a losing battle. Unexpectedly, Bishop reached out and took the stack of books from me. And he carried that stack of books all the way back to Riverton too. Each time I finished reading one, he'd walk me down to the little library in town to return it.

All the small-town libraries connected to the big one in Sheffield. So no matter which one you returned the books to, they made their way back to their home library. I remember thinking that was a slick system, and when I was old enough to get my driver's license, it would be the perfect summer job. I could be the person who drove the bookmobile around to each town, handing out fresh books and collecting all the finished books. Then I'd sit in a park and read them under a tree during my lunch breaks.

The little Riverton library was at the end of Main Street, across from the beauty shop and next to the barbershop. Bishop would wait for me outside while I returned my books and took a lap for any new ones I might want. He liked to amble past the cars parked in front of the barber. He'd circle them slowly as he admired their design and peek inside at the interior, keeping his hands in his pockets to avoid the temptation to touch.

Everyone in town was used to him doing this. Thank goodness, too, because he looked a bit like a car prowler.

Sometimes the gentlemen even showed him the engine if he was looking at their car when they came out from their fresh shaves. It was wonderful how everyone was so accepting of his behavior, and I figured they likely knew what had happened to him, so they understood Bishop meant no harm.

One late morning, Bishop took me downtown to return some of my books, and when I came out of the library, I found him crouched behind a car, peeking his head up over the hood like he was watching someone.

"Who you spyin' on?" I asked.

"I'm not. I'm hiding," he said.

"From whom?" I looked up and down Main Street, but bless his heart, there was no one else around. I kneeled next to him to see his vantage point.

"Them ladies that cut hair. They talkin' 'bout me. Gossipin'."

He said he saw them cupping their hands to each other's ears so he couldn't hear what they were saying.

Couldn't hear? From outside and across the street? I peeked over the hood and looked into the beauty shop. The lights were off. Nobody was inside. It looked like they hadn't even opened yet.

I assumed he was remembering a time when they really did do that to him. "Yep. Those old biddies are mean!" I said.

I grabbed his wrist, and we duckwalked our way down the sidewalk, shielded behind the cars until we were out of sight of the beauty shop.

Bishop may have had a few screws loose, but his imagination made for a fantastic playmate. Still, I found his behavior to be stranger than usual. When we got back to the house, I told Momma about it while we made lunch. Faith scolded me for encouraging his "dramatic episodes," as she called them. Momma didn't seem concerned and told me my imagination was no match for Bishop's. She was right too. I came up with some whoppers of a tale, but Bishop...he lived them.

The Garden

SLOANE, 1948
ALABAMA

I WAS A SMIDGE OFF on my guesstimate of when my baby brother would make his appearance. It was two months after Daddy had left, and I hadn't seen him since. With his limited leave from work, he'd been waiting for Momma to go into labor. So he wasn't there for Osee's birth. But I was. And it was an emotional roller coaster of a day I will never forget.

Papa T woke me and Faith when Momma's contractions started in the middle of the night. I begged to go to the hospital, but Faith offered to stay back and take care of LeLe and Bishop, which I thought was a gracious gesture. I later realized Faith had a way of making it appear like she was doing *you* a favor when she was only doing it for herself. She told me later she just wanted to go back to sleep.

Papa T helped Momma to the car and laid her down on the back seat. I got to sit in front; a rare occurrence. I sat backward on my knees so I could look after Momma, although the best I could offer was holding her hand. She squeezed it so hard I thought I might lose a finger. Watching the waves of pain she endured nearly turned me off from wanting kids of my own.

She asked me to keep time, and if the pains came five minutes apart, Papa T needed to drive faster. Papa T handed me his wristwatch and told me to read it with the flashlight from the glove box. I had an important job and took it seriously. Momma and my new baby brother were depending on me. By the time Papa T screeched to a stop at the hospital's entrance, her contractions were right at five minutes. We barely made it, even with Papa T driving like a street racer. With my view out the back window, I knew he passed at least twenty honking cars.

Momma was in hard labor as the nurse wheeled her from the car. Papa T tried to get me to stay with him as he parked, but I was not leaving Momma. I jumped out and ran beside the wheelchair, hanging onto the arm for dear life. As they took Momma into a room, a rude doctor blocked the doorway and told me to sit in the waiting area, then shut the door in my face to keep me out. So I sat in the chair closest to her room.

Soon after, they wheeled Momma out on a gurney and down the hall. Papa T assured me everything was fine, but I don't think it was. One nurse was holding an IV bag above her head, shuffling her feet to keep up with the gurney. Momma looked unconscious with a mask on her face.

Papa T paced the waiting room. The nurse at the counter told him to stop asking for updates, that she would tell him when there was one to give. I pretended to sleep, watching every hallway movement through the slit in one eyelid. They finally brought Momma back to the room, but Osee wasn't with her. I panicked, waking from my fake sleep, and insisted the nurse tell me where my baby brother was.

She took my hand and walked me down the hallway. I wasn't sure where she was taking me, but Papa T was following behind. She stopped in front of a large window, and Papa T picked me up, then pressed his pointing finger to the glass. It was love at first sight when I saw Osee peeking out from his tightly wrapped blue blanket. He was the cutest baby in the nursery, and I couldn't wait to hold him.

I fell asleep for real, and when I woke, Papa T took me into Momma's room. She was sitting up, snuggling Osee between her forearm and hip. I climbed onto the bed, and she gently guided him into the resting place between us. I touched his tiny hand, and he latched onto my finger, holding it as he slept. My sisterly duty as his lifelong protector was a job I didn't take lightly, and it started immediately. Momma had to tell me more than once it was okay to let the nurse take Osee for his wellness checks.

I watched the nurse like a hawk, asking her what she was doing with each change in task. She played along, trying to ease my nervousness, and let me help weigh and measure him. The way she held Osee so he wouldn't wake up was pure magic. Of all the professions I'd been considering, this was by far my favorite. Who wouldn't love to hold newborns all day?

Momma and Osee came home from the hospital a few days later, but Papa T had already brought me home. I was eagerly waiting for them that afternoon when my daddy's car drove in. I ran out to greet him, the warm sun dancing across my bare feet as he scooped me up and spun me around the front yard. It seemed like a perfect day, but it didn't stay that way for long.

Daddy and I went inside to visit with LeLe. I bounced from the couch to the chair and then back to the couch again, eager for Osee's arrival.

"Katydid, stop it," my father barked as he caught me midjump.

"Sloane, dear, come sit next to me. I wanna tell you a story," LeLe said.

I was usually the one telling the stories, so I was excited to hear hers. She was wearing one of the new headscarves Momma and I had sewn for her, and it complemented her well.

"This scarf is my favorite of the ones you and your momma made," she said. "Do you know why?"

"Because it's a pretty shade of pale pink?" I said.

"That's right. It's the same shade of pink as my runnin' roses in the front yard. Do you know what runnin' roses are, Sloane?

"Roses that grow crazy and run where they ain't supposed to?"

LeLe got a kick out of my answer, coughing through her laugh. "They're called runnin' roses because, back during the Civil War, the ladies of Riverton hid their valuables from the Yankees by burying them under rosebushes. So they called them runnin' roses, as in, 'runnin' from the Yankees.' Just one of the many ways they outsmarted those Yanks, and why roses are so symbolic around these parts. Those roses have as many stories to tell as you do, Sloane. And perhaps a few hidden heirlooms buried beneath."

LeLe shivered. As I tucked her quilt around her legs, she caught my hand and clutched it. "Keep my roses alive for me, Sloane."

LeLe's grip loosened, and her hand collapsed gently to the bed. Daddy rushed over and nudged me aside to check her pulse, but she was gone. It was quiet and undramatic, just like my LeLe. I'll never forget the feeling of her silky-crepe skin as she let go of my hand.

LeLe had become my favorite person to tell my stories to, and my grief as I lost her came pouring out. Faith heard me sobbing and ran to see what was happening. Right away, she knew. Bishop came in from the front porch, where he had been waiting for Momma to get home. Daddy passed me off to Faith so he could comfort Bishop, but Bishop pushed away and slammed out the back kitchen door, leaving it wide open as the brass bell above it rang.

"I'll go find him," Daddy said.

Bishop was sitting outside by the cooking fire, fixated on the lingering embers from breakfast. Daddy sat quietly next to him. Sometimes saying nothing says everything. This was one of those times. Now that I think about it, Daddy had quite the predicament to deal with, being the only parent home when LeLe passed. And the worst part was yet to come—telling Momma and Papa T.

When they pulled in, Momma saw me sitting on the bottom porch step crying, and when I didn't immediately run out to greet Osee, she somehow knew. Papa T rushed past me and up the steps to be at LeLe's side. Daddy kissed a sleeping Osee and whisked Momma into the house, where they all stood around LeLe's bed with their heads bowed.

The lull that came next was the ultimate juxtaposition of life and death. Nobody knew whether to cry happy tears for Osee or sad tears for LeLe. Momma retreated to her bedroom with Osee. Daddy called the church to make funeral arrangements. Faith left to go find her friends, claiming she couldn't deal with the sullen vibe hanging over the house. Bishop stayed by the fire all day. I sat alone on the porch, where the sound of the river branch drowned out my sadness. And Papa T sat in the chair beside LeLe, holding her hand until it was time for her to leave the house and family she so cherished.

Once the neighbors heard of LeLe's passing, we had enough food to last a year. Well, not really, but when someone dies, especially a matriarch, everyone thinks they need to feed her family. As if they're not capable of feeding themselves because that was the role *she* filled. I wasn't complaining, because honestly, it all looked delicious and Momma was in no shape to be cooking, but it was an embarrassing amount of food.

Momma didn't want to be rude and refuse visitors, but she was exhausted and just wanted to sleep. I sat on the front steps and tried to run interference, although most paid me no mind. They marched right into the house to console Momma and Papa T and passed Osee around like he was the offering bowl at church.

Occasionally, I checked on Bishop out by the fire. I was the only person he'd let sit next to him, because besides Daddy

I was the only person who didn't try to talk to him. Everyone else who checked on him wanted him to say he was okay, so they didn't have to deal with a man they didn't understand how to comfort. All they had to do was not talk.

LELE'S WAS MY FIRST FUNERAL. I was well aware of death and what succeeded it after years of riding through the Lafayette Cemetery. I had seen people visiting their loved one's graves as I rode by on my tricycle, careful not to disturb their prayers, and now I was one of those people. It was surreal knowing that was going to be my relationship with LeLe now. As I walked past her open casket and said my goodbyes, I promised her I'd visit every Sunday after church, for as long as we stayed in Riverton, and tell her my stories she loved so much to hear.

A few days after the funeral, Daddy and Momma called me and Faith to the porch and said it was time for him to go back to New Orleans. But there was good news this time. He had changed his route to pass through Huntsville on his way to and from Louisville, Kentucky. Huntsville was still a couple of hours' drive from Riverton, but much shorter than the eight-hour one he was making from New Orleans. So, the new plan was for us to stay put in Riverton and help Papa T a little while longer, and Daddy would drive in from Huntsville every three weeks.

It just made sense for us to stay in Riverton. Papa T couldn't keep tabs on Bishop from the cotton mill where he worked, and he needed help running the house. And now that Osee had arrived, we needed a place to live that was larger than our apartment back in New Orleans. Daddy was saving for a bigger house of our own, but for the time being, Riverton was where we'd live our lives. And I had made peace with that.

Faith, however, had not. She'd been hoping that when LeLe died, we would return to New Orleans. She threw a spectacular fit, screaming at Daddy for not taking her with him while tossing about the colorful porch bed pillows LeLe had made. Bishop pushed off from the corner on which he was leaning and picked up the pillows as if they were priceless works of art, gasping and whimpering as he dusted each one off before placing it gently back down on the porch bed.

The next morning was a near repeat of the first time Daddy left, with Faith muttering a resentful goodbye. Bishop watched from his front-porch rocker. Papa T had left before dawn, opting to distract himself with a fishing pole as opposed to wallowing in sadness at home. So he'd said his goodbyes to Daddy the night before.

This time, though, as I looked up at Momma, it wasn't at her growing belly. It was to see her cradling baby Osee close to her chest. Daddy kissed him sweetly on the back of the head. He hugged Faith and me together as three, with Faith's limp arms messing it up, then gave a wave to Bishop, and that was that. He was gone and would return in three weeks.

Each month, Daddy marveled at how much we had grown. He marked our heights on the back of the kitchen door, and inch by inch, I was catching Faith. With every visit, he'd bring us each a box of Cracker Jack and fresh-cut flowers for Momma. She had a field full of them outside but appreciated the sentiment just the same.

Back then, nothing was more coveted than a Cracker Jack prize. We collected and traded them and used them to barter across the school lunch table. The thrill of finding and tearing open the red, white, and blue prize inside was as sweet as the caramel-coated peanuts clinging to it.

With the days of summer dragging into one another, I needed some new entertainment. There was a garden in the side yard, just outside the back kitchen door. A peeling white picket fence surrounded it, and half an old wood ladder served as an arbor over the entrance gate. It held overgrown pea vines that shaded you in a lush green canopy and tickled your arms as you passed under.

Bishop loved to be out in that garden, and tending to it was his primary chore. Each day, he'd carry two buckets to the water well behind the woodshed and return with them filled to the brim. He walked with no bounce to keep the sloshing to a minimum. Then he'd water the rows of plants and check each section of the garden, snipping off what was ripe and tossing any duds over the fence into the cooking fire. He'd take his pickings into the house, and that's what we'd eat for supper.

Every day I enjoyed the juicy tomatoes and perfectly sweetened strawberries he grew. It intrigued me that someone so inept in most aspects of life was a wizard at bringing life into the world. And I wasn't exactly sure how he retrieved the water from inside the well, but walking the buckets back without spilling a drop looked like a fun challenge.

It occurred to me, however, that I hadn't seen Bishop out in his garden since LeLe had passed, and I worried his broken heart needed help to heal. I thought if I got him out there, he might return to his normal self. Plus, his butter lettuce was wilting. So, after breakfast the next morning, I asked Bishop to teach me how to garden.

He taught using the watch-and-learn method, which I preferred. He showed me how to do things like parting the soil and dropping in the seeds. And watering plants by watering around them in a circle instead of dumping water on top of their delicate heads. Before long, turnips were peeking from my crooked row, and I beamed with pride.

Bishop was intensely protective of his garden and would circle the outside each morning, looking for fence gaps where the pesky bunnies could tunnel in. If he found a hole large enough for them to get through, everything had to stop while we rearranged the "bunny block," as I called it.

The fence perimeter looked like a battlefield trench system, guarded by intricately crisscrossed branches from the woods behind the house. And mostly, it worked. Most bunnies steered clear of that mess and found an easier garden to steal from. But Bishop believed a devious one had outsmarted his bunny block, and he was on a mission to catch him.

One morning, as I was waking up, I watched through my window as Bishop tiptoed out to the garden. He had tried to convince me the day before that the bunny had figured out how to hop up and unlatch the gate. Faith was to blame for that one. She'd left the gate open one night after sneaking a handful of snap peas. Bishop didn't like her in the garden because she didn't watch where she stepped, so he was always chasing her out.

I should have told Bishop that Faith was the culprit, but it was hilarious watching him surveil the yard from behind the woodshed, darting out every time he thought the bunny was approaching. I about fell off my bed laughing when a stray cat wandered into the picture!

My gardening lessons were going as planned. I was learning, and Bishop's broken heart was mending. Although I wasn't great at the water bucket challenge. Instead, I sang "Mary, Mary, Quite Contrary" while he watered. Bishop didn't sing, but his face would light up once I started.

"How does your garden grow, Bishop?" I'd sing.

"With silver bells, Miss Sloane," he'd say.

Toward the end of August, he was showing me how to transplant strawberry runners so they'd be ready to thrive in the spring. But as he reached out to grab one, he reared back and shouted, "Big bug!"

I stepped closer to see it, but all I saw was the last of his vibrant red strawberries with perfectly plumped mini seeds. I told him there wasn't a bug on his strawberries, but he didn't believe me.

"Big bug! Big bug! Big bug!"

He was having a full-on conniption, pantomiming the sheer size of the bug with his hands. It apparently rivaled the girth of our entire solar system.

He grabbed hold of a shovel leaning against the fence and swooshed it above his head like a warrior assuming a battle stance. I had to stop the insanity before he gutted all our remaining strawberries, so I hovered my hand over one of the larger berries and balled it into a fist, pretending I'd grabbed a hold of the giant bug. I conjured my best baseball throw and hurled the imaginary insect over the side of the picket fence toward the cooking fire. He crooked his head over the fence to verify that the bug met a fiery death, lowered the shovel, and leaned it back against the fence, then started pointing out where to divide the strawberry runners.

This was by far the most dramatic of Bishop's episodes that I'd witnessed, and my concern grew over how real the bug was to him. For him it was threatening enough to warrant protecting us with a garden shovel.

As time passed, Bishop's pain over losing LeLe lessened. Mine did as well. It's amazing how a little earth between your fingertips can cleanse your mental state. That's why my gardens have always been so important to me and why every house we've lived in has had one. It's not about the flavorful tomatoes bursting in your mouth, although I love their seedy explosion. It's about leaving your troubles in the dirt and turning them into something glorious. Gardens became a safe space for me to retreat, and I will always have Bishop to thank for showing me that.

It's Jesus!

SLOANE, 1953
ALABAMA

FOR THE NEXT FIVE YEARS, Momma raised us the best she could. We ended up staying in Riverton much longer than anyone expected, as we fell into a rhythm that met everyone's needs, but not necessarily their wants.

Momma spent her days juggling the cooking and canning while helping me and Faith with our schoolwork and keeping tabs on Bishop. He never strayed far from the house, but occasionally he'd take too long coming back from the post office. Momma would get to worrying and venture out to ensure he was okay. She'd find him in a neighboring yard looking at the flowers or petting the goats through the fence.

Every day, at about the same time, Bishop would walk to the post office and pick up our mail. Everyone in town knew his routine and could set their watch by it. We had a mailbox at the house, but Bishop had few sources of pride. Momma didn't want to take one away from him. Plus, it kept him busy for at least an hour.

The postmaster, whom I'd nicknamed Mr. Pink, knew to keep our mail separate from delivery. He had bright rouge cheeks perched atop a long snowy beard, like the bitterness of winter had frosted his gaunt face. He was a friendly man but could look ghostly behind the counter of our dimly lit post office. So calling him Mr. Pink, the least scary of colors, kept me from seizing up whenever he approached. Bishop thought my nickname for him was funny, so he called him Mr. Pink, too, just not to his face.

The exchange of outgoing for incoming mail was usually smooth, but there was one day when Bishop had one of his dramatic episodes. And thank God for Mr. Pink having the kindness in his heart to let it go. Bishop walked inside and slid our outgoing mail into the slot, then waited in line to pick up the incoming mail as he normally did.

When he got to the counter, Mr. Pink greeted him. "I'm sorry, Bishop, you don't have any new mail today," he said.

Well, that was the second day in a row of no new mail, and Bishop became suspicious Mr. Pink was hiding our mail from him. Wanting to see for himself, Bishop tried to go behind the counter. And it was like a switch inside him flipped.

"Gimme my mail, Pink! I know you got it." Bishop said as he rattled the locked gate against the latch to the point of almost breaking it. Other patrons backed away in fright, unsure how to calm Bishop down. And why he was calling our postmaster the color pink.

Mr. Pink kept a cool head and improvised, hurrying to grab a vacation postcard he'd received that morning from his daughter. He'd intended to hang it on the wall with the others she'd sent him but hadn't yet gotten the chance.

"Oh, Bishop, I'm so sorry. Here. You *do* have mail today," he said.

Bishop's demeanor switched from crazed to calm in an instant as he gently took the postcard and politely walked out. Mr. Pink sat down on his work stool behind the counter, relieved Bishop had left. From then on, Mr. Pink kept a stack of postcards behind the counter in case he needed to give one to Bishop in lieu of mail. They were duplicates of postcards he collected as he and his wife took road trips around the Gulf and East Coast. He even wrote amusing messages on them in case Bishop read them.

"Have a great day, Bishop." "Might rain tomorrow, if we're lucky." "You grow the best tomatoes in town, Bishop." Things like that. Momma got a kick out of them and tacked them to the back of the kitchen door, right above our growth-chart hash marks. She had quite the collection going, and I remember thinking one day I would visit every single destination on those postcards when I was older.

By then, I had become accustomed to Bishop's quirks. He'd occasionally throw in a new one, but his normal behavior became part of my life, too, and I no longer found him strange. Faith still considered him an odd duck, though, and continued to avoid him.

Momma couldn't go anywhere without Bishop attached. She was his sister, but when LeLe passed, she transitioned into a motherly role. He was twenty-eight years old, but he would never thrive on his own. He needed a protector and a provider to survive his rudimentary life, and that's exactly who Momma became, alongside Papa T, of course.

Sometimes Bishop's quirks created an issue, though. If you tried to sit next to Momma at church, Bishop would stop and stand in front of you, blocking everyone else from filing in until you moved so *he* could sit next to her. More than once, Faith tested him. And each time, she lost.

Car rides were similar. Bishop insisted on sitting in the front with Momma, squishing her between him and Papa T, with her purse in her lap. Meanwhile, Faith and I had a couple of arms' length between us in the back, with Osee in between us as a buffer, which was probably for the best, since we picked at each other so much.

Bishop didn't have a lot of friends. He helped ladies carry their bags and exchanged pleasantries, but there was only one person Bishop ever visited with. Momma said his best friend, Jack Junior, left for the army right after high school. But for years after Bishop's fall, Junior came to the house every week at the same time to visit with Bishop. He talked about the girls in high school and the car motor he was rebuilding, and Bishop would listen to Junior for as long as he stayed.

The doctors had said Bishop may never remember what happened the day he fell, and they never tried to remind him of it. Papa T had allowed Junior back into the house because he was a God-fearing man and believed Junior needed to be given the chance to atone for his part in Bishop's accident.

Momma said that's indeed what Junior did. Call it atoning, call it guilt, call it whatever you want. The fact was, Bishop and Junior both got something they needed from their visits, and that's all that mattered.

It confused Bishop when Junior no longer showed up to visit, though Momma explained it to him multiple times before his departure. For weeks after Junior left, Bishop would wander out to the porch and wait for him. Momma would remind him Junior couldn't come over and visit, and Bishop would get up to go fill his time. And eventually, he stopped waiting.

When Momma told me that story, I understood another one of Bishop's quirks I'd witnessed that made no sense to me. Occasionally, I'd see him venture out to the porch, sit down and look around, then go back inside not a minute later. I figured he'd changed his mind about sitting on the porch and left to go elsewhere around the house. But after all this time, he was still checking to see if his only friend was out there, and it kind of broke my heart.

Faith and her friends hung out in town every day during that summer of 1953, and when Bishop passed by them for his daily post office duties, he usually ignored their stares and juvenile comments. But one day, as he exited the post office holding a stack of mail, he saw a boy's arm draped over Faith's shoulder. He dropped the mail on the ground and walked straight to them, grabbed that boy's arm, and flung it off Faith's shoulder.

"Bishop, stop that! This is Royce, my boyfriend! Now you apologize to him right now."

Bishop stood tall with a puffed chest, glaring at Royce.

Well, Royce was a sixteen-year-old brat whose daddy owned half the buildings in town, and he didn't take kindly to anyone disrespecting his prestigious existence. His temper flared as he taunted Bishop. "What's wrong, slow boy? Can't remember how to apologize?" Royce said.

Faith's friends started laughing and looked at her to make sure she was too. Bishop grabbed her by the wrist and pulled her away.

"Stop it, Bishop! I'm not going with you!" Faith pushed on his wrist to break his grip, but Bishop kept pulling her down the street as her friends laughed hysterically.

Once he'd gotten her a safe distance away, he stopped and let her go. "He's not a nice one, Faith."

Bishop turned and headed back toward the house. Mr. Pink saw the whole thing from inside the post office and went outside to pick our mail up off the ground. Faith wrote off his behavior as another thing he didn't understand, but what *she* didn't understand was that Bishop had seen Royce with his arm around other girls in town, two that week alone. Faith was too smitten to realize Bishop was, yet again, trying to save her.

From that moment on, Faith's world revolved around Royce. He never came to the house, and Faith claimed it was because of Bishop. But it was because Royce was a coward. He pretended he wasn't scared of Bishop, but he was. People like Royce scare easily over what they don't understand. So instead, he talked Faith into sneaking out to see him. Only she wasn't very good at it.

Momma would catch her trying to climb back in her window and ground her, but she ignored her punishment. So Momma got creative. She hid her shoes before bedtime, so if Faith snuck out, she'd have to walk barefoot. Or she'd lock Faith's window so she couldn't get back in, and Faith would have to try opening the door without jingling the doorbell. Faith may have been smart, but she was no match for Momma.

I DISLIKED ROYCE AS MUCH as Bishop did because he took Faith's attention away from playing with me and Osee. She missed out on some of the funniest stories that happened as we grew up, and I know she later regretted all the energy she gave to Royce instead of us.

I was twelve that summer, and every day she could, Momma would take me to swim at the old locks. It was the place to be. All my friends were there with their mommas and siblings, and we spent all day swimming and relaxing on our blankets. I had the cutest blue-and-white checkered bathing suit with a matching wide-brim sun hat that stood out among the sea of yellow beach umbrellas.

Osee liked to chase the gulls and dig holes to fill with water and then come running up onto my blanket, getting it all sandy. He thought it was funny when I screamed and jumped up to shake out my blanket, and he'd run through the flying sand with his eyes closed as if it were a front yard sprinkler.

For lunch, the ladies made french-fried potatoes over the barbeque pit and served them to us in a cone made from newspaper. We'd wash them down with jars of sun tea and top off our sugar tanks with pies in every flavor you can imagine.

After lunch, the ladies rested under the shade trees away from the water's edge and watched to make sure we didn't swim out too far or that Osee didn't follow us. They gossiped about the latest rumors and planned out whatever the next big church event was in between interruptions from the gaggle of kids they'd claimed responsibility for that day.

One day, J. B., one of the older kids, found an old canoe in the bushes and paddled it out to an old lock that was barely peeking out of the water. J. B. had stringy dark hair, much longer than boys typically wore in those days. Well, he climbed onto that lock with his feet level with the waterline, then stood up super straight with his hands frozen in prayer position, waiting for one of us to notice. Of course, it had to be me who did.

"It's Jesus! Momma, it's Jesus! He's walkin' on the water!" I called out as I jumped up from my beach blanket.

The ladies stood to see what I was clamoring about. They didn't come right away, so I ran to get them.

"I'm not playin'; it's Jesus! He's come back! He's out there walkin' on the water!"

Momma laughed as I practically dragged her into the gentle surf. "Now, Sloane, what I tell you about tellin' these stories?"

She did a double-take when she looked where I was pointing. The ladies saw, too, and scurried across the blistering sand, then splashed into the water.

"I suwannee, Sloane's right. It's Jesus out there walking on water!" one of them squealed in delight, clapping her hands together like she just made bingo.

"He has risen!" another called out as she held her hand to her forehead, on the verge of an overly dramatic faint.

They were beside themselves. The day they'd sung about had finally arrived. Proof their Sundays weren't wasted, and He'd heard every blessing. Not only had He risen, but He chose *them* as His witnesses. More *amen*s and *hallelujah*s flew across that beach than Baptists at a hoecake feed, and I was pretty sure my seeing Jesus first had catapulted me to rock-star status.

But it was hard to pull one over on Miss Patsy. "Grace, you see that old canoe next to Jesus?" she said. "And doesn't that Jesus look a bit like J. B.?"

They both fell out laughing, and J. B. heard them. He clapped his hands up over his head, applauding himself in victory. He had fooled us all! Well, most of us, anyway. He paddled that old canoe back to shore and was still laughing as he landed.

"I wasn't sure anyone noticed me, but then I saw all the runnin'!"

I LOVED OUR DAYS AT the river. When I wasn't there, I was usually four hills over at my cousin Mary Ruth's house in Lane Springs or off with my best friend, Norm. That was her nickname, short for Norma. She and I ended up going to nursing school together, and we were thick as thieves growing up. If you invited one of us somewhere, the other would be in tow.

One day, Elsie Jo, a friend from school, invited some classmates to her house for an end-of-the-summer party. She lived on an old tobacco plantation that was supposedly haunted by the ghosts of Confederate soldiers, and I was hoping to find one.

We wandered the grounds, pretending to be the local socialites dressed in fancy hoop skirts and carrying parasols as we strolled on the arms of our dashing husbands. They puffed away on their freshly rolled tobacco cigarettes and bragged about who had the most wealth.

Inside the main house, we glided down the ornate staircase and sipped lemonade from champagne glasses as we danced our way through the ballroom-size foyer. We were having a grand time until I ruined it by spinning Norm a tad too hard, throwing her catawampus as she stumbled toward the staircase. She hit the knee wall and crashed right through it!

We panicked at the heap of trouble we were in, expecting bedroom banishment for the last days of summer. A few kids scattered to the parlor and hid. Elsie Jo just stood there with her mouth open. It wasn't until after I helped Norm up from the floor that I saw what Elsie Jo was gaping at. Norm didn't go through the wall; she fell through a doorway. Someone had wallpapered over the opening, which led to a hidden room under the stairs.

Elsie Jo's momma had heard the commotion and was heading our way up the front hall. She gasped, then shooed us away so she could see inside. We peered in around her in any open space we fit. From inside the room, she must have looked like a lady with eight heads.

Venturing into the small room, we found a rolltop desk with a wood chair pushed under it and a hurricane oil lamp sitting on top. A coat peg was affixed to the wall. Lying on the desk was a leather-bound ledger with a cord tied around it. Elsie Jo's momma picked it up and unwrapped the cord. She read the first few entries and realized that the ledger contained records from the Civil War.

She said the room was an office once belonging to the plantation's overseer. His job would have required managing the tobacco production and enslaved field hands. Mixed in with the record of deaths and births were the happenings on and around the plantation that he'd meticulously recorded. His words shed light on what it took to operate the business and the tasks the people forced to work there performed.

We spent the rest of that afternoon in the parlor, with Elsie Jo's momma reading the ledger to us. Scattered throughout were heartbreaking accounts of families torn apart and the North's invasion of Confederate homes, of women forced to feed and shelter the very soldiers their husbands and sons fought against, and of poor men, whose only motivation for fighting was to protect their homes and loved ones, not preserving the way of life for rich white land barons.

But the most interesting record was about how one of Norm's war hero relatives stumbled onto the plantation and died in one of the back fields. It was a story her family had passed down for generations, and she knew it well.

In the family's account, their soldier died in a sacrifice of honor. The only way to stop the Yankees from attacking his unit was to reload and fire a cannon, and he had only seconds to do it. But if the embers from the previous fire aren't completely extinguished, you risk the charge exploding upon reloading. And that's exactly what happened. As the soldier rolled the shell into the barrel, it exploded and ripped off his right arm. The shell still hit the Yanks and saved his twenty Confederate brothers from perishing, but he bled out while seeking help in the nearby plantation field.

His untimely death was tragic, for sure, but it didn't happen as the family said. The overseer's ledger confirmed their soldier stumbled onto a back field for help, but it was because he had the mumps, which commonly plagued the front lines. He collapsed and died of fever and dehydration—not in an act of heroics—staring up at the enslaved faces at the very core of the war itself. I suppose his family, stricken by grief over an uninspiring loss, gave him the legacy they thought he deserved.

Elsie Jo's mother gifted the overseer's ledger to a museum a few towns over. For years it was on display behind a glass case, but we were part of an elite few who got to read the compelling details. The families it chronicled lived a harsh life, and the last thing they needed was their legacies tarnished. So we promised each other not to divulge the secrets the ledger held, and to this day, I've mostly kept my word.

When I got home, I couldn't help myself. I didn't spill details, but I told Momma and Faith about the ledger's existence and the hidden room in Elsie Jo's house. Bishop came in a few minutes after I started talking, so he missed the part about the hidden room being under *Elsie Jo's* stairs.

A while later, I heard him outside on the front porch steps knocking on the wood treads. He was calling out, "Hello?" and then mumbling words I couldn't make out. I swear he was having a full-on conversation with someone he believed was in a hidden room under *our* porch steps.

I knew better, but I couldn't help myself. I snuck around and hid under an overgrown camellia next to the steps. When Bishop knocked and called, "Hello," I answered.

"Quiet, Bishop, I'm taking a nap!"

He flipped into a tizzy, yelping as he slipped off the step he was sitting on and bounced off each one below it before hitting the dirt at the bottom. Momma came out and heard me giggling away in the bush. She didn't think it was funny, and neither did Bishop. He stormed off and ignored me for the rest of the night.

Momma was so mad she gave me extra chores the next day, the ones she saved up for punishment. And her choice couldn't have been more fitting. As I was repainting the front porch steps, Bishop watched, grinning in satisfaction as he slowly rocked and snacked on an apple he sliced with his pocketknife.

The Piano Key

SLOANE, 1953
ALABAMA

AS THE DOG DAYS OF summer came to an end, I spent hours in the kitchen helping Momma can fruit for the pies she planned to bake for Papa T's retirement party in the spring. Perfecting her piecrust was also of utmost importance. We must have baked twenty pies before Momma settled on the perfect ratio of butter and Crisco. Momma didn't have a competitive bone in her body, except when it came to pie. Hers had to be the best ones on the dessert table. And her competition? Miss Patsy, Riverton's reigning pie champion for four years running. Course, Miss Patsy's husband was the mayor... and a pie judge...so I think there may have been some favoritism going on there. Her pies certainly were good, though. Can't argue with that.

Between growing it, cooking it, canning it, or eating it, a lot about my childhood revolved around food. My favorite was growing, thanks in part to Bishop teaching me how.

Our garden was nature's grocery store, and pole beans were my pride and joy. There was something cathartic about sitting on the porch with a bowl on my lap, popping beans out of their long purple pods while listening to the white noise of the river branch.

Sometimes Bishop would come out with a bowl and help. One day, he grabbed a handful of beans from my pile. I smiled to let him know I appreciated the extra hands, but as usual, he didn't smile back. He just started shelling, taking time to stop and admire overly long pods.

Suddenly he did something I'd never heard him do; he laughed. Not a giggle or a snicker, but a full-on, belly-grabbing laugh. A bean had gotten away from him and fallen on the floor. Out of nowhere, he snorted and laughed so loud it startled me. I wasn't sure what to do, so I started laughing too. He said a few garbled words to the bean, then stopped mid-laugh. So I stopped laughing too.

We continued shelling our beans in silence, with that one still on the floor. I wanted to pick it up before someone walked through and squished it. It was the strangest thing he'd done since the secret room under the porch steps fiasco, and if I'd learned anything from that, it was that I needed to leave that bean right where it was.

It'd been a fun-filled summer with the legendary stories of J. B. Jesus and the hidden ledger, but Faith and I were ready to get back to school. I was starting seventh grade and had been placed at a higher math level than most of my classmates, and I was excited to have the best teacher at our school, Miss

Maybelle. She and her sister, Maudie, lived next door to each other a few blocks from my house. I had exchanged seedlings with them before, and Maudie ran the summer reading program at the little library, so she knew me well.

Faith was entering her junior year, and all she cared about was her popularity status. She'd fallen completely in love with Royce by that point and knew he was her ticket to being accepted into the cool kid's club. She wrapped her entire persona around him and spent all her free time doing whatever cockamamie things he and his friends dreamed up.

More than once, Faith had to be picked up from the police station. She had a hard time escaping the collateral damage when whatever prank her friends played went wrong. It was never a serious offense, and the sheriff always let Faith off with a warning.

There was one time, though, when Bishop caught her sneaking out of the house. She told me about it the next day after I asked her why she'd gotten extra chores. Once Royce was sure everyone had gone to bed, he tapped on her window. She opened it, and Royce helped her out, but Bishop heard them. He may have retreated to his room every night at bedtime, but he was an insomniac and functioned on very little sleep.

Faith was so upset, telling me how it wasn't her fault and that she couldn't possibly ignore Royce. He was drunk, and she was afraid he'd wake everyone up, so she went outside for only a second to convince him to go home. Well, they ended up making out in the backseat of Royce's car. Bishop flung open the door, grabbed Royce by the hair, and dragged him onto the ground. Faith started screaming at Bishop as Royce scampered back into his car and sped away, flinging pebbles at the side of the house as he peeled out. It caused such a commotion it woke Momma and Papa T.

I slept through the whole thing, and while I usually reveled in watching Faith get into trouble, I felt sad for her. She still didn't see Bishop was trying to save her from that troublemaker. Instead, she worried Royce would exile her and she'd lose all her friends. Well, he didn't break up with her. But he never tried to sneak Faith out of the house again, either.

MOMMA WAS RELIEVED SCHOOL WAS around the corner so her house would quiet down. On the eve of our first day, I was dressing for bed, ridding my hair of the day's tangles. In my bedroom stood an antique white vanity dresser with a big circle mirror in the middle and drawers to either side. Little pink flowers had been stenciled above the brass handles that clinked against a strike plate as you let them go.

It was my nightly routine to sit at my vanity and prepare my thoughts for the next day. I fantasized about my first day back at school as my hairbrush ripped through snarls, and I wondered what book reports I'd get assigned or if I'd get to sit next to Norm. We'd been separated the year before for talking too much. Mostly, I was looking forward to having Miss Maybelle for pre-algebra. At the same time, I was nervous I'd be the youngest in the class, since our school taught kindergarten through twelfth grade. I could outwit the upperclassmen any day of the week and twice on Sunday, but they had a leg (or two) up on me in size.

I saw my bedroom door opening in the mirror's reflection and thought it was Momma coming in to tell me goodnight, but it was Bishop. He paused in the doorway and stared at me.

"What's up, Bish-*op*?" I asked, singsong.

He said nothing as he lifted his arm, cradling Papa T's BB gun.

"Bishop! What are you doing?" I screamed as I ducked my head into my lap.

He fired once and hit my vanity mirror, shattering it into a million pieces. Shards rained down around me and hit my bare feet as I squeezed my eyes tightly shut. After the tinging of the glass stopped, I peeked through a gap at my elbow to see if he'd gone. I saw Momma behind Bishop, struggling to pull his arm toward the floor. Then Faith tugged the gun from Bishop's hand. I scurried to hide on the other side of my bed, piercing my feet with each step.

Papa T grabbed Bishop, wringing his shirt at the shoulders as he pulled him into the hall. Momma came and crouched on the floor, rocking me as I wailed. She had no explanation to give as she stroked the hair from my face.

I heard Papa T's car barrel out of the driveway. Momma looked out the window to confirm Bishop was with him, then she checked on Osee to make sure he had not awoken during the chaos that just unfolded. I could hear Faith crying in the bathroom down the hall, opening and closing drawers and cupboards and blowing her nose in between.

I stayed curled in a ball, shaking, trying to remember what I'd done to make Bishop want to shoot my mirror. But nothing was worthy of such revenge. So why? Why did he shoot my mirror? Or did he mean to shoot *me*?

Faith came in and handed first-aid supplies to Momma. As she tweezed the splinters from my toes and wrapped them in gauze, she finally spoke, chalking up what happened to a misunderstanding.

"Nothing else makes sense," Momma said. "It's no excuse, but something must have happened in the last few days to upset Bishop. Think, Sloane. Did you trick him again?"

"No, I swear, Momma. Everything was fine the last time I saw him."

"I'm not sure how I can let him back in this house," Momma said.

"Good!" said Faith. "He's dangerous, and I'm not living here anymore if you let him come back."

For once, Momma didn't take Bishop's side and tell Faith to stop, to take back her words. She didn't tell Faith she was being emotional and that Bishop didn't mean to cause harm. She didn't say any of those things. For the first time in her life, it seemed, Momma was afraid Bishop *was* dangerous.

Momma slept with me in my bed that night, and when I woke the next morning, Faith was lying on the floor next to us, asleep. She'd dragged in the couch cushions to build a makeshift mattress on the mirror-free side of the bed and was lying halfway off them with her hair flung over her face.

Papa T had taken Bishop to the same hospital that had treated him after his fall. The doctors examined him and kept him for observation. When Papa T returned home that morning, he said Bishop had told him why he'd shot my mirror. He wasn't trying to kill me. Or even hurt me. He said Faith told him to shoot my mirror.

Faith swore to everything holy that Bishop was lying and that she was in her room the whole time. That was true too. We were both in her room before it happened, choosing our first-day-of-school outfits. Plus, Faith was just as scared as I was. So Bishop's explanation left more questions than it gave answers.

Momma assured us it would be okay and to not worry. A little hard to do when all you keep imagining is your vanity mirror shattering all around you. But Bishop was staying at the hospital until the doctors sorted out what happened, so at least I didn't fear him coming home that day. Or even that week. As Momma sent us off to school after we'd nibbled at our breakfast, she came out and trailed behind us. I think she just needed to make sure we were okay.

We weren't.

I shuffled along the road to the bus stop with Faith and Osee, who was silent as a church mouse. Even the river branch couldn't calm my nerves. Faith was right. I was unsure how I could live in that house if Bishop was living there too. Daddy was due back the following day, and I was sure he would never let Bishop return if it wasn't safe. That gave me some comfort.

As I stepped up into the hull of the school bus, its stench hit me like a sweaty sock slingshot to my face. My lungs strained in the heavy air as I plopped myself onto a seat I never sat in. I pushed in the window latches and slid the top pane down, hovering my face in the morning breeze like a dog on a car ride. It was the only thing keeping me from throwing up the apple Momma had insisted I eat half of at breakfast.

Momma tasked me, not Faith, with making sure Osee got to his kindergarten room. I needed to pull myself together for him. I'd been his protector since the day he was born, and I couldn't fail him now. I blocked out the ruckus ricocheting around me and focused on Daddy's return, homing in on anticipating whatever fun surprise he'd bring me from Huntsville. A pittance of hope, but my meditation was working. The apple felt content to remain in my stomach, and as I relaxed into the seat, I noticed Faith and Osee jammed in next to me. Osee sometimes sat by me. But Faith? Never.

The bus's brakes squealed to a lurching stop. Osee trotted on into his classroom, ready to play, so I continued down the hall to my homeroom. I milled outside the door, pumping myself up to enter as if I were a boxer about to go twelve rounds. And for the first time in what felt like days, I finally caught a break. My seating assignment was right behind Norm's.

I came home exhausted from my day of fake enthusiasm. I told no one but my diary about what had happened, embarrassed I had been a part of something so chaotic. Momma had cleaned up the broken mirror pieces I had gingerly avoided that morning while getting dressed. My feet still stung from the nicks, and the floorboards had not yet dried from Momma mopping up my smudged trail. I was thankful she had, because before I left for school that morning, it looked like a cornucopia of bleeding slugs had invaded my room.

I heard a door slam in the hallway and then Faith crying in her room.

"Faith? Can I come in?" I knocked gently on her door.

"Go away, Sloane," she said.

I turned to go back to my room.

"Okay, fine," Faith said, changing her mind.

I sat down on her bed next to her feet. "Are you still upset about what happened?"

"Royce told everyone what Bishop did, and now I'm the laughingstock of the eleventh grade. My best girlfriend wouldn't let me sit next to her at lunch. She acted all dramatic, holding up her shaking hands as if scared of me, begging me not to have Bishop shoot her. The entire table laughed at me, and when I looked at Royce, he wouldn't even look back. What kind of boyfriend tells all your friends something you told him in confidence?"

I thought it best not to answer that question. "I'm sorry, Faith. Your friends should never have done that."

Faith threw her pillow at the picture of Royce on her dresser and knocked it over. "Never get a boyfriend, Sloane. They'll just disappoint you. But you know, none of this would have happened if Bishop wasn't such a retard."

"Faith! Momma told us not to use that word." I got up and retrieved her pillow.

"Yeah, well, it's true. He's a God damned disaster, Sloane. And we have to suffer for it. I hope he never comes back home."

If I'm being honest, I didn't want him to come home, either. I went back to my room and lay down to rest my weary eyes, and the moment I sunk my head into the pillow, I noticed my missing reflection. I had adored that vanity. Now it was ruined, just like my feelings for Bishop. And I still didn't understand why he did it. Or why he lied and said Faith told him to do it. There was no logical reason for any of it to have happened. I had done nothing to upset him, and neither had anyone else that I knew of. I kept playing it over in my head, angered he'd put so much conflict inside me and Faith right before we were to start a fun new school year.

Just as I shut my eyes, I heard Daddy's car pull in, and I bounced back awake. Papa T took him to the kitchen, so I snuck out to the front room to eavesdrop. When Papa T got to the part about Faith grabbing the BB gun from Bishop after he fired it, I emerged from the corner and had a fit. A literal fit.

"How can any of you be okay with all these guns lying around?" I screamed. "If you don't lock them up, I'm going to take every single one and throw them in the big river!"

"Now, Sloane—" Momma started before Papa T cut her off.

"No, Grace, Sloane's right. We can't risk Bishop getting hold of another gun."

In a display of solidarity, Papa T retrieved his revolver from his nightstand. Several in boxes on the upper shelves of his closet. And the shotgun mounted above the kitchen door, along with its shells lining the top of the doorframe. He laid them out on the kitchen table, next to the BB gun, which was usually leaned against the corner by the back kitchen door in case Papa T needed to scare off any wildlife intruders.

I hadn't realized Papa T had so many revolvers and rifles. I don't think he did either until he took inventory. He was always picking them up at yard sales, proving there was no shortage of widows willing to make a deal because she no longer wanted her dead husband's guns in her house. He kept a few loaded for protection, and we knew not to touch them. But mostly he found their manufacturing and history to be interesting.

Papa T and Daddy took the guns to the front room, and with me and Faith watching, loaded them into a cedar cabinet that had two rifles already in it, along with ammo boxes resting on the bottom. Then Papa T locked the double doors.

"Sloane...Faith...there's only one key to this cabinet," he said as he held it up for us to see. "And you're going to help me hide it. Sloane, grab an envelope from my desk."

I crossed the front room, slid up the cover to his rolltop desk, and grabbed an envelope from the stack in the center cubby. "Here you go," I said as I handed it to him.

"Thanks—wait, swap it for one without a stamp already on it," he said, handing it back to me.

As I did, he asked Faith to retrieve his roll of tape, also on his desk. I could have grabbed it as well, but I think he wanted us both to be part of the process.

"Sloane, you put the key in the envelope, and Faith, you seal it," he instructed.

Faith licked the edges of the flap and sealed it, smacking her tongue at the bitter gum, then handed it to Papa T. He lifted the hinged top of the piano sitting next to the cedar cabinet and taped the sealed envelope to the underside. All four edges, so it was securely stuck.

"No one is to discuss where the key is hidden, and the piano top is to remain closed at all times. Come get me or your momma if you want to check on the key, okay?"

"Yes, sir," I said.

Faith looked at Papa T inquisitively. "Papa T? Maybe we should put something on top of the piano? Make it harder for Bishop to just lift it up. If for some reason he wanted to."

"Sure, we can do that, Faith. But I'll leave the decorating up to Grace."

"Angels," Momma said. "It's the perfect place for my angels." She laid down a lace table runner and filled it with her collection of angel figurines, which were scattered around the front room. A porcelain security system, of sorts.

I felt safe from future gunfire, but at some point, I still had to face Bishop when he returned home. And from that, I did not feel safe.

THREE MONTHS LATER, PAPA T pulled into the driveway, and Bishop stepped out of the car. He headed straight for the garden, no doubt to check on the pumpkins he'd planted before the mirror incident.

"Sloane, where's Faith?" Papa T asked as he came in.

"Over at Royce's," I said.

"Okay, I'll fill her in later. Sit down with me. I want to explain some things now that Bishop is back."

"Okay," I said hesitantly.

"He's on a medicine called chlorpromazine, meant to keep him levelheaded. His doctors said the damage from his fall all those years ago had slowly developed into schizophrenia."

"Schizowhat?"

"Schizophrenia. Now listen, Sloane. It's a serious disease. The doctors don't think his case is that bad, but without this medicine, his brain will confuse facts. Make him believe things that aren't true. And his vivid imagination could trick him into believing something he sees is real when it's not. So he has to take chlorpromazine every day for it to work."

I remembered that day shelling beans and how he laughed and talked to the one that fell on the floor. And then it occurred to me—it wasn't just the bean. He'd been showing signs of schizophrenia for a while, but nobody picked up on it.

Accusing Postmaster Pink of hiding our mail. The old biddies at the beauty shop, gossiping and whispering about him. The big bug on his strawberries. His paranoia about the bunnies sneaking into the garden. The person in the hidden room under the porch stairs. And saying Faith told him to shoot my mirror when she hadn't.

After months of anguish, the underlying reason for all of it came to light. His schizophrenia was to blame. He wasn't trying to kill me. He wasn't trying to frame Faith. He was, however, mentally ill. Which caused my anxiety to skyrocket.

Bishop came in from the garden and walked straight over to me. I didn't look up from the table, fearing what was next. I felt my fingernails dig into my palms.

"Sorry 'bout your mirror, Sloane. I'll clean it up."

I ignored him and let Momma tell him she'd already done it. It had been three months, after all. He spoke more clearly, which was promising, but I wasn't ready to forgive him just yet.

Pastor Douglas had said during Sunday service that forgiveness was the key to a happy life. This was my first big test of it. I'd never had to forgive anyone for something this big before. Usually, it was for little things Faith did, like hiding the book I was reading or chasing the river ducks away while I was feeding them. Forgiving her for things like that was easy compared to the forgiving I needed to give Bishop.

The garden was the best place I could think of to start. It's where Bishop and I had always connected. So, after I watched him take his medicine every morning for a week, I made two glasses of lemonade and headed out to the garden. I gave the gate a wiggle to let him know I was coming in, then offered him a glass. He hesitated a moment before thanking me and telling me the brussels sprouts were looking good. It was late November, so there wasn't much growing. Just a ton of cleanup I'd fallen behind on while Bishop was in the hospital.

It was difficult for me to make that first move, but Pastor Douglas was right. The healing began the instant I crossed under the gate trellis.

That winter was brutally cold, and our brussels sprouts and onions didn't fare too well. I spent most of the season inside reading and singing while I played the piano. Sometimes I'd think about the envelope taped inside and feel nervous, imagining it would fall and cause the sound to muffle and Bishop would figure out why.

And So I Ran

SLOANE, 1954
ALABAMA

THINGS HAD SETTLED DOWN AT home. Faith and I were in the back half of our school year, and Bishop was acting as normal as he could. My fear of him still lingered, but I had moved past my anger. Schoolwork took precedence, and I had no spare time to dwell. I prided myself on my straight As, working hard for the one in pre-algebra. It wasn't as intuitive as I'd hoped, but it was still my favorite subject because of Miss Maybelle.

I was becoming closer to her and her sister, Maudie, and frequently helped them with their bulletin boards after school. They loved my creative ideas, and in return, Miss Maybelle would give me private math lessons because she knew I was struggling. Maudie, let me help choose the book lists for the library's reading programs.

I was also busy helping Momma ramp up preparations for Papa T's big retirement party. Every morning, before he left for work, he'd tell us how many days he had left. "Thirty-four more days until I'm officially old," he'd say.

The countdown continued—twenty-seven, then fifteen, until finally, it was one. Papa T had just left the house for his last day of work when Daddy pulled in. That evening, they headed to a poker party and didn't come home until the wee hours. Momma seemed annoyed but let them sleep in a little extra the next morning while we packed the car.

We ate a light breakfast and headed to Rose Trail Park to set up. Gracing the hillside overlooking the big river, the park's borders overflowed with its namesake runnin' roses—the same breed of roses I looked after in our front yard as I'd promised LeLe I would. As I scanned the ground for rocks to weigh down napkins, I wondered if there were still some heirlooms buried beneath them. Still hiding from the ghosts of Union soldiers.

Ladies brought their tablecloths from home and spread a festive hodgepodge of flowers, stripes, checks, and polka dots that popped under the spring sky. To lure the birds and bees from the buffet table, we decorated trees with popcorn garlands and hung soda bottles infused with maple syrup.

As guests arrived, they placed their tightly wrapped casserole dishes and bowls of ambrosia salads and crisp coleslaws on the table. Daddy had brought in smoked ribs and ham from Huntsville, and Papa T couldn't wait to dig in. I'd caught him in the kitchen the night before, sneaking pieces of ham. I demanded two in exchange for my silence, which he happily paid.

It was as if two parties were happening in tandem; one for the adults and one for the kids. We played croquet and hide-and-seek behind the trees, while the adults told the same tired cotton mill stories they'd been regurgitating for years. They basked in the jealousy that Papa T was finally escaping the daily grind and gifted him with a shimmering array of fishing lures. But there were pockets when both parties entwined to enjoy the mayonnaise-laden feast.

Momma's pies were a hit. She had every flavor you could want, even rhubarb. Miss Patsy asked her for the recipes, but Momma was no fool. She had a secret agenda. Papa T's party was a trial run to see which one of her pies everyone raved about most. Then she would enter that pie in Riverton's summer contest and take the championship title from Miss Patsy. The strawberry and cherry were superb, but her peach pie was the clear trial winner. Each bite burst with more flavor than the last, and the fresh whipped cream piled on top was a glorious display of fluffy peaks.

She finally told me years later what her secret was. It wasn't the crust, although it was the moistest, flakiest crust I had ever tasted. It was the fact that she used sweetened canned peaches mixed with enough of Papa T's bourbon that he didn't notice any missing. Miss Patsy ran a dry house, so it hadn't occurred to her to sauce up her peaches a bit. And later that summer, when Momma took the championship title away from Miss Patsy, I giggled as the Holy Rollers raved over how delectable her peach pie was. They had no clue they were sinning!

All of Riverton made their way over to the park to congratulate Papa T, and he thanked each one warmly. Sheriff Hayes, who'd inherited the job from Dossie, even stopped by on his way to the station. He was a hulking linebacker of a man, and it was sweet to see him sit and talk with Bishop.

It was a wonderful celebration, and a much-deserved one too. Papa T had worked at that cotton mill since he was a teenager. It showed me a person could stay in one place their whole life and be perfectly happy. It was the life Papa T wanted, but I knew my path was the opposite. I yearned for the excitement of a metropolis. To see beyond where the Doodlebug train could take me. Even if that meant leaving a world I cherished.

WE CAME HOME EXHAUSTED AND collapsed in the chairs around the cooking fire. Papa T told funny stories about his friends at the mill and teared up at how grateful he was for them and for the family sitting around him. It's a moment I reflect on often, and if someone asked me what home felt like, I would describe that scene to them. Everyone was in a great mood. Papa T was the epitome of relaxed, knowing he didn't have to rise at the crack of dawn the next morning.

As Papa T told his stories, it occurred to me he was surely around when the TVA flooded Riverton, so I asked him if he saw it happen. He did, and he said it was quite the event. The whole town watched from the safety of the hilltop, and although the excitement was palpable, so was the sadness of seeing their town submerged. The town they helped build and called home their whole lives. Papa T said a wealth of history drowned that day, but that one story, in particular, had not met a watery grave.

Papa T sat up straight, and through the dancing flames, he told us the story of Maggie Williams. She was born in 1894 and by all accounts was a beautiful, well-liked young girl. When she was fifteen, she was over in Hog Hollow visiting the Newsom family and fell ill sometime in the afternoon. She complained of a terrible headache and asked to be taken home. Sadly, the next day, the Newsom's learned Maggie had drifted into a deep coma.

The local doctor examined Maggie as she lay still in her bed. She had no pulse and no reaction to reflex tests. As he held a mirror to her nose, the glass did not fog. By his assessment, Maggie was dead.

Embalming was not a practice in 1909, so Maggie's body was bathed, dressed, and looked after until her funeral. The cemetery was full of buggies and wagons. Horses tied to the trees behind Maggie's gravesite painted an eerie backdrop as steam rose from their muzzles.

As Maggie lay still in her coffin inside the little white church, many wondered if she was truly deceased. Her skin lacked the lifeless gray pallor of a corpse, and her frame seemed untouched by rigor mortis. She appeared to be in peaceful slumber, and it rattled those paying their respect—and no one more than the local coroner.

Well, have you ever heard the phrase *dead ringer*? Back then, it was common practice to bury the dead with their hands attached to a safety bell. A night watchman would roam the cemetery, listening for the faintest sound of a bell. And if they heard one ring out, it meant someone was buried alive.

A ringing bell could ruin a coroner's reputation, so the doctor attending to Maggie performed a few more checks to make sure she was *completely* dead.

He pulled a small penknife from his shirt pocket and pricked Maggie's fingertip. No blood dripped from her limp, cold finger. He struck a match and held it to Maggie's palm, which gave nary a shake. The coroner declared Maggie ready for burial but insisted the nightwatchman stay close to her grave and listen for her bell.

For a fortnight, Maggie's bell did not ring. But a few months later, strange things began to happen near her resting place. Maggie's mother commissioned a tall marble tombstone for her grave. It was also customary to plant a rosebush on the graves of the deceased, and Maggie's mother chose the purest shade of white.

That night, as the watchman wandered the aisles of the dead, he noticed a light above Maggie's grave and assumed it was a lantern. He wandered over to see who was visiting at such a bewitching hour. As he approached, the light slowly floated up Maggie's tombstone and disappeared into the darkness above.

In the spring, when the roses were in bloom, every gravesite in the cemetery burst with vivid color. Every site except Maggie's, that is. The tender new leaves had shriveled and fallen to the earth. The branches held no buds or blooms, only thorns. The puny bush looked starved of sun and water, even though Maggie's mother tended to it weekly. She replanted bush after bush, but none made it to bloom.

The nightwatchman wasn't the only one to report seeing the strange light above Maggie's grave. Three hunters followed it into the woods, where it vanished as an owl flew through its path and screeched so loud it spooked their coonhounds. And Mrs. Newsom said she saw the light one night when she stopped by to visit Maggie's grave. As the light slowly traveled up Maggie's tombstone, a faint outline of her face formed in the marble's white veins. Mrs. Newsom stood paralyzed in fear as Maggie's face stared back at her, the light growing brighter. It was almost blinding her when…

"Heavens! What is that?" Papa T's face shuddered as he pointed at the woodshed.

I fell off my chair as a glowing orb slowly traveled up the side of the shed. Faith let out a blood-curdling scream, and Bishop looked the same as he did when he saw that big bug on his strawberries. Momma roared with laughter as Papa T flipped his flashlight in the air and caught it with his other hand, overly satisfied he'd scared us all.

I will never forget the story of Maggie Williams—and not only for the fright Papa T gave me. To this day, people still report seeing a strange light hovering above her grave. I've never seen it myself. But then again, I know better than to wander around cemeteries in the dead of night.

THE NEXT MORNING, DADDY DROVE me, Faith, and Osee to school. I loved riding the school bus, but nothing beat a ride in Daddy's car. Plus, he needed to go into Sheffield to run some errands, so he didn't mind taking us on his way. And when he returned that afternoon, he picked us up from school and took us to the five-and-dime for ice cream and trinkets. Osee got a matchbox car, Faith chose a strawberry lip gloss, and I picked a rhinestone barrette that shone so bright I felt like a glamorous movie star with it clipped into my hair. We felt so spoiled that day. I should have sensed there was a catch.

Before supper, Daddy called everyone to the porch. I was hesitant since he didn't have the greatest track record for announcing good news out there. As Faith and I sat on the porch bed, she leaned over and whispered, "I bet we're about to be big sisters again," which got my hopes up. But she was way off.

Daddy had waited until after Papa T's retirement party to tell us his news. He didn't want to steal any thunder away from his father-in-law's big day. "Everyone, I've taken a new route, as lead engineer for the City of New Orleans train. It runs between New Orleans and Chicago, and I'm pretty excited about the change in scenery. This is a huge promotion for me. For all of us."

"Oh, Hardy!" Momma said as she hugged him. "What a wonderful surprise. When do you start?"

"Day after tomorrow. But there's more," he said.

"Grace, after six years of saving, I have enough money to buy you the new house of your dreams. But it needs to be in New Orleans. It's time to go back, Grace," he said.

"Oh…Hardy. I didn't expect you to say *that*," Momma said.

"Think about it. With Tom retired, he can look after Bishop now. You and the kids can finally come home, just like we'd planned."

Momma's face sank, and the corners of her smile flattened. "It's just that…it feels wrong to leave right now. Papa's only been retired one whole day."

"Grace? You *do* want to move back, don't you?"

"Yes, but—"

"No!" said Bishop. "Her home is here."

Papa T put his hand on Bishop's shoulder. "It's okay, Bishop. Remember what I told you? She was always going to leave, someday."

Bishop looked at Papa T, then at Daddy. He flung open the porch screen door and stomped halfway down the staircase, standing with his back to us.

"Hardy, I'm so proud of you for landing that promotion. But perhaps this is all happening a bit too fast," Papa T said.

"Too fast? Tom, it's been six years…"

I tuned out while they continued discussing. I loved New Orleans, and for the longest time, I'd wanted to move back. This was the moment I'd been waiting years for. At first, eagerly. But I hadn't thought about New Orleans in quite some time.

I remembered the apartment. Its yellow kitchen cabinets and the blue bedroom I shared with Faith. Daddy still lived there. And I remembered the streets of the city. The way one block smelled of boiling crawfish and the next of powdered sugar. And how it took forever to walk anywhere because you had to stop and talk to anyone who was out on their front porch.

Then I realized that, unlike Faith, I hadn't written letters to anyone there. I had no friends to send them to. I was only seven when we left, and it hadn't occurred to me until that moment that the only people I knew in New Orleans lived in Lafayette Cemetery No. 1. The only living soul waiting for me to return was my daddy, and that was enough to make me want to move back.

I wanted to jump up and hug him. Tell him how excited I was for our new house and to be going home. But that's just it. New Orleans was no longer home to me. It may have been the place I was born, and I will always cherish my memories of it, but Riverton is where my heart took root. It's where I learned how to garden and where I learned to survive river branches infested with snake nests and hollows full of things you could hear but not see. It's where I helped Momma perfect her pie recipe. And it's where secrets hidden beneath staircases bonded me forever to the friendships I'd forged. And that was more than enough to make me want to stay.

"I'm not leaving. I refuse!" Faith said suddenly, crossing her arms like a five-year-old being denied cake.

"I thought out of everyone you'd be the happiest," Daddy said.

"Well, you thought wrong!" Faith got up and stormed away. I followed her to her room, where she threw herself onto her bed.

"Sloane, I'm not leaving Royce! I love him!"

"Don't you miss Daddy?" I asked.

She rolled onto her side and pulled a pillow into her face to muffle her blubbering. I felt bad for her, seeing how much pain she was in. Then she kicked at my hand as I squeezed her foot, and I didn't feel so bad for her anymore. I left her there to cry it out, softly shutting her door as I made my escape.

Bishop was sitting in the new recliner Papa T had bought himself as a retirement gift and placed in the spot once occupied by LeLe's makeshift hospital bed. His fingers gripped the varnished chair arms as he chomped his teeth together so loudly I thought he might crack them in half.

"Are you okay, Bishop?" I asked.

He stopped midchomp and looked at me, then got up and paced, carving a pattern through the furniture. "He can't take Grace. She's supposed to live here."

He walked to the window between the front room and porch and fidgeted with the window lock, peering at Daddy as he flipped it back and forth, locking and unlocking it until Papa T came in and snapped at him. "Stop that, Bishop. You're going to wear out the lock."

Bishop glared at Papa T before retreating to his porch rocker, banging it against the side of the house over and over as he pushed against the floor to propel it.

"Hardy, it's time to start supper. Let's give Bishop some space, shall we?" Momma said. "Sloane, you come too."

Daddy poured himself a jar of sweet tea and sat down at the kitchen table. I drained the bowl of hominy soaking on the table, then set out spices to take out to the fire. Momma reminded me how much salt to measure out of the canister. The last time she'd left me in charge of the hominy, it was barely edible.

The three of us ended up outside by the cooking fire, with Daddy and Momma discussing the pros and cons of moving back to New Orleans. They weren't fighting, but their elevated voices took on a tone I'd never heard from them. Like when a political guest on a newscast is trying to convince their counterpart of something, and their voices keep getting louder as each takes a passionate stance on their position.

I kept quiet, stirring the hominy as they talked. And whenever the decision seemed to lean toward New Orleans, Bishop would appear. "Riverton, Hardy. Grace lives here," he'd demand with a firm jaw.

Papa T had another retirement party to attend that night with his friends from the mill. He stopped by the fire on his way out and told Daddy he didn't think pulling us kids out of school when we had only a few months left was the best idea. Honestly, I think Papa T wanted us to live in Riverton forever. With LeLe gone, he would be alone with Bishop, and he would miss the gleeful chaos that filled the house each day.

Papa T's comment about school made me realize even more how much I wanted to stay. I didn't want to leave before the school year ended, and I knew I'd get Miss Maybelle again next year. Faith was going to be a senior. I was positive she didn't want to transfer schools, even if it meant attending one with her old friends in New Orleans. I gave Papa T a big hug and told him to have fun at his party. A hug that doubled as a grateful thank-you for planting a seed in Daddy's mind, perhaps prolonging our time in Riverton.

After Papa T left, Momma asked me to fetch the salt I'd forgotten in the kitchen. Daddy wanted more tea, so he joined me. The path to the house from the cooking fire was a short walk, so he set a slow pace, affording himself the time to tell me how luxurious his new train was.

"It's beautiful, Katydid. And the route runs along the Mississippi River, so there's lots of action to watch outside the windows," he said.

He told me about stops in cities I'd heard of but had never seen, which fed my desire for adventure. Then he described the house he'd picked out for us in New Orleans.

"It's even bigger than Papa T's house. Everyone will get their own bedroom with windows that overlook a large community garden. And the front porch has those gas lamps your Momma loves. But the best part, Katydid—it's only a few blocks from the French Quarter. We can have beignets every Sunday!"

I had to admit the thought of weekly beignets and watching the Mardi Gras parade every February was alluring. He almost had me convinced to leave Riverton as we approached the bottom of the kitchen steps. I heard the dainty chime of the kitchen door's bell and looked up to see Bishop standing on the top step. From below, his normal hunch looked more pronounced. I waited to let him down the stairs first, but he just stood there.

"You comin' down, Bishop?" Daddy asked.

Then I heard the panic in his voice.

"What the hell are you doing? Bishop, no!"

My ears flooded with a high-pitched ring. Blood raced to my legs, and it took a few pounding heartbeats for me to grasp what was happening. I knew what that deafening sound was. I looked down to see where the bullet hit me, but all I saw was my frozen, moonlit shadow stretched out in front of my feet.

I looked back up at Bishop as he was lowering the gun to his side. The ripped screen on the kitchen door behind him was flapping in the breeze. Time slowed as I turned toward Daddy. He let go of his empty tea jar, and it fell to the dirt, rolling in a half circle and stopping against the toe of his shoe. He folded over, hands to his abdomen, then lifted his head and grabbed onto my sweater as he whispered in one strained breath, "Run."

And so I ran.

My mind blanked, and I didn't know where I was running to, but my feet were moving beneath me. I found myself alone in the front yard, staring back at the house. The crickets had halted their evening symphony. The leaves had stopped mid-rustle. No shadows danced beyond the front room window.

Was I the only one aware something horrific just happened?

"Harts," I said aloud to myself as I took off running again. Papa T had left. Momma was by the fire but had surely looked up as the shot rang out. I begged Jesus not to let her go to the kitchen door and prayed Faith was still in her room, crying, and would ignore her curiosity. I swore I'd never again take His name in vain if He spared them both from harm.

Our next door neighbor, Harts Barnett, was already outside when I burst through the shortcut in our property line hedge.

"What's goin' on, Sloane? We heard a shot." Harts held out his hands and pushed against my shoulders to stop me from running straight into him.

Jack Senior, Junior's daddy, lived on the other side of Harts and was standing next to him, as he'd come straight over when he'd heard the shot. "Christ, Sloane, is that your blood on your sweater?" he asked. "Are you shot?"

This was 1954, and 9-1-1 didn't exist yet. I knew Harts and Jack were my best chance at saving my father's life. "Not mine. Daddy's. He's been shot! Please, can you take him to the hospital? Momma can't drive and Papa T's not home."

I panicked upon hearing myself say the words out loud. Harts did, too, pacing around, grabbing his head in disbelief.

"Come on, Sloane; I'll drive him," said Jack.

We tore back through the hedge and rounded the corner of the house. Momma was on the ground next to Daddy, pressing a towel against his side, trying to calm his agony. Faith was on the top step, folded into her lap and begging Jesus to help Daddy. I spun in circles looking for Bishop, then fell to the ground at Daddy's feet.

Jack ran over to Daddy's car. The key was hanging from the gear shifter, the spot Daddy always left it, and Jack drove it over to the steps. He crouched down next to Daddy. "Hardy, you tough old bird. You ain't dyin' on my watch," he said.

He draped Daddy's arm over his shoulder and lifted him into the back seat. Momma got in beside Daddy. "It's gonna be okay, Hardy. It's gonna be okay," she kept repeating, as I clung to the shutting door.

Sheriff Hayes's police car came barreling to a stop next to Daddy's car. "Harts and the girls will tell you what happened," Jack said as he slammed the gear shifter into reverse. "I gotta get Hardy to the hospital."

"I called 'em already," said Hayes. "They're gonna have the ambulance meet you on the way. When you see it, flash your lights so they know it's you."

"Roger that," said Jack.

In seconds, my father's car was gone. I stood there, swallowing the bile burning in my throat, wondering what to do next. I avoided the bloody towel as I rushed up the steps to sit with Faith, where I fell into a trance as I watched blood drip from the bottom step and pool next to Daddy's tea jar. It was so fresh it hadn't sunk into the earth yet. I didn't know a lot about gunshot wounds back then, but I remember thinking the amount of blood covering the bottom step and the ground below didn't seem possible.

Hayes stopped short of the steps. "What the hell happened, girls? Faith? Sloane? Sloane, answer me!"

I started bawling. Inconsolable bawling. I'd held my fear inside long enough to get Daddy help, and it was time to let it out. I strained to speak. All that came out was a string of broken vowels.

Faith wiped her eyes and cleared her throat. "I wasn't out here when it happened, Sheriff. I came outside to see what the loud noise was and found Momma bent over Daddy. She told me to call you, then get towels because Daddy had been shot. So I did. When I came back out, she stopped me. Told me to stay up top and throw the towels to her. I haven't moved since."

Faith's voice broke as she continued. "I asked Momma what was happening, and she told me..."

"It's okay, Faith, you're safe now," said Hayes.

"No, we're not," she said. "Bishop shot Daddy and he ran off into the woods behind the house. He's still out there!" Faith pointed towards the ominous black sea of Dark Hollow.

"Okay, I can talk now," I said as I fumbled to wipe my face with my skirt. "I was with Daddy by the fire, and I forgot the salt. So he went to the kitchen with me because he wanted more tea. Then Bishop was on the top step. The one Faith and I are sitting on right now. He just held up a gun and shot Daddy. I don't know why! Daddy did nothing to him. So I ran to Mr. Barnett's house. Jack was there too. We ran back here, and well, you saw. Jack took Daddy to the hospital."

Harts nodded to Hayes as if confirming my sequence of events.

"So, none of you know why Bishop shot Hardy?"

"No." I started crying again as I noticed the blood on my shoes. "He didn't say a word. Just shot him."

"No?" said Faith.

"No? As in, maybe?" asked Hayes.

"Well, sir, he was pretty upset earlier because Daddy wants us to move back to New Orleans, and Bishop doesn't want Momma to leave. So maybe he thought Daddy *did* do something to him. And he's on this medicine he's supposed to take every day because he shot out Sloane's vanity mirror, and the doctors said he has this mental disease called skitsoplaneya. So maybe he didn't take his medicine today?"

"You mean schizophrenia?"

"Yeah, that's it," said Faith.

"Christ. Do you know where the gun is? Or where Bishop got it?"

"No, sir," said Faith. "I haven't seen Bishop or the gun. I don't know how he got one, either, because after he shot Sloane's mirror, we put all the guns in the cedar cabinet and hid the key."

"Faith, I want you to show me where you hid that key," he said.

We all went inside, and Faith took the angels off the piano. Hayes lifted the top and confirmed the envelope was still taped underneath. He jiggled the cedar cabinet doors to make sure they were still locked.

Hayes scratched his head. "So *all* the guns are in this cabinet?" he asked.

"Yes, sir," said Faith. "They used to be everywhere. The kitchen, Papa T's desk, his nightstand. But mostly up in his closet."

"His closet, huh?"

We followed Hayes down the hallway, and there, on the floor in front of Papa T's closet, was an empty gun box. They had missed one, and Bishop had found it.

"Well, that solves one mystery," Hayes said. "Now we gotta find where Bishop is with that gun."

Hayes called all available deputies to the house on his CB radio, and at my request, Harts fetched Maudie and Miss Maybelle. What I needed at that moment was to feel safe, and even though two protective men were standing in my kitchen, I needed the type of comfort only a close confidante could provide.

Faith had to get out of there. It petrified her to stay at the house, no matter how many armed men filled it. So she asked Hayes to get a message to Royce. He showed up a little while later and took her back to his house. His mother adored Faith, even more than her own son, so I knew she would be safe.

Miss Maybelle lay down with me on my bed, and I curled into her side, weeping. She stayed with me all night. I woke several times in a panic, and she was right there to reassure me I was safe. That Faith was safe.

But the night was far from safe.

Merciless Fate

SLOANE, 1954
ALABAMA

HAYES SAT AT THE KITCHEN table, took off his hat, and placed it upside down next to the salt I never got the chance to use. He slicked back his dark, greasy hair with his hand. Pulled a handkerchief from his back pocket and wiped his brow, then dropped it into his hat as he leaned into the table, palms cradling the temples of his weary head.

"Harts, you think Bishop's gonna hurt himself?" Maudie asked.

"Well, if what the girls said was true—that he's a lunatic—I guess anything is possible at this point. Why didn't Grace tell us he was schizophrenic? Or about that whole mirror shooting incident?" he said.

"Probably because people would call him a lunatic. Sorry. I didn't mean that. It's just—"

"I know. This whole thing is bad, no matter how you look at it," Harts said. "And I'm worried Hardy's not gonna make it. That was a *lot* of blood. Sheriff? You ever seen that much blood from a shot?"

Hayes barely heard the question. He was thinking about the day of Bishop's fall in the Ginhouse Hollow and how Sheriff Dossie had rappelled that cliff side without hesitation. He'd forcefully taken the helm like the captain of a storm-battered ship and led his men, and Bishop, to safety. But he was the sheriff now. He needed trust in himself to guide *his* men through this. They were counting on him, just as he'd counted on Dossie.

Hayes pushed his chair back from the table and swiftly snatched his hat, then stood and adjusted it on his head as if about to give a campaign speech. "Maudie, Harts, my deputies should arrive any minute. We gotta find Bishop before this thing gets worse. And we better clean that mess up before somethin' comes lookin' for easy prey."

Maudie grabbed the cleaning bucket from below the kitchen sink and filled it with water. Her stomach churned as she headed down the back steps. She'd seen blood before, of course. But not like this. Not spilled in an act of violence. And once she got a good look, she shared Hart's worry. That was too much blood.

She poured the water onto the bottom step and powdered it with Borax, then got down on her knees and started scrubbing. Red suds covered her hands as she gagged back her supper. As Hayes poured a fresh bucket onto the step, she rinsed her hands under the falling water.

Harts grabbed a shovel leaning against the garden fence. He picked up Daddy's tea jar and handed it to Maudie, then turned over the dirt below the step until it formed a gritty slurry. He scooped up the blood-soaked towel with the blade of the shovel, walked it over to the fire, and dropped it in.

"There. That should keep scavengers away from the house," Hayes said as Maudie intercepted the whisky flask he'd extended to Harts.

Harts leaned the shovel back against the garden fence where he'd found it. Maudie went inside with the bucket and tea jar. And Sheriff Hayes rested his shoulder against the side of the house, planning his manhunt as he looked blankly toward the trees.

Bishop had the advantage. Dark Hollow was his daily stomping ground, and he knew every nook and cranny. Every animal den to avoid, every cottonmouth nest along the stream inside, and every path to freedom. He was an armed man in the middle of a psychotic episode. And Hayes had to find him before he hurt himself. Or others.

Backup came speeding into the front yard. Hayes grabbed his flashlight from his squad car and stationed one man at the house, in case Bishop returned. The others met at the tree line and prepared themselves.

Hayes reminded them of what lurked inside Dark Hollow. Dense vegetation led to a creek, then shifted to a hillside. The men knew their reaction could mean the difference between life and death if they should happen upon one of the wood's deadly inhabitants. Bobcats tended to avoid human interaction but could be unpredictable. And a panther's stealthy ability to stalk a trespasser was unparalleled. But it was what they couldn't see, or hear, in the cover of darkness that most threatened to take a man down. Between the poisonous water hemlock hiding in the streambed weeds and brown recluse spiders who hate being disturbed, the men had to be extremely careful where they stepped and what they touched.

The men spread out and faded into the trees, flashlights drawn beside their revolvers. They scanned in front of each step, careful not to trip. With each crackle of snapping sticks, they made their presence known. Hayes signaled the deputies, zeroing in on the faintest cry. They set a wide perimeter, holding their position as Hayes motioned to freeze with his fist held high. Hayes alone trekked forward, careful not to make a sound, but a limb cast a strobe of his flashlight, and the cry stopped.

One deputy screamed as his pant leg shifted. "Christ almighty, he just ran past me! Sheriff, over here!"

Hayes caught its path with his light. "Just a kit, deputy."

The men continued deeper into the woods until halted by a blaring car horn. "Sheriff Hayes! I got him! I got him!" the deputy stationed at the house howled.

Hayes could barely hear him, but the horn echoing off the hillside was clear as day.

Bishop exited through the garden gate and dropped the gun on the ground.

"Hoo boy, you stop right there!" the deputy commanded.

Harts took cover behind Hayes's patrol car, astonished he hadn't noticed Bishop when he grabbed and returned the shovel. Maudie peeked through the rip in the kitchen screen door and backed away slowly when she saw him.

Hayes and his deputies emerged from the trees and sprinted back to the house. The stationed deputy stood stiffly, with his legs spread wide apart and his gun pointed steadily at Bishop. Bishop was squatting like a toddler, covering his head with his arms in an act of surrender.

Hayes reached down, grabbed Bishop by the shirt, pulled him up straight, and spun him around. "Put your hands on the gate, Bishop."

He kicked the gun to slide it away from Bishop, then patted him down to make sure he didn't have more. Bishop struggled to stand as Hayes cuffed his trembling hands, led him by the arm to his squad car, and shoved him down onto the back seat and slammed the door with a burst of adrenaline.

Hayes couldn't take Bishop to the local jail. Deputies weren't trained to handle someone with his mental condition. So he decided the hospital in nearby Sheffield was the best place for him. The same hospital that had treated Bishop after his fall and after the mirror incident. And where Jack was speeding to that very moment, racing to save Hardy's life.

Maudie checked on Miss Maybelle, who had watched and heard everything through my cracked bedroom window. "Is she sleeping?" Maudie asked.

"I don't know how, but yes," said Miss Maybelle. "Are you okay, Maudie?"

"Ask me again tomorrow."

"Lord, Maudie, go find Tom's bourbon."

Maudie asked Harts to stay with her after Hayes and his deputies left. She didn't want to be alone while Miss Maybelle guarded my sleep.

And yes, she and Harts found Papa T's bourbon.

HAYES WATCHED BISHOP THROUGH THE rearview mirror. His internal struggle over what Bishop had done was crushing. How could the kindhearted boy he'd helped rescue all those years ago turn into the crazed man sitting behind him in handcuffs?

It was a quiet drive for the first forty minutes until Bishop caught Hayes's stare.

"Hi, Sheriff," Bishop said. He checked his surroundings as if waking from a sleepwalk.

"Hi, Bishop. Can you tell me what happened tonight?"

"Hardy was tryin' to take Grace."

Because of what Faith had told him, Hayes understood what he meant.

"Where you takin' me?" Bishop asked.

"Someplace safe."

When they arrived at the hospital, a nurse took Bishop and Hayes to the top floor—the psychiatric ward. Bishop remembered the hallway as the nurse pushed him from behind. It was the same hallway he'd been wheeled down after the mirror incident. He thrashed to free his cuffed hands and lurched himself forward, nearly falling face-first onto the cold vinyl tile. The nurse gave Bishop a shot, instantly rendering him powerless.

Hayes hunched over to remove Bishop's handcuffs and whispered into his ear, "I'm sorry it's come to this for you."

Hayes requested that Bishop stay committed until the judge said otherwise. As Hayes signed the intake form, the doctor assured him Bishop would get the best care possible.

Bishop understood what that meant. Locked in a medicated jail, same as last time. To him, this place was anything but safe. The doctor's muffled words sifted through Bishop's memory of pills in white paper ketchup cups and restraints buckled around his wrists and ankles. He tried to speak. To tell Hayes he couldn't leave him there. But the sedation was overpowering.

Hayes retreated down the long, sterile hallway to the elevator. He marveled at the bleakness of the dismal white walls. An orderly inserted a key into the call-button panel and twisted it until the elevator door opened. As it closed, Hayes turned his energy toward finding my father.

The nurse stationed at the emergency room counter motioned to Hayes as the elevator door opened in the ER. He made his way across the hall, pausing briefly for a passing gurney.

"I'm sorry, Sheriff, I don't see a Hardy Morgan on our patient list," she said. "And I radioed the ambulance. The medics say they never connected with Jack. They're headed back to the hospital now."

Hayes knew something was wrong. There was only one road out of town, so the plan for Jack to flash his lights should have worked. Even if it didn't, and Jack missed seeing the ambulance, he should have arrived at the hospital by then.

"Ma'am, have the medics pull over and wait for me, please," Hayes said.

Hayes ran to his car and backtracked toward Riverton, taking it slow at every bent guard rail along the road. He was approaching the city limits when he saw the ambulance sitting outside the Texaco station. He pulled in alongside and told the medics he had a bad feeling Jack never made it past Cherokee.

Hayes pulled out to continue toward Riverton, with the ambulance following. Three miles outside town, Hayes spotted fresh skid marks disappearing through the grassy berm. He slid his car to a sideways stop and jumped out, flagging the medics with waving arms overhead. From the front of his squad car, he could see a faint glow rising from the gully. He ran to the edge of the roadway's shoulder and peered down.

There it was. Daddy's car, resting against the trunk of a tree, with one headlight still shining up into the night.

Hayes ran down the embankment, sliding on his backside to keep from tumbling forward. The medics followed with their gear, albeit at a slower clip. As Hayes approached the car, steam slowly billowed from the radiator. Looking through the back window, he saw Momma's head resting against the back passenger-side window. Hayes continued around to the driver's seat. Jack's folded body covered the dashboard, head projecting through a hole in the windshield. Hayes cringed and looked away, then scanned the car for Hardy. There was no movement inside. No noise, but for the sound of Hayes's own labored breath.

He opened the back door and fell to his knees. Daddy's lifeless body splayed across the backseat, with legs crumpled on the floorboard and head on Momma's lap. The medics pulled Jack and Momma from the car and laid them side by side on the ground. Hayes searched for Daddy's pulse, but to no avail. Between the gunshot and the car accident, he didn't make it.

Momma opened her eyes, and through her clouded vision, saw Jack lying dead next to her. She turned her head toward the car. Hayes sat on the ground below the open back door, sobbing into his hands, with the outline of Daddy's legs in the shadows.

As the medics lifted her onto a stretcher and into the air, her heart crushed into as many pieces as my vanity mirror. The image of Daddy's body blurred in her vision as tears dripped from the bridge of her nose. She didn't want to leave him, but nothing more could be done. Daddy's merciless fate had been sealed.

A Closed Book

SLOANE, 1954
ALABAMA

SHERIFF HAYES HAD SENT A deputy to retrieve Papa T from his retirement party. When he arrived back home, Maudie and Harts told him everything from the time he'd left for his party until the sheriff left with Bishop. And when Hayes returned to the house in the middle of the night, he filled everyone in on the tragedy that befell Jack and my father.

As the morning sun peeked through the sheet curtain covering my window, Miss Maybelle woke me from my turbulent slumber. She led me toward the kitchen, passing the chiming clock atop Papa T's desk. Six-thirty. It sounded like it skipped half a note.

I walked in a daze, questioning if the night before was real. And if *this* was real. Papa T was sitting at the kitchen table with Sheriff Hayes, Maudie, Harts, and Faith. They were wearing the same clothes from the night before and their eyelids hung low, propped open by the coffee in front of them.

I was wearing my nightgown and felt uncomfortably underdressed, crossing my arms across my chest like I was cold. Miss Maybelle noticed and wrapped the sweater she was wearing around me.

My eyes stung with each elongated blink. In the pulsing darkness was an image of *my* sweater. The one marked with my father's blood. Last night was real. Not a nightmare or my imagination taking a twisted turn. Real. Faster I blinked, recalling the gore I'd witnessed as if advancing through a View-Master horror reel. And when I stopped blinking, I realized who was missing from the table.

Panic set in as I scanned the room, crooking my neck to check the blind corners. "Is Daddy okay? Where's Momma?"

Faith started crying.

"Your Momma's okay," said Papa T. "She's at the hospital, and I'm gonna take you there soon. But Sloane…it pains me to tell you this, but your daddy didn't make it."

Didn't make it. Didn't make it. What does that mean, didn't make it?

"But…Jack took him—"

"Jack's gone too, Sloane. Only your momma survived a car crash that happened on the way to the hospital," Papa T said, his eyes filling with tears.

My scream nearly shattered the coffee cups littering the kitchen table. Faith dropped from her chair, wailing in a child's pose. Miss Maybelle pulled me to her side. I grabbed hold of her waist to keep from falling to the floor as well. *Didn't make it.* The devastation those three words conveyed was like nothing

I'd ever felt. No antivenom could stop the pain paralyzing my heart. No love could replace the one I'd now lost. *Didn't make it.* Those three short words irrevocably destroyed me.

Faith and I lay on her bed with our eyes closed but not sleeping. I couldn't fathom my life without my daddy in it. His monthly presence may not have been the parenting norm, but I always knew he'd be back. It made the time we had together more meaningful because our relationship didn't include the minutiae of life. He was the distance that made my heart grow fonder.

Papa T came in to fetch us. The next thing I remember was sitting beside Momma in her hospital bed. I don't remember the drive there, save for one gut punch of a moment. We were just outside town and approached the scene of the car accident. I saw Sheriff Hayes's car parked on the shoulder. He was talking to a tow-truck driver who had Daddy's car hooked to the back of it. Papa T slammed on the brakes and told me and Faith to lie down. My stomach sank, and my mouth watered, same as it always does before filling with vomit.

Papa T's head traced right as we passed by, and his awestruck expression told me I'd made the right decision not to look. It was bad enough the last memory I had of my father was of him doubled over, bleeding, telling me to run. I didn't need to add the image of his mangled car.

I lay next to Momma as she slept in her hospital bed. I tried sleeping, too, but hospitals are the least restful place on the planet. Between the beeps and buzzers and nurses coming in and out at all hours, it's impossible to nod off without sedation.

Faith was looking for something to pass as breakfast at the candy machine down the hall when Momma woke. She looked around the room, and as her eyes fixed on mine, she let out a whimper.

"Sloane, your father—"

"I know, Momma."

I had to spare her from saying the words aloud. I told her I was okay, an obvious lie, and that everyone was safe. Faith came in eating a Clark Bar and rushed over. Papa T was miraculously napping in the bedside chair and jolted awake as Momma's heart-rate monitor beeped faster. She frantically ripped at the cords, trying to escape their tethered hold.

"Jack didn't make it, did he?"

"No, Momma. He's gone," I said.

"Who's watching Osee?"

"Maudie. She's at the house with Miss Maybelle and some others."

"Did the sheriff find Bishop?"

"He's here at the hospital, too, Grace. On the top floor," Papa T said.

We answered all her questions, though easing her mind was impossible. Her night of horror had finally ended, but grief took hold once the pain of losing Daddy set in. I never left her side. She was always there for me, and it was my turn to repay her. She mostly slept, but the nurses woke her every two hours on the dot to check her pupils. As the blinding light seared her vision, she'd remember where she was and cry again.

Remarkably, the only injury she suffered was a concussion from when her forehead hit the back of the front seat. The doctor said the weight of Daddy, practically lying in her lap, had acted like a seat belt and likely saved her life. Momma's doctor gave her a prescription to help her sleep and another to help her function, and then released her the following night after she begged the doctor to let her go home.

She knew Bishop was on the top floor of the hospital. She had to get out of there, as far away from him as possible. He'd caused the death of her husband, and she said Bishop was now dead to her too. But when someone dies, you can't just instantly stop loving them. It takes time for the bond to wane, if it ever does.

When we got home, Momma slept for two days. Only Papa T attended Jack's funeral and paid respect on behalf of our entire family. Junior was still in the army, stationed overseas and unable to fly home in time for the funeral. So Papa T escorted his mother to the cemetery. She feared we blamed Jack for the car accident, but Papa T assured her everyone had lost two great men that night. And if anything, our family was to blame for *her* loss.

Daddy's funeral was the day after Jack's. We buried him next to LeLe in our family's section of the Riverton Cemetery. Sheriff Hayes escorted our car to the church, just as he'd done for Jack's wife the previous morning. Faith sat up front with Papa T, and Osee and I sat in the back with Momma. She was blindly going through the motions of funeral etiquette, numbed by the pills her doctor gave her.

After Daddy's funeral, I had nothing to focus on but my emptiness. I needed closure, and not knowing what caused Jack to wreck or what was next for Bishop kept me in a state of blind confusion. I spent my nights rereading the diary entries that led me to this point. And the new ones I penned would have surely concerned anyone who dared read them. No longer was I afraid of Bishop shooting me or my new vanity mirror. Not because he was committed, but because he'd already shattered everything I knew and loved. The only thing gluing the shards of my life back together was the ink that filled my diary. And once I filled every page, I lifted the loose floorboard where my diary lived and buried my pain.

After weeks of hiding in my room and distracting myself with the schoolwork Miss Maybelle dropped off every few days, I emerged. Through the kitchen window, I saw Momma sitting in the garden, feathering her fingertips across the tops of the butter lettuce, as her toes dipped in and out of the iron-rich dirt. It looked as though she was trying to make sense of where Bishop hid before he surrendered to Sheriff Hayes.

I opened the kitchen door, and Momma looked up as its bell chimed. "Come on, Sloane, we need to water."

As she sprinkled around the thyme, she told me what happened after Jack sped away from the house. He drove as fast as he could, weaving around cars. Daddy passed out soon after they hit the main road out of town, but before he did he told Momma what she needed to do to take care of us. He knew he wasn't going to make it. I think Momma did, too, but she tried to stay strong for both of them. The ambulance was on its way, and she prayed he'd survive if they could just intersect it.

Daddy told her who she needed to call at the train yard to get access to his retirement, and he told her that the money he had saved for the house was at their bank in New Orleans but their bank in Sheffield could help her access it. He told her how much he loved her and loved their life together, even though they'd spent most of it at a distance. He kissed her knee and then passed out, as she stroked his curls and told him she loved him too.

Just as she reached to check his pulse, a thunderous boom blasted the front of the car. Jack cursed in fright as he struggled to keep control of the car. Momma clutched Daddy's chest, holding him tight as the car screeched sideways. As the tail end spun around, Momma saw the deer they'd hit limp off into the woods alongside the road.

She saw no other lights on the road. No cars to hit as Jack spun the steering wheel in opposing circles, trying to regain control. But the cracked windshield blinded his view. Panicked, Jack hit the gas instead of the brake. The tires rumbled across the gravel shoulder, then launched into the air as they left the pavement. With a hard slam, the car came crashing down, vibrating through the patchy crabgrass as it careened down the gully. And when it hit the tree, Momma's head banged against the back of the front seat, then whipped back hard against the door window. The next thing she remembered was Jack dead to her left and Sheriff Hayes sobbing at Daddy's feet to the right.

IT HAD BEEN A MONTH and five days since the funeral. The judge assigned to Bishop's case summoned everyone to the courthouse for a recorded interview. At Momma's request, Faith and I told our pieces with Papa T in the room, since we were minors. She wasn't yet ready to hear what I was about to say. Although by the end of the day, she had no choice.

I sat in one of two tufted leather chairs in front of the judge's overly polished oak desk. Papa T sat in the other. A well-dressed lady in a pencil skirt and perfectly coiffed hair sat at a small table off to the side; the judge introduced her as his court reporter, Sissy. Her table held a black, half-size typewriter with long skinny keys. I'd never seen one like it, so when the judge asked if I had questions before we started, I asked what kind of typewriter it was.

He smiled at my youthful curiosity. "It's a stenograph. Would you like to see how it works? Sissy, show Sloane how it works." *Yes. Anything to delay my deposition.*

Sissy gave me an inviting wave. "Sure. Come on over here, sweetie."

She asked me for my full name and typed it onto the receipt-size paper. It was a cipher of missing and oddly spaced letters, and for a while after, I aspired to be a stenographer. I'd get to type the secret code while listening to stories like the one I was about to tell and mingle with judges and lawyers every day. It seemed so distinguished.

The judge called me back over to my chair. "Sloane, out of everyone telling me their pieces of the story today, yours counts the most, because you're the only one who saw your daddy get shot. So take your time—as much as you need—and tell me everything you saw, heard, and even smelled. Understand?"

I nodded and sat forward, pulling the hem of my dress taut over my knees while I relayed every detail surrounding the moment that had wrecked my peaceful life. And when I was done, I let go of my dress hem and looked at Papa T, who smiled at me approvingly.

The judge thanked me and Papa T and told us we could leave his chambers. As Papa T and I exited into the courtroom, Sissy handed me one of those red lollipops with a stiffened white cord looped into a handle and told me how brave I was. I didn't feel brave, but her saying that helped me relax enough to enjoy my reward.

Everyone in the courtroom watched as we entered. Momma came over to ensure I was okay. Oddly, I was. I never again had to retell the story aloud unless I wanted to. And until today, some sixty-six years later, I haven't.

After everyone told their piece of the story, the court reporter and judge came out of his chambers and sat at the stately podium. It reminded me of a church, with a pastor front and center and a pianist off to the side. Right down to the black robe hiding the judge's bulging waistline.

"Sissy, please stand and read the events for all to hear," the judge asked.

She stood and carefully read each person's statement aloud, prefacing each with the names of those who said them. That's how I learned the full, unabridged storyline of what occurred that night from each person's point of view. It was as if Sissy had been floating above the house, watching it all unfold, following each one of us, simultaneously, and stitching together the threads that bound our tragic story as she typed away on her stenograph.

Included was the professional opinion of Bishop's doctor. Bishop had only pretended to take his chlorpromazine for over a month, citing a dry mouth and drowsy existence. His brain chemistry upended, and his hallucinations intensified, resulting in an inability to separate what was real from what was fantasy. Ironically, his next appointment was for the day following the shooting. His doctor would have noticed Bishop hiding his meds.

"Thank you, Sissy," the judge said. "Are there any corrections to what Sissy read?"

With no one speaking up, the judge was ready to make his ruling. "Typically, a person charged with a crime has their day in court. Because of the illness of the accused, he is unfit to be here today. I will rely on the expert opinions of the doctor and lawyers present in the courtroom, as well as my own, in deciding what's in the best interest of everyone involved. Under Chapter 16 of Title 15 of Alabama State Law, I declare Bishop Medford not guilty by reason of insanity and remand him to the Alabama State Psychiatric Hospital in Tuscaloosa."

He ordered Bishop's doctor to facilitate an immediate transfer from his temporary stay at the Sheffield hospital and for the psychiatric hospital to hold Bishop for the remainder of his life or until such time a review saw him fit to reenter society.

Papa T stood up alarmingly fast and fled the courtroom. Momma sat still beside me, with her eyes closed and hands holding her Bible.

Faith grabbed my leg and leaned into me, so no one would hear. "He's finally going to the looney bin and never getting out." I wasn't sure if I was supposed to smile at that statement or not, so only half of one formed.

It was as if the judge had quietly closed a book he finished reading. There was no murder trial with media fanfare. No newspaper reporters rushing the courtroom steps to get quotes for their articles. The only public trace of what happened was a blurb in the *Sheffield Times* about an out-of-town man dying from a gunshot wound on the thirty-first of March. To the rest of the world, that night never happened. But for me, it replayed for years.

A Second Scotch and Soda

RYNN, 2020
WASHINGTON

MY MOTHER HELD UP HER glass and swirled the slivers of ice at the bottom. "Rynn, I think it's time for another drink."

I went into the kitchen and leaned against the island, exhaling more air than a surfacing orca. *That. Was. Intense.* The quarter chime from the clock sitting on top of my mother's china hutch rang out, skipping a full note. I'd heard that clock my entire life. Marveled at how hypnotizing its four spinning brass spheres were. Laughed over how each dog we owned listened intently for the fifth suppertime chime. Watched as my father carefully lifted the glass dome on the first of each month and wound it. I'd always assumed, since it was called an anniversary clock, that my father had gifted it to my mother. It had never once occurred to me it was *someone else's* anniversary clock. A priceless heirloom that echoed not only throughout the house I grew up in but in the one where my mother grew up, as well, chiming in the background during everything she had just told me. It was Papa T's desk clock.

I poured a second scotch and soda for my parents, then poured one for myself. My nerves needed the type of soothing only a smooth single malt can provide.

I set my parents' drinks on the coasters between them and sat back on the couch. I watched the tiny bubbles simmer in my glass as the warmth of the elixir coated my throat. It reminded me of the warm coke Bishop had given me and Leigh that day in 1986 as we drove away from my grandmother's house, back to Dallas. Away from the most awkward summer vacation I'd ever had. A kind gesture from a rail-thin man with a soft step and fondness for chewing gum. It was hard to believe the person I had met caused the damage my mother described.

"For the longest time, I'd focused on Hardy's destiny. How his life choices had caused his death to happen. I see now, it was never *his* destiny that caused it. It was Bishop's," I said.

"How do you mean?" my mother asked.

"Bishop was guilty of shooting Hardy. But take away his fall in the Ginhouse Hollow. Take away his schizophrenia. Would it still have happened?"

"No, I don't believe so," she said. "Because of both those things, Bishop didn't always understand right from wrong. And he didn't know how to handle the threat of losing Momma to Hardy, as he saw it. But if he had never fallen—never gotten sick—I'm positive none of it would have happened."

"Is that why you were able to forgive him? Because it wasn't really his fault?"

"Ultimately, it was part of the reason."

"Part? So…that's not the end of the story?"

"Not even close."

The Trigger

SLOANE, 1954
ALABAMA

THAT MONTH LEADING UP TO the judge's ruling was the quietest the house had ever been. While I sat in my bedroom, trapped by memories destined to haunt me forever, Bishop sat trapped in that tiny wardroom on the top floor of the Sheffield hospital. Per the judge's orders, and despite Bishop's repeated pleas for Momma, no one was permitted to visit him. Although I'm not sure Momma would have visited if she'd been allowed to. Bishop had broken her heart clean through, and as much as she prayed each night, she had not found peace.

I overheard Papa T relaying hospital updates to Momma, but her blank stare and lack of response told me she wasn't yet ready to care about Bishop's well-being. She'd sit there at the kitchen table, pressing crumbs into her fingertips, then rubbing her fingers until the crumbs cascaded back to the table. Again and again, until the crumbs were near dust. So completely lost in grief that even the tidiness of her kitchen became irrelevant.

Now, Rynn, some of what I'm about to tell you I learned from those Papa T updates I overheard. And the rest, well, you'll understand how I know everything I'm about to say by the time I'm done telling you the rest of the story. Just bear with me, because it might seem like there's no way I could know all this.

THE DAY AFTER THE JUDGE'S ruling, Bishop found himself alone in the second row of a short white bus, not too unlike the one our local milkman drove. He watched through his small window as his doctor and the bus driver conversed, glancing at him periodically to make sure he was still in his seat.

"Don't be gettin' any crazy ideas, crazy man," the bus driver said as he jumped in and adjusted his rearview mirror on Bishop.

"I'm *not* crazy," Bishop said and turned his head toward the window.

The driver shifted in his seat, realizing Bishop wasn't as sedated as he'd thought. He knew what Bishop had done. He also knew the only thing Bishop wanted was to go back home, and if he somehow got out of his restraints, there was no telling what Bishop would do to get there.

Moments later, Sheriff Hayes slid into the passenger seat. "Let's go," he told the driver, then turned around to face Bishop. "I know your doctor told you about the new hospital you're being moved to. That's where we're going now."

"I don't want a new hospital," Bishop said.

"Look, Bishop, because of what you did, you can't stay at Sheffield. It's not set up to house violent patients long term. But because of your…unique personality, a normal prison is no place for you either. So the judge ordered you to be treated at a place that's a combination of both. A hospital you can't leave."

Hayes took a pull from the flask he hid in his pants pocket and continued, "Consider yourself lucky. I've seen where they send people who did what you did. You wouldn't last a day in prison."

Bishop didn't speak for the rest of the nearly three-hour drive. He was trying to figure out what Hayes meant by "what you did." Bishop's memory of the last few months was so clouded by medications he didn't remember his own birthday had passed. So the fact that he'd repressed shooting my father was no surprise.

As the bus slowed to a stop, ornate iron gates crawled open. Hayes had made it clear this was the only time he'd be passing through them, and as the bus crept through the entrance and the gates began closing, the distinction between them and a jail cell door blurred.

Looking out his window, Bishop took in the beauty that ran along the long gravel driveway. Rose beds, with the first blooms of summer peeking from their buds. Beyond, an explosion of color seemed moments away from surrounding the benches and birdbaths sprinkled between towering oak trees. The gently winding drive reminded Bishop of the entrance to the Grand Gulf Hotel in Alabama. One of his favorite postcards hanging on the back kitchen door. He saw fence lines that seemed to go on for days, and a grove of trees, poking their tops above a third story, disappeared as the bus neared the stately main building.

"Alabama State Psychiatric Hospital," read the sign filling the grassy knoll in the middle of the circle drive. The bus stopped and Sheriff Hayes got out.

Pristine white columns stretched to the eaves, framing thick marble steps leading to solid double doors. They opened to a doctor in his white coat and a nurse with her white hat and dress. He was only slightly taller than her, and they both had the same dishwater blond hair. From afar, they looked as if they could be fraternal twins.

They descended the marble steps to greet Sheriff Hayes. The driver looked at Bishop through his rearview mirror and sneered, "Welcome home, killer."

Bishop was used to being called names. Slow boy. Retard. Dummy. And lately, crazy. He'd heard every slur people's intolerance could think of. But *killer* was new.

Bishop may not have remembered what he'd done to Hardy, but he did remember a time when he could beat any kid on the playground in a foot race. He was lightning fast and briefly considered making a break for it as soon as the bus door opened. But he'd run *this* foot race before and always lost. If he made any attempt to flee or resist, he'd find himself on the ground with a needle pricking his arm, then wake up hours later in restraints. So he quietly followed and did as instructed.

Once inside, Bishop heard the doors lock behind him. He turned his head and upper body around, while clumsily still advancing. An orderly stood with his back to the doors, chest puffed like a no-neck bouncer at a nightclub. Bishop turned back around and recognized the same bleak white paint that had surrounded him at the hospital in Sheffield.

"I'm Doctor Matthews, and this here is Nurse Parker. We're happy you're staying with us, Bishop. I know this is all new to you, but I think you'll find it comfortable here. And if you work with us, Bishop, I know we can help you feel better."

Dr. Matthews was careful not to use the word *cure* or make any promises about one day going back home. He had treated several schizophrenics in his tenure at the psychiatric hospital, and rarely did they improve enough to leave.

A center stripe of carpet ran the length of the long hardwood hallway and morphed into a red staircase at the end. Bishop stopped at the bottom and lifted his leg, gently tapping the first step with the tip of his slipper. His foot sank into the velvety carpet, and with every step, an amber glow from the chandelier above bounced off the glossy cherry banisters, lighting the way like an airport runway. It was much more lavish than the Sheffield hospital, but the posh appearance of the entrance, as he would soon see, was misleading.

They stopped at a second-floor foyer lined with benches resembling church pews. Dr. Matthews paused for an introduction at the nurses' station. A young nurse looked up from her paperwork and flashed a brief smile. Her wavy red hair was in a tight chignon, and her blue eyes beamed above a faint peach lip.

"You must be Bishop. I'm Nurse Dixon," she said. She grabbed her clipboard and came out from behind the counter. Leaving Nurse Parker to man her post, Nurse Dixon continued with Bishop and Dr. Matthews.

They passed through two locked doors and into a common area. "This is the sunroom," Dr. Matthews said as he took off his horn-rimmed glasses and wiped them with a paisley pocket square.

Meant to foster hope in an otherwise dim setting, the sunroom was flooded with light from a wall of fixed windows, and the furniture arrangement resembled the sun, with rays of couches shooting away from an inner circle of chairs. There were no rugs. No decorative pillows to lend life to the plain gray furnishings. No curtains to soften the coldness of the thick glass panes. They were an impenetrable fortress with a teasing view of the rose-lined entrance and gates to a world no longer accepting of Bishop's presence.

A dozen or so male patients filled the sunroom. Some sat on couches talking, while others sat alone. Half of them didn't notice Bishop, and the other half seemed excited he was there, as if a new player had entered the schoolyard playing field. One even waved, but as Bishop raised his hand to wave back, Nurse Dixon caught it midlift and told him to *never* wave back at Jerry. Bishop didn't understand why, but he understood Nurse Dixon meant business. So, he didn't resist as she lowered his hand to his side.

Two counters ran along the back wall. Next to one was a utility cart holding rectangular food trays, the kind with molded sections to keep peas from invading mashed potatoes. To the right was another service counter, but Bishop couldn't yet tell what it was for.

On the wall opposite the windows was a doorway. Nurse Dixon led Bishop through it and down an even longer hallway than the one he'd walked along a story below. Doors ran parallel on both sides. Each had an etched placard below a small window, and a wood spindle chair was stationed next to each doorway. Some chairs were occupied, presumably by the patients who lived in the rooms.

They stopped at the fourth door on the right, number 204. "This is your new bedroom, Bishop," said Nurse Dixon as she opened the door.

Bishop peered in at the sizable space, bigger than the room he'd had at the Sheffield hospital. A twin bed and nightstand with three shelves were against one wall. There was no dresser. Only a chair under yet another sealed window with a small side table next to it.

It wasn't so bad, really. The movies tend to give psychiatric facilities a bad rap. The rooms aren't as dank and haunted as the movies lead you to believe. At least, not the rooms in Bishop's hospital. His was more like a cross between a youth hostel and hotel room but without the private bath.

Nurse Dixon set Bishop's duffel bag on his new bed, then left the room. It had come with him from Sheffield, where Papa T had dropped off some of his clothes and a few belongings.

"Bishop, get yourself settled," Dr. Matthews said. "Nurse Parker, who you met when you arrived, will be by in a few minutes to take you to meet the rest of your new caregivers."

Bishop sat on his new bed to see how bouncy it was and sank his fist into the pillow to check its plushness. It was flat, and the stained pillowcase threadbare. The metal springs holding the sagging mattress scraped together in a shrill harmony.

He reached into his duffel and, to his surprise, found the quilt LeLe had made for him when he was a child. As he spread it across his bed, he heard a thud behind him. Then another. He turned to see a man's face in the little door window and met the man's caring gaze. After a few moments, the man backed up and flashed Bishop a crooked smile through his scruffy beard. Bishop smiled back, and the man went away. He thought it strange, but he'd been in the psych ward at Sheffield long enough to know odd behavior was normal.

Bishop peeked outside his bedroom window as he put away his clothes. Below was a concrete courtyard with a red rubber kickball and a basketball hoop with no net. A dirt trail led to the fence line, turned to follow along in front of a grove of trees, then looped back toward the building.

He traced the path with his eyes, and when he reached the point of return, he saw the best sight he'd seen in over a month—a garden. It wasn't as big as his garden back home, and no picket fence or bunny block protected it. He was wondering how he could get down to it when two knocks on his door interrupted his planning.

"Hi again, Bishop. I'll always knock twice before coming in. That's how you'll know it's me," Nurse Parker said.

She led him into a small room with a single chair in the middle facing a table with five chairs behind it. A blackboard covered the back wall. No chalk, no erasers. Nurse Parker told Bishop to sit in the single middle chair as the door shut behind her. She took a seat at the far end of the table and clicked her pen as she flipped to a new sheet of paper on her notepad.

One by one, the remaining chairs at the table were filled. "Hi again, Bishop," said Dr. Matthews. "You've met me and Nurses Dixon and Parker, and now we'd like you to meet two more doctors."

He pulled a stick of chalk from his coat pocket and wrote all their names on the blackboard, reminding Bishop of what few first days of school he'd had.

Dr. Daniels spoke first and introduced himself as a colleague of Dr. Matthews, then Dr. Holcomb took his turn and explained he was visiting from New York and was there to teach Dr. Daniels and Dr. Matthews some new therapies. Bishop remembered Momma's advice to always be polite when first meeting someone, because you never knew when your paths might cross again.

"Nice to meet you," Bishop said.

Dr. Daniels was an overly assertive man of short stature. Achievement pins weighted his lapel, and he stood to speak when the others had not. "My specialty is anesthesia, and I'll also be ensuring your daily medicines are appropriate for your treatment. I want to make it clear right now that hiding medication or refusing to take it, as you previously did, will not happen here. Do you understand?"

He didn't mention any punishment, but Bishop got the implication there would be one. "Yessir," Bishop said.

Dr. Holcomb was more clinical. Not one wrinkle marred his long white coat, and his jet-black hair was the same color as Bishop's, only thinner and combed over to fake the hairline he once had. "I'll be assisting with new therapy techniques and conducting your private therapy sessions on Tuesdays and Thursdays. Dr. Matthews will lead daily group therapy in the sunroom circle every morning after breakfast."

Nurse Dixon explained how he would spend his days and what time meals would be served in the sunroom.

"Art supplies and games are available at the window next to the food counter but only after dinner each evening."

Nurse Dixon continued, describing what behavior she expected during lights out and what the bells over the loudspeaker meant. Bishop nodded after each instruction but worried he might not remember everything in the correct order.

"Any questions before we introduce you to your housemates?" Nurse Dixon asked.

"Yes, ma'am. How do I get to the garden?"

"Oh! Do you like to garden? Ours needs someone with a green thumb," she said.

"I do. I miss my garden back home."

"Well, if you do everything asked of you—everything—Nurse Parker will take you to the garden every day after lunch. Does that sound good to you, Bishop?" she asked.

Bishop smiled for the first time since arriving, and Dr. Holcomb took note. He was particularly good at figuring out what was important to each patient, and Bishop's smile told him all he needed to know. That garden was leverage.

The adjustment was uncomfortable, but Bishop settled into his new surroundings. He was taking his medication, and after a few mistakes, the bell schedule sank in. The food was devoid of any flavor, and he rarely finished it unless it was spaghetti night. It was the only supper that tasted as it should. And while he was making small strides during therapy, he was not too keen on socializing. The only interaction Bishop entertained was the daily door-window smile from the gentleman whose bedroom was three doors down from his. He'd seen him sitting in his doorway chair but hadn't officially met him.

Bishop found comfort only in talking about Momma. He often spoke of her during group and private therapy sessions, so everyone knew "Grace" was his sister, whom he desperately missed. But no one knew why he was so deeply connected to her. They didn't know about his fall as a teenager or that Momma was his caretaker after LeLe passed away. They didn't know the only thing he had ever accomplished in life was a bountiful garden Momma helped him create. And they didn't know that hiding below the chlorpromazine and a slew of other medications was a man capable of murder.

ONE SUMMER MORNING, DR. HOLCOMB filled in for Dr. Matthews during group therapy and sat next to Bishop. The scent of pipe tobacco lingered on his breath, and it reminded Bishop of the tobacco fields in Riverton. When it was Bishop's turn to share, Dr. Holcomb asked if he thought Grace had forgiven him for what he'd done or if he knew she'd tilled under his garden as punishment. That was a complete lie, and the harshness of the question caught everyone off guard.

The stares of the other men bore through Bishop as they homed in on what he'd done to his sister. Their jittering eyeballs circled him like a slowly churning twister, thirsty for gossip and tormenting fodder. Faster they blinked, until Bishop reached out with both arms to part the air, scattering their eyeballs to the corners of the room. "Enough!" he shouted.

Panicked at the thought of his plump strawberries and sweet snap peas composting under the rusty soil, Bishop sprang from his chair, knocking it to the floor. "He was taking her!" The other patients shifted their bodies, crossing and uncrossing their legs and arms. One stood up and threw his chair across the room in blind unity, smashing it into the cart of clean food trays.

"I had to stop him! I had to save Grace!" Bishop said as he ran for the door to the nurses' foyer.

As the stinging needle entered the back of his arm, Bishop remembered firing the gun. The trauma had been suppressed by so many drugs it took the threat of a tilled garden to surface it, ridiculous as that may sound. But Dr. Holcomb knew questioning Momma's love and threatening the life of his garden was the push Bishop needed to face what he'd done, to break past the stabilizing effects of the chlorpromazine and into a paranoid outburst. It was exactly what Dr. Holcomb wanted to happen.

The FDA approved chlorpromazine for use that year, but the doctors were still learning its side effects. Especially when mixed with other medications. Bishop already had the experience of being on chlorpromazine and then having an extreme event occur as a repercussion for stopping it, so Dr. Holcomb had decreased his dose two days before group therapy. It was all part of his bigger plan.

Schizophrenia had developed differently for Bishop than for the other patients in the hospital. His was the outcome of the traumatic brain injury he'd suffered when he fell in 1939. At least that's what the Sheffield doctor's diagnosis was. No one would ever know if that was true or if it was Bishop's destiny to develop schizophrenia from the start. But Dr. Holcomb was fascinated by Bishop's case. He felt strongly that chlorpromazine wasn't the answer to curing Bishop, but he'd been unable to convince the other doctors to try alternative methods.

You see, Dr. Holcomb wasn't at the Alabama State Psychiatric Hospital just to teach. He was there to experiment with a new psychotherapy technique he'd learned abroad. One that was gaining popularity as a potential treatment for schizophrenia. All he needed was a few disruptive patients to convince the other doctors to let him administer it.

A Gap in Time

SLOANE, 1954–1955
ALABAMA

IF YOU LIVE IN A psychiatric facility, the last thing you want is for other patients to find out what triggers you. Thanks to Dr. Holcomb, that's indeed what happened. Every day during group therapy, Jerry the Waver, as Bishop called him, asked him what he'd done to Momma. Then he'd whip up some fantastical story about how Bishop took scissors to all her dresses because they walked around the house at night watching everyone sleep. Or that he'd burned down her house because the Wild Thang got inside. Jerry would rile the other patients, and they'd pile on to his story as if it was a delusional game of telephone.

Over time, Bishop found their fables revealed their own missteps that had landed them in the hospital. Even though their lunatic babble wore on him, nothing their twisted imaginations came up with was worse than what had actually happened. But Bishop didn't even know the extent of the damage he'd caused.

He remembered only pulling the trigger and that he did it to keep Momma from leaving. But he couldn't recall *deciding* that's what he'd do. He had no recollection of finding the gun in Papa T's closet, loading it with bullets, or opening the kitchen door and stepping outside. And he'd yet to be told about the gruesome crash that took the life of his best friend's father. As far as Bishop knew, Daddy was the only person who died that night, at the base of the kitchen porch steps.

It was hard for Bishop to ignore the taunting from the other patients, but his increased dosage of chlorpromazine was helping, along with the daily moments of normalcy that fed his sanity. There was the man in the window, who greeted him each morning with a smile. He was checking on Bishop, the same way Momma did if he hadn't made a timely return from the post office. And the garden out back, which he'd been restoring every day after lunch, patiently waiting for the sun to reveal his edible masterpiece. He had created a safe space that felt like home to him. A home he longed to return to.

One fall morning, Nurse Parker knocked twice and came in, but Bishop wasn't in his room. She figured he'd gone to the sunroom earlier than usual and was pleased he'd become more social. But when she opened the door to the sunroom to make sure, she saw Jerry on top of Bishop, pinning his waving wrists to the floor. Nurse Dixon struggled to pull Jerry loose while an orderly hovered above, frantically filling a syringe.

Patients were jumping on the couches. "Get him, Jerry! Get his wave!"

Others camouflaged into the bare white walls, shuddering at the chaos.

"What on earth is happening?" asked Nurse Parker.

"Bishop came in, whistled at Jerry, and waved at him with both hands," said Nurse Dixon. "Help me get him back to his room!"

The orderly subdued Jerry and carried him off, feet dragging, but he didn't have to sedate Bishop. Instead, Bishop willingly got up from the floor and with a satisfied smile retreated. Nurse Dixon asked Bishop why he'd provoked Jerry.

"He had it comin," he said.

"For what?" asked Nurse Dixon.

"For being in my garden!"

The day before, Bishop had found Jerry shuffling his feet through the dirt, right where Bishop had planted new seeds. But instead of confronting Jerry, he planned a retaliation. He'd had enough of Jerry's bullying and knew exactly how to set him off. So that's what he did. He walked into the sunroom, whizzed a sizzle through his teeth in Jerry's direction, and began waving feverishly at him with both hands. He never let up, even as Jerry launched at him from across the room and tackled him to the floor.

Nurse Parker called for the doctors, and they appeared at Bishop's doorway shortly after, whispering to each other. Dr. Holcomb entered and dragged Bishop's window chair across the room. The legs made a high-pitched squeal across the waxy floor. He positioned the chair in front of Bishop, then sat down and rested his elbows on his knees.

"Bishop, I don't think your increased dosage is helping you, so I'd like to try something in addition to it," he said.

"Me? What about Jerry? That fool needs wave therapy."

Nurse Parker returned with the wheelchair she'd left to retrieve.

"It might help you calm down, Bishop. And you'll get to see a new area of the hospital," said Dr. Holcomb.

Bishop didn't want to calm down. He wanted to burst into Jerry's room and wave at him more. He had no idea why Jerry hated it so much, but he didn't care. The only thing he cared about was making Jerry hurt as much as he'd hurt him. However, seeing an unknown part of the hospital intrigued Bishop, so he put revenge on hold and willingly got into the wheelchair.

Nurse Parker pushed him down the hall, through the sunroom, which was completely vacated, and out the main door to the nurse's foyer. She pushed the call button for the elevator. It was small, and they all barely fit inside. Dr. Holcomb pushed the number three, and as the elevator door closed and the floor lifted, Nurse Dixon gave Bishop a shot. Before he could ask why, he was completely out.

Bishop's eyes opened to the ceiling above his bed. His whole body ached as if he'd slept in the same position for days without rolling over. A high-pitched tone, like the one that filled his head after Junior hit him, swirled through his throbbing brain. He turned his head to look out his window and a slow trickle fell from the corner of his mouth as he gazed at the sky, pink and faded. Was the sky going to sleep, or was the sky waking up?

He couldn't recall what happened to him after Dr. Holcomb pushed the number three button in the elevator or how he'd gotten back to his room, but a familiar sound comforted him when three short bells rang. Supper. Three was for supper. Two for lunch. And one was for breakfast. He pushed himself up and swung his legs off the side of his bed, but that's as far as he made it. When he didn't appear in the sunroom for supper, an orderly brought it in and set it on the small table under his window.

Bishop glanced over to see a plate of spaghetti. He stared at it, salivating over how good it smelled and imagining the comforting taste of the warm tomato sauce. He lay back down and watched the sun finish its plunge below the treetops, then shut his eyes.

The next morning, in group therapy, Dr. Matthews asked Jerry and Bishop to apologize to each other. Neither of them meant it, but both had gone to bed the night before, not having touched their spaghetti. Whatever happened to them would likely repeat if they didn't make amends.

"Sorry," said Bishop.

"Fine, me too," said Jerry.

And that was that.

THE NEXT DAY WAS FAMILY day, and almost everyone was excited to see their loved ones. There were a few forgotten souls who never had visitors, who stayed in the sunroom and watched TV.

Papa T was the only person who visited Bishop, and once a month he made the Saturday drive to Tuscaloosa. He never asked me or Momma to go, figuring we'd tell him if we wanted to, but one day I got curious and asked him what it was like. He said the outside looked like the postcard of the Grand Gulf Hotel tacked to the back of the kitchen door, but he'd only seen the first-floor visiting room inside.

Through the tall entrance doors and to the left, wood tables and chairs filled a sparsely decorated parlor. There were round serving trays with water pitchers and plastic cups on an antique sideboard, and Bishop always waited at the same table with three filled cups, hoping Momma had come with Papa T. Each time, Papa T had to create new excuses for why she wasn't there, as he drank the water from the extra cup.

His explanation for November was that it was my birthday and Momma needed to set up for my party. It was my birthday all right, but the pain of losing Daddy was still too fresh for any celebration. Momma made my favorite coconut cake, but that was all that marked my fourteenth birthday.

When Papa T returned home, he told me and Momma that Bishop had become increasingly distant and spoke of only one person at the hospital, a man who smiled at him every morning through the tiny window in his door. He still didn't know the man's name and never talked to him, but he liked the consistency of his appearance.

Papa T said Bishop couldn't remember what he'd done in the days preceding family day, and he was worried Bishop's medicine was causing memory loss. His hands shook when he drank from his water cup, and his words were slurring again. Momma tried to put her concern aside, but she knew Bishop would never thrive estranged from her.

No amount of time was going to heal her pain. Nothing could undo what had happened. So at what point has someone like Bishop suffered enough? Momma was a good Christian and knew that was not up to her to decide. She had to find it in her heart to help Bishop survive, and the rest was up to the Lord.

I like to think I'm a good Christian, too, but there was no hiding my feelings for Bishop. I even said it out loud a few times, trying to rid myself of the hate. I'd never gotten the chance to speak my mind and damn him to hell for taking away my daddy. Curse him for ripping our family apart. Anger raged inside me, churning like an overdue volcano. And no matter how many books I read, no matter how many diaries I filled, I couldn't run from it.

Those months after Daddy died were the worst of my life. I did my best to picture only happy memories with him, like riding the carousel giraffe or being filled with happiness over the surprise he'd brought me from Huntsville. But I couldn't shake the image of him doubled over, blood smeared on my sweater, tea jar rolling in the dirt, and him telling me to run.

For weeks I woke up soaked in sweat. I'd change my nightgown, then lie there waiting for the sun to rise, so I'd have an excuse not to fall back asleep. I'd hear Momma up at all hours, milling around and coming in to check on me. And sometimes when I woke, Faith was next to me, and I'd always make sure the sheet was covering her.

The days weren't any better. At school, I panicked if someone yelled "run" on the playground. Hiding in a bathroom stall, I'd stand frozen in fear until the bell sounded, telling me it was okay to come out. And at home, I could smell the faintest hint of gunpowder every time I reached for a tea jar in the cupboard. I broke so many Momma finally switched them out for plastic cups.

I tortured myself with questions I couldn't answer. The actions I couldn't change. There weren't rabbit holes deep enough to find the answers I was searching for. What had I missed? What could I have done to stop it from happening? I was spiraling into a deep depression, and nothing anyone could say gave me solace.

Then one Sunday after church, Pastor Douglas read me a Bible verse about letting go. "Trust in the Lord with all your heart and lean not on your own understanding." Proverbs 3:5.

He explained I wasn't meant to understand why Bishop acted on his impulses. It was in the Lord's hands, and I had to trust that His understanding would guide me past my pain. I needed to let go of the hatred inside me and move on, or I'd be stuck in the grip of its talons forever. And the harshness of my memories would fade in time, but they had to be given the chance to do so.

I knew he was right, because he always was, but I didn't know how to accomplish what he was telling me I needed to do.

I wandered over to visit Daddy's grave, and with no forethought, I said the words I didn't know needed to be said. "I'm sorry, Daddy. What happened wasn't my fault, and I know that. But I need you to forgive me for not running faster."

As soon as those words left my mouth, it became clear my hatred included self-imposed guilt. Even though I had zero control over Bishop's actions, I blamed myself for not having done more to save my father. For not succeeding. And I know how this sounds, but at that moment when the guilt left my body, a whip-poor-will landed on Daddy's marker. He didn't stay long, but I swear that little bird picked up all my guilt with his stubby stick feet and carried it off for me.

WHILE I WAS EMERGING FROM my darkness, Bishop was entering the depths of his. By spring, he was on the highest dosage of chlorpromazine the doctors could legally administer, as his tolerance kept overtaking any effectiveness. He spent most of his time in his room or the garden, which was waking from its long winter nap.

Every week, Bishop woke in his bed, not knowing what had happened in the hours or sometimes days prior. And with each gap in time, his confusion intensified. The progress he'd made in Sheffield—the smidgen of his former self that had reappeared—was now lost again.

During one visit with Papa T, Bishop said he was growing suspicious of the man in his door window. He said he was the reason he couldn't remember things in the morning and that his smile was erasing his memory of the day before.

After visiting hours were over, Papa T requested a meeting with Bishop's doctors.

"There's no reason to be alarmed," Dr. Matthews said. "We increased Bishop's dosages last week, and his system will take a few weeks to stabilize. We're also trying a newer therapy on Bishop to see if the combination of medicine and ECT is beneficial."

"What the hell is ECT?" Papa T asked.

Dr. Holcomb tried to explain in layman's terms. "ECT stands for electroconvulsive therapy. We administer a small amount of electricity into Bishop's brain to trigger seizures. Those seizures may change his brain chemistry and yield an increase in serotonin and a decrease in dopamine, which are key to keeping schizophrenia in check. It may never cure him completely, but we're optimistic it can help Bishop live a more productive and nonviolent life."

"Oh, and don't worry," he continued. "Bishop is under anesthesia and sedation the whole time and can't feel or remember a thing."

"You're shocking his brain? What kind of doctors are you? You can't expect me to believe this is safe. How do you know it won't kill him?" Papa T said, flinging his arms around as he paced.

The truth is, they didn't know. ECT was a newer technique, and Bishop's case differed from the other patients receiving the treatment. His was the only case of schizophrenia developed from head trauma, and doctors had only a suggested protocol to follow for the number of shocks and duration of them. There was no guarantee it would help. And there was no guarantee it wouldn't harm.

"I did not sign off on this, and I demand you stop immediately," Papa T continued.

Dr. Holcomb calmly reminded Papa T they didn't need his permission. The judge ordered Bishop into their custody for rehabilitation by whatever means they saw fit.

ECT is a beneficial therapy, scary as it sounds. But in the 1950s, it was just gaining popularity in America's medical circles. Doctors didn't fully understand its effects or how best to administer it.

Papa T told Momma about the ECT and his worry about it doing more harm than good. "What if the doctors are torturing Bishop and frying his brain?" he said.

That was the Lord's push she needed.

The Man in the Window

SLOANE, 1955–1956
ALABAMA

MOMMA WAS NERVOUS AS SHE rode alongside Papa T. This would be the first time she'd seen Bishop since watching him run into the woods, and she had three hours of staring out a car window to think about the first thing she'd say to him. Would she tell him how angry she was with him? Would she tell him how much he altered her life by taking away her husband? Or would she extend an olive branch because that was the Christian thing to do?

She replayed each scenario as the mile markers passed, with alternate endings and new beginnings, each not lending itself to a satisfying outcome. So, she did what she'd always done when faced with the unknown. She left it to the Lord to decide.

When Papa T pulled up to the open gates, Momma was awestruck by their imprisoning mass. The front flower gardens were as lovely as Papa T had described, and their dainty aroma masked the pain that lived inside the massive estate. Staff lined the circle drive, ready to receive visitors as if they were royalty arriving home after a stay at their country house. It was otherworldly to Momma.

Papa T parked in line with the other cars around the circle and escorted Momma up the marble stairs. Bishop was at his usual table, and when he saw Momma, he looked at Dr. Matthews to verify she was real.

Bishop nearly knocked Momma over with his embrace, and at that moment, the Lord told her the answer: He could not heal Bishop without her help.

Bishop clung to Momma's hands as he told her about his days at the hospital and how proud he was of his garden. "My garden! Come and see it, Grace," he said.

Dr. Matthews had been standing in the hallway, observing Bishop's reaction to seeing Momma, and when Bishop dragged Momma toward the hall, he stepped in to offer a private tour, something that was not normal protocol. He was curious about what kind of effect showing her his garden would have.

Bishop described how pitiful the garden was until he came along and how he had worked the previous fall and winter to get it ready for spring. Dr. Matthews was impressed that despite Bishop's many memory gaps, he remembered every detail about bringing that garden back to life. And it occurred to him that perhaps the best therapy for someone with Bishop's condition was giving them exactly what they loved most.

Dr. Holcomb, however, wasn't convinced. He was of the mindset that the ECT was showing its positive impact and that's how Bishop remembered his garden with such vivid detail. Week after week, he subjected Bishop to shock therapy sessions while varying his medication to observe the results of each combination.

In contrast, Dr. Matthews noted a strong positive influence in the days immediately following his visits with Momma, only to watch it disappear after his next ECT session. He gave his findings to Dr. Holcomb, who rejected his theory and held steadfast in his belief that the cocktail of ECT and medication was why Bishop was showing improvement.

That November, Momma went alone to visit Bishop. Papa T had taught her how to drive his car at her request, but I don't think she enjoyed driving. It reminded her of the accident that took Daddy's and Jack's lives. That was the guilt *she* harbored. Guilt over the precious time wasted because she didn't know how to drive a car—moments that may have changed the outcome of that night.

When Momma arrived at the hospital, Bishop was eager as usual to see her, but she had news for him she wasn't sure how he'd take. She filled Dr. Matthews in before she entered the visitor's room, and Nurse Parker was on standby with a sedative. Papa T had passed away quietly in his sleep shortly after their October visit.

Bishop was silent. His father had died, and for that, he was visibly sad. He picked up the cup of water he had poured for Papa T, stood up, and walked over to the sideboard. He poured the water from the cup back into the plastic pitcher. Hand shaking, he spilled a little on the tray. Then he sat back down at the table.

"Papa T always came for me," he said.

Momma reached across the table and pulled his clasped hands to her lips, then kissed them once. "I'll still come for you, Bishop," she said.

And she did, every month she could. She kept Papa T's memory alive by retelling stories that happened before Bishop's fall and before the shooting. Times that were sentimental to Bishop or particularly funny. When he and Papa T went bank fishing on the big river and caught the biggest catfish of the summer. And when Papa T caught his lucky fishing hat with his hook midcast, only to have it returned to him by the fish he caught. Bishop laughed when Momma reminded him how that fish came out of the water wearing Papa T's hat and how his cotton mill buddies gave him a fake trophy for "Best Dressed Bass" as a joke.

JUNIOR CAME HOME FROM THE army in late December. He had been overseas on special assignment, training the South Vietnamese army for a conflict that eventually escalated into the Vietnam War. During a training exercise, a Vietnamese soldier didn't understand his instructions and shot in the wrong direction, hitting Junior in the back and leaving him paralyzed from the waist down.

Junior had built a commendable career working his way up the ranks, but his injury stopped his climb and earned him an honorable discharge. His mother still owned the house two doors from ours, but it needed some modifications to accommodate his wheelchair. So, the church organized a build day and made Junior a wheelchair ramp beside the front porch steps.

Momma hesitated to go. She had made peace with her feelings toward both Jack Senior and Junior. Neither of them meant the harm they caused her or her family. In fact, they were both doing everything they could to help. But Momma was unsure how Junior felt. Did he harbor ill will toward her or Bishop over his father's death? Or had he also made peace?

As the congregation hammered away, Junior asked if he could speak to Momma privately. They sat under the oak tree in his front yard, as the breeze nuzzled the tire swing Junior and Bishop played on as kids.

Junior looked down at the ground to hide his shame. "I should have been here, Grace. I should have been here for Bishop."

Momma reached for his hand. "There was nothing you could have done. It was the medicine and the situation. Bishop didn't know how to understand it."

"No. I shouldn't have chosen my country over my family. Your family," Junior said. "And if I'm being honest, ma'am, I stayed gone so long because it was hard to face the pain I'd caused Bishop. Every week I sat visiting with him was just another reminder of what I'd done, and I ran from my shame like a coward. It took a bullet to my back for me to realize that."

"Well, you're here now. And I reckon you ain't got many plans," Momma said, nodding to his wheelchair. "How 'bout you go with me to visit Bishop next month?"

She remembered how much Junior's visits meant to Bishop. Starting them again might help with his "Positive Reinforcement Therapy," as Dr. Matthews called it. And it was obvious Junior needed those visits now more than ever too. A chance to no longer feel like a coward.

"Yeah. I'd like that, Grace. I just hope he remembers me."

Momma was thankful for Junior's company during the long drive, but she realized she was doing all the talking. So she asked him what Vietnam was like. He gave vague details that led her to believe he'd seen things he'd rather forget, so she didn't press. Mostly, he talked about how being in a wheelchair affected every aspect of his life. He drew parallels to Bishop being trapped inside his own mind, just as he was now trapped in a chair. They both ended up reliant upon others to help them through life, and Junior was not coping well with seeing his independence stolen. Momma told him he'd do well to talk to Pastor Douglas.

When they arrived, Momma parked the car and opened the trunk. An orderly came over and assisted with Junior's wheelchair. He helped Junior into his chair and then wheeled him up the ramp that ran alongside the marble steps.

"I can take it from here," Junior said.

"I got you, sir," said the orderly.

"Just let me do it!" Junior took hold of the wheels and pushed himself the rest of the way and through the open double doors.

"Apologies," said Momma. "He's not adjusted yet to being in a wheelchair."

"It's okay, ma'am. I shouldn't have assumed," the orderly said.

Momma joined Junior in the entryway. "You ready?"

"Not entirely, but I hope Bishop is," Junior said.

Momma had called ahead and let the nurse know Junior was coming. That was an instruction they'd given her. They needed to understand who any additional visitors were and how they fit into Bishop's life, so when they observed him, they had context.

Dr. Daniels came over and introduced himself to Junior. "How long has it been since you've seen Bishop?" he asked.

"Too long. I'm not sure he even remembers me," Junior said.

"He does. He's talked about you in therapy sessions, but his memories of you seem to be from before his fall," Dr. Daniels said.

As Junior wheeled into the room, he saw Bishop sitting at the first table, holding a plastic cup in each hand. Momma picked up her pace and moved a chair to the next table over, so Junior had space to roll under.

Bishop had not yet noticed Junior because the second he saw Momma, he jumped up to give her a long hug. Momma softly grabbed Bishop's arms and pushed him away from her body. She told him she'd brought a special visitor with her and tilted her head down at Junior.

Staring up at Bishop was a man he'd seen before. With that same scruffy beard. That same crooked smile. That same tall man who visited him through his door window each morning was sitting directly in front of him, paralyzed in a wheelchair.

"Hi, Bishop, I'm sorry I was away in the army for so long and couldn't visit with you," Junior said.

Bishop's face drained into a shade of sheer fright. He screamed, slapping himself on the head. Dr. Daniels grabbed the handles of Junior's wheelchair and whisked him back out to the hall. This was not the reaction Junior had hoped for. He took Bishop's distraught head-slapping as his way of yelling at him for what he'd done to it all those years ago.

Nurse Parker took Bishop's arm and led him past Junior, past a mortified Momma, to the elevator where Dr. Holcomb was waiting. When Bishop saw him standing there, he thrashed and scratched to get away. Dr. Holcomb all but dragged Bishop into the elevator and pressed the number three button. Bishop collapsed onto the floor as a needle drove into the back of his arm. And as the door slowly closed, Bishop watched as a tear-faced Momma grabbed hold of Junior's hand.

When Bishop opened his eyes later that evening in his room, he had not forgotten. This time he remembered everything from the time he woke up that day until Nurse Parker sedated him in the elevator. He remembered what he'd had for breakfast. That he never had lunch or supper. And he remembered the horrified look on Momma's face as the elevator door slowly closed. He struggled to comprehend how the man who lived three doors down from him—the man he saw every single morning—had gotten out of the hospital. And was now visiting him with Momma.

He fell back asleep, feeling worse than he normally did after Dr. Holcomb pressed the number three button, and when he woke to the sound of the morning bells, he knew he had seconds before the man in the window would appear. He stood in front of his door, stared directly into the glass, and waited for him to show.

Without fail, there he was. The man from the wheelchair, standing outside his door and staring right at him. Eyes locked, smiling gleefully through his scruffy beard, as Bishop's breath fogged the glass. Bishop flung open the door, bolted into the hallway, and spun to see which direction he'd gone. But there was no trace of him. He ran to the third door down and looked through its window and saw Jerry the Waver getting out of bed.

Bishop banged on Jerry's door, pressing his face to his door window. "Jerry! What'd you do to my window man? You bury him in my garden? I told you—stay out of my garden!"

Jerry cowered in the corner of his room. Bishop dropped to his knees, slapping his head to knock some sense into it. Make it remember correctly. But it was no use. The man in the window was yet another hallucination. The sense of comfort he'd felt from the man's visits day after day was a farce. He fell to the floor and sobbed so tragically Nurse Parker had to wipe her own eyes dry to see the syringe she was filling. Bishop held out his arm, practically begging her for sedation.

She gave him enough to calm down but still be conscious. His head bobbed to stay upright, focusing on Dr. Holcomb across a room he didn't remember. As Nurse Dixon readied the anesthesia and muscle relaxers for Dr. Daniels, who had not yet entered the room, Dr. Holcomb grabbed her arm and stopped her as she passed.

"Wait. Nothing else has worked. Let's try something different this time. Let's do it unmodified," he said.

"You mean *don't* give him the anesthetic or succinylcholine like we normally do?" she asked.

"Yes. That's exactly what I mean. That's how ECT was originally conducted, without anesthetic or muscle relaxers. Just sedation."

Nurse Dixon hesitantly went along with Dr. Holcomb's instructions, hoping Dr. Matthews or Daniels would walk in and either agree or disagree to let this happen. She helped Bishop onto the padded table. As he stared blankly at the light on the ceiling, she fastened his wrists and ankles to the table and lowered the headset to his temples.

"Shouldn't we wait for the other doctors?" Nurse Dixon asked.

"*I'm* the expert here, remember?" Dr. Holcomb said as he pressed the red button to begin.

Every muscle in Bishop's body clenched with the force of a thousand charlie horses, and the taste of wet leather flooded his mouth. His torso shook, and his legs and arms bounced against their restraints. His jaw seized, and his fingernails dug into the butts of his palms.

"That was the lowest time setting. Let's try a little more," Dr. Holcomb said.

Before Nurse Dixon could contest, he hit the red button. And after Bishop stopped convulsing, he turned the time duration to the maximum.

"If this doesn't cure him, nothing will."

He pressed the red button, but this time, Bishop's body didn't move. Nurse Dixon batted the headset off Bishop's temples, crashing it to the floor. "Stop! You're killing him!"

Dr. Matthews heard her from the hallway and rushed in as Dr. Holcomb was storming out.

"There. Now he's fixed," said Dr. Holcomb as they passed in the doorway.

Nurse Dixon frantically checked for Bishop's pulse and let out a cry of relief when she found it.

Dr. Matthews chased after Dr. Holcomb and lambasted him so loudly Nurse Dixon heard every word, including the part where he told him to get out of his hospital and that he was reporting him to the medical board.

BISHOP WOKE IN YET ANOTHER new room. There were beds lined neatly in a row to either side of him, and a nurse was changing linens. He made eye contact with her, and she swiftly left the room. Minutes later, Dr. Matthews and Nurse Dixon came in and sat on the empty bed next to Bishop's.

"How are you feeling?" Dr. Matthews asked.

"Bishop, do you know where you are?" asked Nurse Dixon.

"You're in the infirmary, Bishop. The treatment Dr. Holcomb gave you didn't go as planned, and he's been relieved of his services here," said Dr. Matthews.

For the second time in his life, Bishop had been in a coma for two weeks. His doctors were unsure what damage he'd suffered, so he remained in the infirmary for a few months for observation. During that time, he wasn't allowed any visitors. He had no outbursts. And he didn't appear to have any hallucinations. Dr. Holcomb's final ECT session had rendered him completely docile. He seemed to have been cured of his schizophrenia but at an enormous cost. For better or worse, Bishop was no longer the same man who had arrived at the hospital two years prior.

When Bishop left the infirmary, he did not return to his previous bedroom on the second floor. His new room was an identical arrangement on the first floor. It was as if they had picked it up and moved it downstairs, even placing the tiny pillow Momma had made for him on his window chair where he always kept it. He closed his eyes and pressed the pillow to his face. It smelled like home. And as he opened his eyes and looked out his new window, right there in front of him was his garden, bursting with glorious spring blooms.

A Lasting Impression

SLOANE, 1957
ALABAMA

DADDY HAD BEEN GONE FOR over three years. I visited his grave, as well as Papa T's and LeLe's, every Sunday after church and filled them in on the previous week's occurrences. It was just me, Momma, and Osee at home by the fall of 1957. Faith had started her second year of nursing school at the University of Alabama, so we hardly saw her. But I knew she had visited Daddy on the anniversary of his death.

Each year, a Mason jar filled with lilacs and adorned with a dainty blue ribbon around the rim rested at the base of his marker. I knew Faith had left them. Daddy's favorite color was blue, and lilacs were her favorite flower because the first four letters in 'lilac' spell Lila. A flower as beautiful and full of life as the baby sister between us she'd lost so many years ago.

UA was a couple of hours away, so Faith's secretly coming home from college, just to leave a bundle of flowers on his grave, told me she still missed him every bit as much as I did.

Momma was getting by, but when Faith turned eighteen, the money from Daddy's retirement payout decreased. She had done exactly what Daddy had told her to do right before he passed out on her lap and the car crashed. But his benefits were from a railroad retirement plan, and it stipulated Momma would get only so much a month for each child under the age of eighteen. Once we all reached that age, the benefits would end. Of course, Papa T had left Momma the house and car when he passed, so at least she didn't have any big monthly payments to make.

Momma was already skilled at making ends meet, but with a limited retirement income and no training for a job, she became an expert. We grew and raised most of what we ate, and although we never went without, the Doodlebug trips to Sheffield for new dresses weren't as frequent as they'd once been. My passion for sewing was a byproduct of that. Momma taught me how to sew the dresses we could no longer afford, and for years I made the latest fashions for myself and as gifts for others.

Momma also had the money Daddy had saved for our new house, but she'd earmarked it for helping us kids through college. She was adamant about her desire that we would receive the education she never got the chance to have. I'd toured the University of Alabama when we dropped Faith off in the fall of 1956 and decided I would go there as well. It was only a few hours' drive from Riverton, and their well-respected nursing program all but guaranteed you a job upon graduation. So it seemed like a fail-safe route. Plus, Faith got straight As, and if she could pass the classes, so could I.

It was a wonder Faith went to college, though. That summer after Daddy died, she ran off with Royce and lived with him in a rundown apartment in Cherokee that his father paid for. Momma tried her hardest to get her to come home, but she couldn't bear to be in our house. The memories were too fresh and too painful for her.

Royce was supposed to be managing the building they lived in since his father owned it, but all he did was drink and throw parties and keep Faith up all night. She'd finally had enough when she came home after working a double shift at the diner next door to find him kissing some trollop against their kitchen counter.

Faith came home shortly before her senior year of high school started. And once Royce's friends found out she'd broken up with their illustrious leader, they made her life at school a living hell. Royce turned every friend she had against her and dubbed her "Unfaithful Faith."

Thankfully, Faith really did have faith. In herself, that is. She finally saw that those hoodlums she ran with would never amount to anything. And that Royce would never be husband material. Their teasing was relentless, but once she stopped reacting, they all but forgot she existed. So she buckled down and graduated with straight As. She even made a few new friends.

Her senior year nearly crushed her, but it ended up empowering her instead. And it's the only thing I can thank Royce for.

MY SAVING GRACE DURING MY darkest times was Miss Maybelle. Her willingness to help me with my schoolwork for the rest of that year after Daddy died gave me focus, and it gave me a reprieve from thinking too hard about the things I couldn't answer. Any time I started tunneling down a rabbit hole again, I threw myself into another assignment and finished the school year with a perfect grade-point average. And that gave me something positive to be proud of during my darkest days.

When I look back on my life, many moments stand out as pivotal. Watching my daddy being shot was certainly one of them; it showed me what utter helplessness feels like. The next would happen in the fall of 1957, at the front end of a new school year. Sometimes there are moments where the gravity of what's happening doesn't resonate until much later. You don't realize at the time that the lessons you learned from it have become part of you. This was one of those moments.

Math was still not my strongest subject, in spite of Miss Maybelle's continuing guidance. I could eke out an answer when I had a formula, but the theory behind the formulas never quite clicked. Miss Maybelle, however, always seemed to be familiar with the theory, as if she was fluent in an exotic foreign language few people knew. She could solve any math problem from our textbook without reading the lesson, and she took great joy in creating her "Friday Freebie," as she called it. She'd write a problem on her blackboard before class on Monday, and the first student to solve it by the end of class on Thursday got an automatic A on her Friday quiz.

Kids would line up outside her classroom each morning, waiting for the door to open so they could race in and propose their solutions. You had exactly two minutes, so you had to be quick. She made math fun and challenged us to learn more than the curriculum she'd been assigned to teach us, and while I may have never earned a Friday Freebie, that didn't stop me from trying.

Miss Maybelle liked that about me. She knew I would always try and she could count on me to help whenever needed. One day, she asked me to stay after class. I was sure I had bombed a homework assignment, but that wasn't the case at all. She was hosting a group of people at her house that evening and asked if I was free to help serve cookies and Cokes to her guests. I jumped at the chance and arrived at her house promptly at four o'clock, as she'd requested.

I set out the trays of assorted cookies she and Maudie had baked the night before and placed bottles of Coke in the ice bucket on the front porch.

There were no decorations or appetizers and salads, so I knew it wasn't a party. "Are you hosting our church group, or is this a teacher's meeting?" I asked.

"You'll see," she said.

My job was to greet her guests as they arrived and offer a Coke to anyone who ventured out to the porch during the evening. I found myself intrigued, wondering who would show up, but never in a million tries would I have guessed correctly.

Half an hour later, I heard cars coming up the lane, so I manned my station on the porch to start my job. Once they came into view, I saw they weren't just cars. There was a black limousine leading the way, with a small convoy of army trucks following it.

Miss Maybelle nudged my arm with her elbow as she stood at my side, then gave me a wink. "Get ready. You're about to see something incredible, Sloane."

The limousine pulled in and the back door opened. Four polished gentlemen stepped out wearing suit jackets with crisp collars and color block stripes. One of them stayed back to converse with the drivers of the trucks, and the other three men walked to the porch to greet Miss Maybelle. They spoke as if they'd known her for years. She shook their hands and offered them a Coke. That was my cue, which I completely missed because I was standing there speechless, mouth agape.

"I'll take a Coke, sweetie," a man said.

I snapped out of my trance, grabbed a Coke from the ice, wiped its glass with a tea towel, and popped the top. Miss Maybelle took the men inside, and I turned my attention toward the trucks.

Cloth canopies covered their beds, and each cab contained a driver and one passenger. They were army men dressed in fatigues, and together, they hauled one large storage trunk from each truck. They set the trunks in the yard, in front of the porch. As they opened them, my eyes were glued to what was inside, expecting a cache of weapons. That made about as much sense as what was actually in them.

Each trunk held three stacked blackboards, separated by a built-in wood rack so the surfaces wouldn't rub together in transit. As the men took them out, the man in the suit reminded them to be careful not to touch the writing surfaces. The men attached wooden legs with casters to the bottoms of each board. One by one, they took the boards inside the house, passing right by my befuddled face.

Miss Maybelle's house wasn't small, but fitting all those blackboards inside looked to be impossible. I peeked in and watched as they looped them in a chain that started in the parlor, extended back toward the rear hallway, came out where the hallway met the kitchen, then continued through the dining and front rooms to arrive back at the front door.

The men turned on work lights and shone them up from the floor. As they lit up the parlor, I finally saw what the boards contained. They were math formulas, and each board had a circled number in the top left corner. It was one continuous math problem that was placed in sequential order. The formulas reminded me of Miss Maybelle's Friday Freebies. Only our class would never have solved the complex problems written on these boards.

What happened next was like watching the most gracefully timed waltz you've ever seen. Miss Maybelle picked up the chalk, stepped onto the footstool she had placed in front of her, and started at the top left corner of the number-one board. As she finished with one, she'd go on to the next, solving the equations, telling the men where they'd gotten things wrong, and giving them ideas for how to make improvements. Chalk dust drifted through the light beams as she toiled away. It was the most beautiful display of intelligence I had ever seen, and I knew I was witnessing something extraordinary. I just didn't know what.

It took her the evening to work her way through the nine boards and explain the theory behind her calculations and modifications. Men would come out to the porch with a cookie in hand and ask for another Coke, and I'd engage in small talk about how Miss Maybelle was my favorite schoolteacher. They'd tell me how lucky I was to have her, which I already knew.

The men's fatigues had a Huntsville Redstone Arsenal arm patch. I'd heard of it before, but it took me awhile to remember where. Daddy had told me Huntsville had an army base that was working on rockets and spacecraft for the USA's space program. It's called NASA now, but back then it was called NACA, the National Advisory Committee for Aeronautics. We were in a space race with Russia to be the first country to launch a manned mission, and I remembered Daddy telling me we were getting close.

That's when it hit me. It was entirely possible the equations Miss Maybelle was inside solving had something to do with the space race. That epiphany was one I'll never forget.

After they stacked the blackboards back into their trunks and the caravan left, I asked Miss Maybelle if she was working with NACA and if those formulas had anything to do with going to the moon. She said I'd find out one day, and that I was welcome to help serve cookies and Coke every month as long as I kept her job helping the army a secret.

I kept my word until 2014, when I accidentally let it slip while talking to Norm on the phone. She was as dumbfounded as me that night on Miss Maybelle's porch and shocked no one saw a limousine-led army convoy rolling in and out of little old Riverton every month. But she wasn't surprised that Miss Maybelle was their secret math weapon.

It was one of the most defining experiences of my life and left a lasting impression that has carried me through some of my most doubt-filled days. Each month until I left for nursing school, I served cookies and Coke to the army gentlemen and watched in awe as Miss Maybelle worked her magic. She showed me that intelligence meant strength and that even a schoolteacher from Riverton, Alabama, could make a difference in the world. Even if nobody knew about it.

So, did Miss Maybelle have a hand in the great space race? I'll never know for sure, but twelve years later, in 1969, we landed on the moon.

Hostess Twinkie Truck Day

SLOANE, 1959
ALABAMA

I WAS SEVENTEEN THAT SUMMER of 1959. Five years had gone by since my father's death, and I had become a young lady he would be proud of. As planned, I was headed to the University of Alabama's nursing program in the fall. I had received enough scholarships to cover most of the cost, and Momma helped where she could. Faith was happily married and lived across the Tennessee river, where she worked at the local hospital. We saw her often, as she was pregnant with her first baby and needed Momma's help to prepare.

Momma continued to visit Bishop nearly every month, but I still had no interest in going with her. She never said much when she came home, just general statements about him doing fine and carrying on. I think all those years of her visiting helped her forgive him for what he'd done. Not because she felt sorry for him, although she did. But with every passing month, his appearance reminded her of how much he'd suffered and paid for his mistake. Especially during those first few years at the psychiatric hospital.

Hate no longer filled my heart like it once did, but I had not yet forgiven Bishop. I was finally in a good place mentally, and I'd spent way too many years letting him affect my life. It had taken awhile, but I'd let go of my internal struggles and focused on my dreams and goals.

I spent most of my summer before nursing school with my cousin Mary Ruth, who lived four hills over in Lane Springs. One day, she invited me over to hang out and see where the day took us. It was getting hot outside, so we headed to the river to swim and explore the Georgetown Caves. Mary Ruth had a fascination with all the caves in the Tennessee River Valley and was always wanting me to go spelunking with her, since I wasn't a fraidy cat like her sister Carlyss.

We put on our swimsuits and shorts and packed our river bags with a towel and other things seventeen-year-old girls can't live without. My aunt was nowhere to be found, so we rolled a note like a scroll and shut it in the screen door. The last time we'd left her a note the wind blew it under the table where she couldn't see it and we got into a heap of trouble. From then on, we made sure our notes were wind resistant.

The river was a two-mile walk down the main road. And by main, I mean the only road through Lane Springs. It was barely wide enough for two cars to pass without sliding into the ditch on either side. We knew the times and days for every scheduled delivery and used them to our advantage.

The mail truck arrived every morning at seven. Every Friday evening at eight, the ladies in town left for their church meeting. At least, that's what their husbands thought. If they were to peek through the stained-glass windows, they'd see their wives sipping sherry and playing bridge. But most importantly, we knew what days the delivery trucks came to town and stocked the shelves at the Lane Springs corner store. And that particular day was Hostess Twinkie truck day.

Mr. Glenn, the Hostess truck driver, knew us well. He saw us walking down the road one day and made the mistake of stopping to ensure we were okay and didn't need a ride. We thanked him for the offer but explained that the walk to the river was half the fun for me and Mary Ruth. So, he kindly offered us a cold drink from his cooler and gave us a Twinkie before driving on into town.

After that, whenever we walked the main road and heard his noisy old truck coming, we'd do different things to make him stop and give us a Coke and a Twinkie. We'd pop out from behind trees with our finger guns pointed, or we'd lie in the middle of the road and play dead. He'd curse us, trying not to laugh, but he always came through and gave us what we wanted.

As we walked along the road that day, we planned our greatest heist yet. Chiffon scarves were all the rage back then, and we had brought ours with us. We had four or five each, in different colors and patterns. We'd tie them to the shoulder straps of our bags as adornments or use them to keep our hair intact if we caught a ride somewhere. Summer in Alabama meant windows down, so you had to be prepared.

Our grand plan for that day's felony was to tie our scarves together into a rope and hold it across the roadway so he couldn't drive through. We roared with laughter, as only teenage girls can, and mimed how he'd play along and let us rob him once again. I could already taste the warm whipped cream and spongy sweetness of the cake, mixed with the burning bubbles of a chugged Coke.

Mary Ruth found a narrow spot in the road with two trees across from each other. We climbed high enough to hide and hold our scarf rope at the same level as the truck's windshield. We were giggling away in our trees and singing across the roadway our improvised "Hostess Heist" song to the tune of "Yakety Yak."

Here comes the Twinkie truck again,
That poor old driver, Mr. Glenn.
Take all his loot, but not his cash,
Then get away just like the Flash.
Hostess Heist… oh, so nice.

It was the silliest song, but we had endless fun singing it. Especially the low vocals on the "oh, so nice" part.

Before long, we heard the noisy truck coming. "This is it! Get ready, Sloane!" said Mary Ruth.

"Okay, hold the rope tight!" I said.

The two trees were over the crest of a gentle hill, so we couldn't see the truck as it approached. We could only hear it. But our plan worked, and the truck stopped.

Laughter billowed from below. High pitched, low pitched, even a snort. Then I heard Mary Ruth denying guilt, so I knew something had gone wrong with our plan.

"Sloane, is that you up in that tree?"

It was a familiar voice asking.

"No!" I rustled the leaves to get a better look below.

I couldn't believe it. That wasn't the Hostess Twinkie truck at all. It was Bubba, Mary Ruth's next-door neighbor. He was with his cousin Ray, who had an old Mercury that was so loud it sounded exactly like the Hostess truck.

"Yes, it is. Now come down from there. And what the hell are y'all doin'?" Ray said.

I climbed down from my tree, and Mary Ruth and I exploded in laughter. "You don't want to know," she said.

Ray and Bubba shook their heads at us. They were used to our hijinks and didn't find them as funny as we did.

"Well, get in the car. Mary Ruth's momma needs y'all back at the house," Ray said.

Carlyss was with them. My aunt had sent them to fetch us after finding our note. She was missing from the house when we left because their dog had run off, and she wanted us to help find him.

We never made it to the river that day, but we did find Mary Ruth's dog. He'd been hiding under her porch the whole time, scared because some boys were playing with firecrackers in front of the house. It was probably Ray and Bubba. But if all those things hadn't happened, if Ray wasn't visiting Bubba that day, and if someone hadn't scared Mary Ruth's dog, Ray and I might have never started dating.

It had been a while since I'd seen Ray. He'd become a handsome young man, wearing his dark hair in the typical crew cut and dressed in James Dean-esque rolled jeans and a white T-shirt. I caught him glancing at me in his rearview mirror, and I blushed like I never had before. Most of the boys at school annoyed me, but he wasn't from my school. He complimented me on my shorter hair, too, when most boys preferred longer locks.

We had played together as kids whenever I was at Mary Ruth's and he was at Bubba's. My strongest memory from those days was at the park across the street from Mary Ruth's house. They lived in a neighborhood called Village One. If you looked down at it from the sky, you'd see that its roads were in the shape of the Liberty Bell. The houses were all different but painted the same shade of putty. The village's original purpose was to house the workers constructing the nearby Pickwick Dam, but it had since become a nice place to raise a family. And there were four more identical villages in the neighboring towns.

A community park and playground filled the center of the bell. It also had a tennis court, where we loved to play. Not tennis, just on the fenced-in court. Ray and Bubba said the court was their fort, and they would hold anyone caught trespassing prisoner for all eternity. So, of course, I strutted on in. They were off in the corner, climbing the chain link to snag tree limbs hanging over the top.

I snuck up behind them and lowered my voice as far as it would go. "What do you two boys think you're doing?"

They slipped from the fence, startled, thinking Bubba's daddy was behind them.

"Ha! Some soldiers you are!" I said.

Well, they didn't think it was funny. They got on either side of me and lifted me under my armpits and set me down in front of one of the fence posts. Bubba pulled out his shoelaces and tied them together. He used the laces to tie my wrists to the pole as Ray held me in place, giggling as I tried my hardest to wriggle loose. I thought it was funny, too, until they took off and left me there. A tiny ant crawled across my sandal. Then another, and another, until they covered my feet.

I screamed as the ants pierced the tops of my feet with their burning venom. "You dummies, get back here and untie me! Get back here!"

They ran out the court gate and across the park. I thought I was a goner. I'd spent so many years afraid of snakes when turns out I should have been worried about ants. Fortunately I realized Bubba wasn't good at tying knots, and it took only four more bites to free myself.

I didn't see them again until later that evening. Mary Ruth and I were sipping lemonade on her front porch swing. They came flying into Bubba's front yard on their bikes, and when they saw us, they came over.

"Oh, you finally got free?" Bubba said.

"Finally? When my feet stop itching, I'll show you how to tie a *real* knot," I said.

Then I pointed to my feet, propped up on Mary Ruth's lap and covered in calamine. "And next time you take prisoners, make sure you don't put them on top of a damn anthill!"

Ray looked at my pink feet and chomped his teeth together with a frown, but they were boys and did what they normally did—laughed as if they didn't care and took off before their daddies could get their belts off.

THOSE TWO WERE ALWAYS IN trouble. Bubba attended school with me and Mary Ruth, but Ray lived in Sheffield. In the fall of their senior year, Ray suddenly showed some school spirit. Sheffield's football team was playing at their rival school's homecoming game, so Ray, Bubba, and three other boys from Sheffield decided they were going to do something no one could miss during the game. They piled into their friend Dean's car and set out for Florence High School.

Dean drove around to the back of the school near the football field and parked in a dark spot, then they waited to make sure no one was around. They had it all planned out. Well, everything except for what to do if they got caught.

They got out of the car, retrieved a gas can from the trunk, snuck onto the center of Florence's football field, and poured a giant *S* for Sheffield in the middle of it. With one flick of a match, the *S* erupted in glorious flames. They went primal, dancing around like characters in *Lord of the Flies* as the flames lit up the entire field. And as they watched it dwindle to a soft glow, red strobing lights came up over the hillside.

Everyone but Dean took off running for the trees. He jumped into his car but failed in his attempt to speed away, narrowly missing the patrol car blocking his exit. The other boys watched from their bellies as the Florence sheriff handcuffed Dean and threw him into the back of his car, then drove off, with a deputy following in Dean's car.

Ray, Bubba, and the other two boys hid in the trees for hours before crawling out. They made their way to the service station where they'd filled the gas can. Bubba and Ray had a friend in Florence, so he told the station attendant his car had stalled up the road and asked to use the phone to call his father. The attendant remembered the boys and didn't believe a word Bubba said but still let him use the phone.

Bubba called their friend, pretending he was talking to his father, and within the hour, the friend picked them up and drove them to the police station. But when they arrived, neither the sheriff's nor Dean's car was there.

"I bet they took him to the judge since we're minors," Ray said.

That's exactly where they found the cars, parked outside the judge's mini-mansion a few blocks from the courthouse. The boys knew they couldn't let Dean take the fall, so they walked up the cobbled pathway to the front porch and knocked on the door. The judge's wife, who was used to being woken up in the middle of the night, refastened her silk robe and ushered them inside to her husband's study. Dean was sitting in front of the judge's desk, with the deputy standing behind him, ready to tackle him should he make a break for it again. The boys stood next to Dean and owned up to their part in the prank.

Well, they got about as lucky as they could. Turns out, the judge went to Sheffield High, so he felt a soft spot for the boys.

Plus, he was impressed that they fessed up to being part of the prank and didn't let their friend take all the blame. The judge warned them all not to do anything stupid like that again and let them go.

That next Friday, Florence not only beat the crap out of Sheffield and won their homecoming game, but they blocked Sheffield from a perfect season. Nobody knew who burned the *S* in the middle of the football field, but ironically, it fueled the Florence players' fire to win rather than snuff it out like Ray and the other boys thought it would.

The Unexpected Letter

SLOANE, 1977
TEXAS / ALABAMA

FAST FORWARD TWO DECADES. I was a registered nurse at Dallas Presbyterian, the same hospital you were born in, Rynn. Ray and I lived in Garland with you and your sister, and I worked the graveyard shift on the top floor—the psychiatric ward. I think by now you can understand why I became a psych nurse, but I can assure you my reasoning was much more deeply rooted than it appears.

The 1950s weren't a high point for mental health. The decade that ushered in ECT and lithium also gave way to the 1960s when state hospitals and private institutions across America suffered for their experimentations with them. Bishop was living proof of that. But there was also just more awareness of it. Thanks to books like *One Flew Over the Cuckoo's Nest* and a generation fueled by flower power, there was an uprising against ECT for what the public perceived to be its unethical use as punishment. By the late 1970s, funding for state hospitals had become a low priority, and private institutions had to lock their doors when benefactors responded to the fallout by withdrawing their generous support.

There was also an underlying stigma in the fifties attached to anyone who saw a psychiatrist of their own free will. When I was a kid in 1954, going to therapy was almost unheard of.

People bottled their pain and prayed it would never escape. Our elders led us to believe that the Lord provided everything they needed. All we had to do was flip a coin into the collection basket each Sunday as payment. When general hospitals didn't know how to treat a person's mental instability, that person likely ended up in a psychiatric institution because doctors didn't know what else to do with them. Hope was coming with new medicine and proper therapies, but it wouldn't be until the 1980s that the stigma attached to mental health turned a corner.

I left for nursing school in the fall of 1959. Ray and I had been dating since the day Mary Ruth and I tried to rob him instead of the Twinkie truck, and he's the one who drove me to the University of Alabama and helped me move into my dorm. My best friend, Norm, got into UA as well, and we were ecstatic to be going to nursing school together.

Ray visited me when he could, and as I worked my way through school, he climbed the ladder of the department store where he worked. He was uniquely romantic, and I could always count on him to do something memorable when we were together. Like the night he asked me to marry him, for instance.

He said later that he knew I was the one for him the day he dropped me off at UA for my freshman year. As he drove back to Sheffield alone, he missed my talking. He's probably tired of my talking by now. But he waited patiently until I finished school to propose, knowing how important it was to me. He didn't want our marriage to derail my goals. So, after my last final was over, he took me to Eddie's Diner to celebrate. And to propose.

Eddie's was your classic drive-in diner, complete with carhops that served the best malts in town. Ray loved their homemade hamburgers and strawberry malts, and it's what he ordered every time we went. It was our special place, so I went there only when he came to visit me.

It was a popular place for college kids, and watching them interact from the front seat of Ray's car was like watching a free drive-in movie. Girls dressed in their best skirts, trying to catch the eye of a cute boy. And the boy would be oblivious until the girl's best friend ran over and whispered to him, tired of waiting for him to notice.

The night Ray proposed, he was so nervous he didn't finish his food. He had a ring hiding in his front jeans pocket, and he planned to wait until one of my favorite songs was playing on the jukebox inside, which you could also hear outside. Ray thought having a song I enjoyed playing in the background would make his proposal more memorable.

But this was Ray we're talking about, and he had a history of messing up the best-laid plans. The fire ants on my feet. The burning *S* on the football field. He didn't have the best track record for thinking things all the way through. Well, he'd seen a TV show where the cool guy would rather kiss the girl sitting next to him in his expensive sports car than finish his milkshake, so he tossed his shake out the window and passionately kissed her. When I got giddy as "He's So Fine" by the Chiffons started playing, he looked at me and reached for his pocket with one hand as he threw his strawberry malt backward out the window with the other.

Only his window wasn't rolled down. It splashed back into his hair and streaked the inside of his window, then trailed down the door and pooled into a pink puddle on the floorboard.

"What the hell, Ray?" I leaned back, annoyed that some of it splashed on me. As I blotted my dress with my napkin, there, in the palm of his outstretched hand, was a gold band holding a speck of a carat. I stopped wiping my dress and looked up at him, pink sludge dripping from his black hair, then leaped across the car and passionately kissed him. Not *exactly* what he'd planned, but it ended in a kiss and me saying yes, so I guess it worked out in the end.

We didn't have any money for a wedding, and I didn't want to put financial pressure on Momma, so we eloped the night before I graduated. A few days before my graduation, Norm and I pulled an all-nighter sewing my wedding dress. The pattern wasn't anything fancy, but I bought the nicest white satin fabric I could afford, and the dress turned out every bit as pretty as the ones in the dress-shop windows.

The day before my graduation ceremony, Ray and I filed for our marriage license at the courthouse, and that afternoon we were married. Norm stood right beside me as my maid of honor, and Bubba drove down to be Ray's best man. Afterward, we all had dessert and coffee at a little cafe by the courthouse. Then Ray and I strolled through the UA campus, dreaming about the type of house we wanted and hoped to afford a better car than that old, noisy Mercury Ray kept reviving.

We planned to tell Momma we'd eloped right after the graduation ceremony, but she saw my new ring as I walked across the stage to receive my diploma. Ray was sitting two seats away from her, and I swear her purse hit his leg, but she wasn't truly mad. Just ticked that we didn't tell her first. She would have at least gotten me new shoes or an appointment at the salon, she said.

I KNEW FROM THE START of my freshman year I wanted my focus to be on psychiatry. Because of my personal experience with Bishop, helping others in mental distress was where I felt I could make a difference in the world. But I also chose psychiatry so I could get the therapy never offered to me after Daddy's death. I still needed to understand and release the lingering pain bottled up inside me and move on with the next chapter of my life. And what better way to self-diagnose than to learn the craft myself?

I finally understood that my flashbacks and confusion were a form of shell shock, which was rebranded "Post Traumatic Stress Disorder" in 1980. With each new revelation, I felt empowered. I was finally healing, and my skills as a nurse flourished. By the time I graduated with a nearly perfect grade-point average, I had secured an entry position in the psych ward at the Sheffield hospital, the same hospital that treated Bishop after his fall and after he destroyed not only my vanity mirror but my family.

Sheffield wasn't exactly my first choice, but it was the closest hospital to Ray's job in Florence. It was surreal being back there again, each day riding the elevator that had taken Bishop to the top floor as a patient. But in a way, I felt like I'd come full circle. I had been in so much distress the last time I was in that hospital. And now I was there to help ease it.

Ray and I built our careers and moved to different cities along the way, eventually landing in Texas. But for all the progress I'd made, something was about to thrust me back into the painful memories I'd worked so hard to release.

In 1977, Ray and I had a rhythm of switching off parental duties. As he came home from his office downtown, I left for my graveyard shift at Presbyterian Hospital. He'd grab the mail on his way in and sit at the table to sort it, and as I finished cooking supper, we'd chat about his day and my previous night. When everything was ready, we'd eat together as a family before I left for work.

One evening, as Ray sorted through the stack of letters and junk mail fliers, he paused his shuffle and called me over. "Sloane, there's something here you should read right now."

As he handed me the letter, I saw the return address for the Alabama State Psychiatric Hospital. My fingers trembled as I opened what I thought was a death notice. Instead, it was a letter explaining the hospital was releasing Bishop due to staffing shortages and a lack of state funding.

Then I read the words I had hoped no one would ever type. "We are releasing Bishop Medford to the custody of Grace Morgan."

I crumpled the letter and dropped it from my hands. Bishop was never supposed to be released. He was never supposed to reenter our family, and he was never again supposed to set foot in the house he crumbled. Ray picked up the letter and skimmed it to catch up. I hadn't yet read the part that described Bishop as being no danger to himself or anyone else for the past twenty years, but I wouldn't have cared. My ability to move on and feel safe was based on him staying locked up and never being able to harm me or my family again. And I felt that sense of security slipping away.

Ray finished making supper so I could call Momma. She told me I needn't worry and that she'd agreed to take in Bishop and assume responsibility for him. She'd visited him as much as she could for the past twenty years and knew he was no threat. He had the IQ of a fifth grader and had been on the same dose of lithium for years without issue.

I hung up the phone, still in a panic. I knew one little thing could, without warning, trigger a schizophrenic. It might be as simple as the sound of the bell above the front door. Or the smell of hominy cooking in the kitchen. I feared for Momma's safety. What if something in the house he grew up in would cause an episode when she brought him home.

I had told Ray shortly after we started dating that Bishop had shot my father and was in the psychiatric hospital, but that's all I'd told him. He said he'd heard enough details from Bubba to keep from being curious, and that was fine by me. He understood it was a time in my life I never wanted to discuss. So, when he read the letter, he knew my pain was about to return and force me to face something—and—someone, I'd disowned so many years ago.

I was a nervous wreck leading up to Bishop's release date. Momma promised she'd call as soon as she got him home and settled, and she did. She said the car ride home mesmerized him, and when you think about it, I suppose it did. He had lived in the hospital for twenty-three years, and even though there was a TV for the patients to watch, it wasn't the same as firsthand experience. Everything from clothes to cars had changed, and that could have caused him distress, but it didn't.

The house had barely changed since the last time Bishop walked through its front door. The furniture was in the same spot. The couch was a different color, but it still sat where the old one had. He wandered around and looked at the photos hanging in the hallway. Momma helped him put a name to each face and introduced him to the new ones. She told him stories about each person to help revive any memories he had of them, but when he got to Momma and Daddy's wedding photo at the end of the hall, he looked puzzled.

"Where is Hardy, anyway?"

Momma hid her astonishment and told him Daddy had died in a car accident, which wasn't a lie, but it wasn't exactly the truth either. He stared at Daddy's face, processing what she'd said. Momma was afraid he would suddenly remember what he'd done, so she drew his attention to his bedroom.

Momma opened his door. "Let's get you settled in, Bishop."

He reached into his duffel bag and pulled out the tiny pillow Momma had made him. The one he'd kept on the chair in his bedroom. He smiled at the model airplanes he'd made so many years before, then placed the pillow gently on his bed. He was finally home.

The only thing different about the house was the kitchen, which Momma had updated with the money Osee never used for college. He got on with the Pickwick Dam's electrical apprenticeship program right out of high school and worked his entire career there. He was still living nearby in Cherokee and helped Momma whenever she needed him.

Osee was six when Daddy died and didn't witness any of it. He was a few blocks away, playing at a neighbor's house. Momma had planned to walk over and get him before supper that night, but everything unfolded before she could. His friend's mother brought him back when Momma didn't show up, and Maudie took care of him until everyone came back home.

Osee had no ill feelings toward Bishop because he had no memory of him. So when Bishop came home from the hospital, Osee was essentially meeting him for the first time.

Faith still lived across the river, and when she got her letter in the mail, she called me to make sure I was okay. She had the same worries I did and promised to be there when Momma brought Bishop home.

Faith wasn't there the second they arrived, but she'd gotten there shortly after and stayed the whole evening to make sure he was okay and not showing any signs of odd behavior. She said Bishop was a completely different person, meek and childlike. I took her word for it but still wasn't okay with him being home. I was perfectly fine with him living out his life in that hospital, and unless someone made a request for release, that's usually what happened to residents like him.

I regret not flying home to Alabama to help Momma transition Bishop. It was hard to find time to visit her, working the graveyard shift on top of keeping up a house and raising a family. But if I'm being completely honest, there was a part of me using that as an excuse to avoid a world that once again included Bishop.

Faith called out of the blue early one afternoon, but I was sleeping. Leigh answered and pinned the message to the corkboard hanging by the kitchen wall phone. When I walked into the kitchen later that evening and saw 'call Aunt Faith TODAY' scribbled across a discarded envelope, I froze. Faith knew I worked the graveyard shift and slept during the day. And she'd never left me an urgent call-back message before. My first thought was that Bishop had done something, and I felt petrified. Twice I had to hang up the phone and start over, spinning the dial for her number. Faith answered with the frailest voice, and I knew right away my fears were coming true. But it wasn't Momma who was in trouble; it was Faith.

She had been sick for a few months with fatigue and had lost some weight, so she asked a doctor at her hospital to run a few blood tests. After he followed up with her a few weeks later, her life would never be the same. It was leukemia, and she needed to start treatment right away to have a fighting chance at surviving it.

We cried for a long time, trying to mix in cheerful stories to offset the horrible one unfolding. As a nurse, she'd seen countless kids come into the pediatric wing where she worked and never leave and feared she'd succumb to the same fate. I made her promise she would fight it, and she did. After multiple rounds of intensive chemotherapy, she was in remission.

It was hard not being there to help her through her treatments, but she had Momma and her husband and kids to help take care of her. I was her long-distance support and always told her I'd be on the next plane if she asked, but she never did. She didn't want to disrupt our family, but honestly, I think she just didn't want me to see what she looked like. Momma said she was ghastly thin, and it might be a good year before she was strong enough to go back to work.

I was just thankful my sister was alive and getting well again. But her being sick helped me realize I could no longer be selfish. I needed to find the strength to return to Riverton. It was time I stopped alienating myself from my family over fear of dredging up painful memories, and acclimate to Bishop's return home.

Home

SLOANE, 1985
ALABAMA

BY 1985, RAY AND I were both thriving in our careers. I believe you were in sixth grade, Rynn. So Leigh was in twelfth. We shuffled you and your sister between the softball field and ballet studio, intent on giving you girls the best childhood we could afford. Ray and I both grew up in households without a lot of extra money, so when each of your talents showed up, we forwent things like new cars and fancy houses so you girls would have what we felt was missing from our upbringing.

Momma and Bishop were doing fine back at home, active in their church as ever, and Faith was back at work. But during a routine checkup, Faith's bloodwork showed abnormally low levels of red blood cells. She started treatment immediately, but her leukemia returned with an aggressive vengeance. And by fall, she'd left it in the Lord's hands.

She called me shortly after Halloween and asked me to come home. She wanted to see me one last time before she died and needed my help to get her affairs in order. So I took a leave of absence from work and flew home that week.

Ray stayed behind in Dallas with you girls. You'd met your aunt Faith only a few times, Rynn, when she came to visit us in Dallas. I didn't want your last memory of her to be at her funeral. Also, there was a part of me still scared Bishop might have violent tendencies, even though Momma and Faith assured me he wasn't capable of harming anyone.

It's a dreadful feeling, knowing your sister is going to die within the month. You get to skip the denial stage of grief because you already know it's coming, but you end up going through the depression and acceptance stages twice—once on the front end and again when they're gone. You can get mad and bargain all you want, but what's done is done. Death is brutal. Not only for the one who suffers it, but for the ones left to accept it, as well.

As I sat on the plane at thirty-two thousand feet, I thought about all that Faith had accomplished. We had taken similar paths but in different towns. She got the education and career Momma wanted for her, and she was proud to be a pediatric nurse. She raised her family in a comfortable house with a swimming pool, and her husband tended the bountiful acreage surrounding it. Faith had everything someone could want, and it gave me peace knowing she built her happiness.

But there was one thing I never asked her about. I had role models like Miss Maybelle and Maudie and lifelong friendships to help me back on my feet. I retreated for a while, scared of trusting those around me, but eventually, I let people back in. But Faith didn't. And her personality changed the day Daddy died.

She had no friends left because of Royce. Outside of family, she had no positive influences to uplift her. I don't know what coping mechanisms she used to get through the pain we suffered, and she seemed stuck mourning Daddy for years longer than me. She was productive and achieved her life goals, but a hint of sadness always showed on her face, and I could hear it in her voice when we talked on the phone. Many times, I tried coaxing her into opening up, but she never did.

When my plane touched down in Huntsville, I had another two hours of driving ahead of me. It was the same route Daddy had taken each month on his layover, and as I drove along, I imagined what the sights must have looked like back then. It was easy to tell which buildings were new, so I replaced them with wheat and cornfields instead. I saw the remnants of a drive-in diner like the one where Ray proposed to me, and it gave me such a warm feeling of nostalgia. I didn't want my road trip to end.

I passed through Cherokee without stopping at Osee's house. He had lunch planned for everyone at his house the next day, so I'd see him then. It looked like the town had shrunk, and its once lively square was now a vacant relic. I took a few photos and drove past some of my old haunts, several of which were boarded up. I realized the town hadn't shrunk; it just never grew.

As I continued to Riverton, my stomach turned sour. My grip tightened around the steering wheel as the sheen from the old Texaco sign reflected the afternoon sun. I was approaching the spot where Daddy's car crashed into the gully, helping that bullet finish the job.

I didn't know the exact spot, but my mouth began its salivatory prep for vomit, so I knew I was close. I pulled over and walked across the road to the other side. I wasn't sure where the accident happened since Papa T had me and Faith duck our heads as we passed by. So, I picked out a tree that looked like it could have stopped Daddy's car, closed my eyes, and said a prayer.

Lost in meditation, I heard a man call out. "You okay, miss?"

It startled me, and I turned to see an old man and woman stopped on the road. They'd seen me standing on the shoulder, with my rental car parked on the other side.

"I'm fine, sir. Thank you for checking," I said.

"You know where you are?" his wife asked.

"I do. I'll never forget this spot as long as I live," I said.

She looked at her husband like I was crazy, since there was nothing around but a grove of trees, then motioned to him to drive on.

I knew they meant well, but I wished they hadn't seen me. I had driven past that spot a million times, ignoring its existence. I just wanted a few invisible moments to connect with anything spiritual that may have been waiting for me. To finally stop and let it find me. It's not like I expected to see my daddy's image, but I yearned for a sign he knew I was there. A bird, like the one on his grave marker that carried away my guilt, or a breeze that engulfed me like one of his hugs.

I got back into my rental car, and just as I started easing the gas, it hit me. That old man was driving a restored Hudson, just like Daddy's.

My whole body shivered in goose bumps as I cried my eyes out. I had passed event signs near the fairgrounds advertising a classic car show, so it made sense that the man and his wife appeared in that exact car. But I was also sure they were the sign I'd hoped for. That somehow, the man who pulled over and asked if I was okay was my daddy asking if I was okay. And his wife's question about me being lost was the nudge I needed to realize I no longer was. I was exactly where I needed to be.

I was a mess, mascara streaming down my half-powdered face, and it took me a good fifteen minutes to compose myself. As I wiped my eyes with a tissue, an overwhelming calm replaced my anxiety. That entire trip, from the moment I stepped foot on the plane in Dallas to the moment I stepped back into my rental car on the side of the road, I was holding my breath, fearful of seeing my dying sister and seeing Bishop for the first time in thirty-one years. That cry was the release I needed to breathe again. To know I was going to be okay.

I DROVE STRAIGHT TO FAITH'S house. Her husband was there but happily gave us time to reconnect. She told me all the things she needed my help with, like going to the bank to make sure her accounts were in order and picking up her burial dress from the dry cleaners. We stayed up and reminisced for as long as she could keep her eyes open. I was glad I'd come because she was fading fast.

As she slept, I watched over her until I finally fell asleep. After all those years of her protecting me as I slept, I felt I owed it to her. Even though my nursing background was not with cancer patients, I had seen what the disease did to LeLe. And what it could do to an otherwise healthy body. The person inside is not what's reflected on the outside, and Faith was no different. Her body was at peak frailness, and her face looked nearly drained of life. I kept picturing the Faith I remembered. The one with long, lustrous black hair and gloss-kissed lips. Turning the head of every boy she passed.

The next morning, we finished her errands and headed to Osee's for lunch. I'd seen pictures of his house, but they didn't do it justice. It swallowed a quarter of its huge corner lot, with a swimming pool twice the size of Faith's. White columns flanked the front door, adorned with orange pumpkins and green gourds at their base. He may have grown up without a father, but he didn't lack the skills needed to build a picturesque homestead.

Faith and I arrived first. Osee moved his most comfortable chair into the parlor for her, and she relaxed while he gave me a tour of his home. We ended in the kitchen, and I helped his housekeeper prepare the sandwich trays while he received guests. Osee's wife had died in the parking lot of the Piggly Wiggly one stormy afternoon, when a bolt of lightning hit the grocery cart she was pushing. It was a total scene, with smoking vegetables and blackened soup cans scattered across the wet pavement.

No one could figure out why she attracted that bolt. If anything, the tall metal light posts should have taken the hit. Osee always said she was one in a million, in more ways than one, and I guess he was right. At least her death was quick, and she gave him two brilliant sons before it happened. But can you imagine? Dying right there in the parking lot of the Pig?

Anyhow, the last time I'd seen Momma was the year before, when I flew her out to Dallas. She was not fond of flying or the fast-paced life of a big city. So when she came into the kitchen at Osee's house, I needed a long hug to make up for the year's worth I'd missed. I felt her thinning gray hair as I held her close.

The worst part about not seeing a parent for a while is the awareness of how much they've aged. Momma was shorter, not that she was ever tall. Her upper back was showing signs of osteoporosis, and age spots freckled her tan skin. She had always worn comfortable cotton dresses that hit just below the knee, and today was no different. She was a proper southern lady, after all.

Faith's impending death weighed on Momma differently than it did on me, as you're not supposed to outlive your children. First Lila, now Faith. It was the second time she would bury a child, but Momma held in her sadness and focused on the time she had left with my sister. I decided to do the same.

It was a good thing I had all that positive energy from hugging Momma because the moment I'd been dreading was about to occur. Bishop appeared in the kitchen doorway, and at first, I didn't look directly at him. I stole glances while I slathered pimento cheese on Wonder bread, and all the fear I'd had seemed so silly now.

"I'm right here," Momma said. His arm shook as he gave her the bag of apples they'd plucked from the yard.

He was still tall, but one shoulder rested lower than the other, and the stiffness in his posture kept him from hunching like he once did. His hair was salty, easy on the pepper, and the corner of a black plastic comb peeked from his back pocket. His jaw opened like he was going to yawn but then stopped before completing it. And he twisted his neck from left to right as if trying to crack it.

As a psych nurse, I had seen these mannerisms before. He had tardive dyskinesia, a side effect of the antipsychotic medicines he'd been on for years. There was no cure for it, but at least his case wasn't the worst I'd seen. It should have been, but the near-lethal doses of ECT he'd received that burned out part of his brain left him with only a few of the telltale traits.

My heart all but stopped when he walked toward me. "Hi, Sloane. Your hair used to be brown."

Only someone who knew me as a child would know that. I'd been a blond for years by 1985. "Hi, Bishop. How does your garden grow?"

"With silver bells," he said with a lopsided smile.

It warmed my heart that he remembered we used to say that out in the garden. It was our only exchange, but I continued to observe his body movements and tics. Everyone else ignored them. In fact, they ignored him. Like he was an invited ghost, allowed to listen in on the conversation, but not cause a stir. Occasionally, someone would ask him to help perform a simple chore, like taking the trash outside to the burn pile, and he'd oblige.

With each arriving person, Bishop would pull out a package of Wrigley's Doublemint gum and offer them a piece. Some said no thank you, and others accepted his offer. I watched as he carefully slid a piece out for them. I had seen this before too. Offering something to people as a greeting lessens their hesitation to interact with someone like Bishop. The repetitiveness of the action also helps with motor skills. He was intriguing to watch from a medical standpoint, but it saddened me to see what had become of him, even after years of animosity.

Around midafternoon, Bishop started pacing. Not hastily, just with a twinge of nervousness.

"In a bit, Bishop," Momma said, knowing why he was pacing without asking.

"Grace, it's time to go on home. It's gonna be gettin' dark soon. It's time to go home. You don't see good at dark," he said. His tongue moved like it had fallen asleep.

Momma leaned into my side and whispered. "His sense of time isn't what it used to be. But I really don't drive good in the dark, so he's not wrong about that."

I had a wonderful day catching up with Osee. He wasn't a fan of air travel and had never come to Dallas for a visit. Instead, we kept in touch with handwritten letters and obligatory holiday phone calls. A few of our cousins and longtime family friends had come to the luncheon as well, and I could have predicted how their lives would turn out. Every one of them still lived within a twenty-mile radius of Riverton. I was the only one who had to board a plane to be there.

As it was time to leave, Faith asked me to drive her to all the old places we went to as kids. She wanted to see them one last time, and she wanted to see them with me. I drove her past the swimming hole by the old locks, past our school, and up to the church. She attended one closer to her house across the river, but she wanted to go inside and pray for old times' sake.

I gave her some privacy and went outside to the cemetery to visit Daddy, LeLe, and Papa T. There was a bench beside them that hadn't been there before, and I was thankful for it so I wouldn't get my dress dirty. Faith came out and joined me, and we sat listening to the leaves tumble across the crabgrass.

"How do you like the bench? I put it here for Momma to visit with everyone," Faith said.

"It's lovely. And when no one's around, I can picture Daddy sitting here with Papa T and LeLe, laughing together," I said.

"Soon, I'll be able to join them."

"Faith, don't say that. But tell them hi for me, would ya?"

"Oh, Sloane. You always know how to lighten a mood."

Faith thanked me for the trip down memory lane, but there was one more place she wanted to stop on the way back to her house—Rose Trail Park. It's where Papa T had his retirement party and the last place we were all happy together before Daddy died. So, we said our goodbyes to our resting kin and headed to the park.

It was breathtaking as ever, with its hillside views over the river. We walked as far as Faith could go before needing a rest, then sat on a bench overlooking the river valley. It was chilly as the afternoon sun faded but not too shabby for early November. The only other creature in sight was a lonely mallard, who gladly took the last of Faith's purse crackers.

"Sloane, I have to tell you something," Faith said.

"Oh? What's that?" I asked, paying more attention to the duck than her.

"I have a secret I can't die with."

Ruthless Guilt

SLOANE, 1985
ALABAMA

A LOOMING DEATH CAN INSPIRE people to make amends for past indiscretions, but I had not expected Faith to say that.

"Whatever it is, the Lord has surely forgiven you by now," I said.

Faith insisted she needed to tell me. That it was the only way for her to be forgiven. "Do you remember when Bishop shot your mirror?" she said.

"Yes, I will never forget that," I said.

"Do you remember how he kept saying I told him to shoot the mirror but no one believed him?"

"Yes, but—"

"I did. I told him to do it," said Faith. "I'm not proud of it, but I did. I have to make things right and tell you. He wasn't lying. Or confused by his illness."

I wanted to scream and remind her how much anguish that incident caused me. Months, years actually, of confusion that strained the relationship I had with Bishop. Aside from the grave robbers and that nasty water snake, it was the first genuine moment of fear I had experienced. And to find out all these years later, she was the one who caused it?

"Faith, why the hell would you do that? Faith? Answer me, dammit!"

She started crying. "I wanted him to do something crazy, so he wouldn't live with us anymore. He was always following me and telling on me when I snuck off with Royce. And my friends made fun of me for being related to him, like I was part of a tainted gene pool. We were starting school the next day, and I couldn't survive another year of them teasing me over Bishop. I just wanted him to scare you, so they'd send him away. I honestly didn't think the BB gun could break the mirror, but obviously it's possible. And the next day, when I told Royce what Bishop did, I left out my part in it. But the whole thing backfired when Royce told all my friends and they teased me even more. I did all of it to myself. And I'm so sorry I did that to you, Sloane. And to Bishop. I tried to apologize to him once, but I don't think he even remembers it happened."

I wanted to lay into her. But what could I say that she didn't already know? She was on death's door trying to make amends for her wrongdoings, and I needed to find the strength to forgive her. I uttered something about finally understanding why he would do something like that when I had done nothing to provoke him. By no fault of his own, Bishop wasn't a smart man. But I didn't think someone could manipulate him like that. I guess because I didn't have that kind of deviousness inside of me to find out. So part of my astonishment was that Faith did.

"I'm not sure what you expect me to say, Faith. I guess, how did you get him to do it?"

"I told him you and I were having a scaring contest and I needed his help to win. We were always scaring each other, so it wasn't that unbelievable. And he liked the idea of being the hero, like he was with the water snake. So he asked me what he had to do. I told him to retrieve Papa T's BB gun from the kitchen, then go into your bedroom and shoot at your vanity mirror. So he did. But Sloane, you gotta believe me. I didn't know you were sitting in front of the mirror. I had nightmares about that for years. The BB hitting you, instead of the mirror."

I guess she got what she wanted. Bishop went away all right, and the aftermath of that incident uncovered his schizophrenia. I suppose that's the silver lining, but Jesus, did it have to be so traumatic? That incident changed the way I saw him and put a reason behind all his odd behaviors, but the comeback from it was arduous.

"Sloane, please say something. I know I'm springing this on you, but I needed you to know the truth. And there's more. You may never speak to me again after I'm done telling you the next part, but I have to make peace with myself and the Lord."

"Faith, obviously I need time to get over this, but I forgive you, okay? You made a mistake, and it was a long time ago. Whatever else happened, let's just let it go. Can we just consider it forgiven too?"

I didn't want to hate her right before she died. Whatever else she did was apparently worse than the mirror incident. And I wasn't sure I could handle it.

"Sloane, I can't let it go. I have to tell you. You need to know that—"

"Seriously Faith, just let it—"

"It's my fault Daddy died!" She burst into tears, gasping to pull the words she'd spoken back inside her mouth.

"Why would you say—Jesus, Faith. That wasn't your fault. It was Bishop's," I said. I paused for a moment. Then it hit me what she was trying to say. "Wait. Oh my God, Faith, what did you do? Did you tell Bishop to shoot Daddy too?"

She slumped over, wailing. "Yes, yes, I got him to do it. Just like I got him to shoot your mirror. It was all my fault, Sloane. I ruined our family, and I ruined all of our lives!"

"No. Take it back. Take back those words right now, Faith." Maybe the cancer had spread to her brain, and she was talking nonsense. I even considered the possibility that she'd developed schizophrenia too. It is hereditary, after all.

Without me saying another word, Faith explained the one piece of that night's puzzle that was never divulged during the judge's interviews. The piece I assumed Bishop held. But that Faith had hidden in the pit of her gut for thirty-one years.

"I didn't want to go back to New Orleans because it would mean I'd have to leave Royce. It would mean leaving my friends, all of whom abandoned me in the end, anyway. But on top of that, I knew something about Daddy you and Momma didn't, but Osee did. He was just too young to understand it.

"The day before Papa T's retirement party, Momma sent me to the store for more flour for her piecrusts, and I took Osee with me. I saw Daddy talking to the new hairstylist behind the beauty shop, twirling her hair with his finger. Their bodies were close to each other. Too close.

"I rushed Osee in the other direction. But he started shouting, asking why we were going the wrong way. He wouldn't shut up, and Daddy heard him. Daddy turned around, and we made eye contact, but I just kept going, dragging Osee along while he shouted. Then I circled back to the store a few streets down.

"I was so hurt and confused by what I saw and didn't know what to do. Daddy said nothing to me about it, and it made me feel like I was part of whatever dirty lie he was hiding. And when Daddy had the nerve to paint the idyllic family picture of us all moving back to New Orleans to the fancy new house he was buying Momma, I snapped. I wanted him removed from our family picture. I wanted to protect Momma and protect myself from having to leave Riverton and Royce. I was a stupid teenager, infatuated with my no-good boyfriend and making bad decisions left and right with our no-good friends. My level of selfishness was through the roof, and I've lived with this guilt my entire life. But I can't die with it, Sloane. I have to rid myself of it, and telling you is the only way to do that.

"Bishop was on edge that whole night. After Daddy told us we were moving, you left me in my room crying. I eventually calmed down and walked out to the porch where Bishop was sitting in his rocker, listening intently to Momma and Daddy discuss options by the fire. He even stormed out there twice to tell Daddy he couldn't take Momma away. That she had to stay in Riverton with him. After Bishop came back that second time, I told him I had a way to stop it from happening and save Momma from moving.

"That hero angle had worked before with the vanity mirror, so I knew it would work again. All I had to do was get Bishop a loaded gun out of the locked cedar cabinet. So, I took Momma's porcelain angels off the top of the piano, peeled off the envelope taped underneath, retrieved the key, then unlocked the cabinet. I grabbed a revolver lying across the upper shelf and flipped down the cylinder lock. No bullets. I set it down and grabbed another. And another. Until I found one still loaded. It was a single-action Peacemaker, which the irony of that hadn't hit me until just now. I knew enough about guns from Papa T's endless history lessons on them, and Royce always screwing around with his, to know what kind of gun it was and how it worked. I'd even shot that exact gun a few times with Papa T the day he brought it home from some rummage sale. So I knew it would be easy for Bishop to fire and that he likely knew how because Momma had said he and Junior hunted rabbits and plinked cans when they were kids.

"I laid the gun front and center on the shelf at eye level, with the handle hanging off just a little. I called Bishop in from the porch and pointed to the opened cabinet. He reached for the BB gun, but I told him that one wouldn't work this time. And when his eyes landed on the revolver I'd made hard to miss, he went straight for it. I told him to take the gun to the front porch and wait for me there.

"A split-second later, Papa T walked into the front room from his bedroom, and I froze. He told me he was off to his next retirement party, and that he'd see me in the morning. Somehow, he didn't notice the wide-open gun cabinet behind me. I heard the chime of the brass bell as he left through the back kitchen door, then I hurried to his bedroom. Seeing him come from there had given me an idea. I pulled down one of the empty gun boxes from his closet shelf and left it lying open on the floor in front of his closet.

"I went back to the front room and grabbed a new envelope and tape from Papa T's desk. Then I ran over to the cedar cabinet and locked it. I put the key into the envelope, sealed it, and taped it back to the underside of the piano top where it was before. I carefully replaced all the angels precisely where Momma had them and put the tape back on Papa T's desk, and as I walked out to the front porch, I saw Papa T driving away.

"I told Bishop it was time, and he got up and followed me to the kitchen. I wasn't sure how the next part was going to play out, but I saw you and Daddy coming up the path to the back steps. I grabbed hold of Bishop's arms and told him to do like he'd done before. Only this time, the mirror was Hardy. I pushed open the screen door, pushed Bishop out onto the top step, and watched from inside as he lifted his arm. Then the shot rang out.

"Daddy doubled over, and you ran off. Bishop stumbled down the steps and out toward the trees as Momma was running up the path to the house. I waited until she reached the bottom of the steps, then opened the screen door, pretending

I'd just gotten there myself. But I'd been standing there the whole time. You and Daddy didn't notice me behind Bishop. But I was there. Watching in horror as my plan played out.

"Momma looked up at the sound of the brass bell. She told me to call the sheriff and grab towels, so I ran back inside and called Hayes. I told him something happened, that someone shot Daddy and he needed to come over right away.

"When I stepped outside, Momma stopped me and told me to stay put. So I tossed the towels to her. I sat on the top step crying, realizing what I'd just done. I'd manipulated my mentally ill uncle into shooting my father, and the pure disgust that filled me at that moment has never left. I wanted to go unlock the gun cabinet again and make things even by my own hand, and for years I had to fight the daily urge to do it.

"I don't know how Bishop ended up inside the garden, but clearly he circled back and hid in the only place he felt safe because that's where he emerged from. He'd stopped taking his medicine, and I didn't know that. I'm sure he was terrified. I can only imagine what he was thinking as he watched my performance and the utter hurt he must have felt over what I did to him. I wish he'd stood up and shot me too.

"Sloane? Please say something. Curse me…anything."

I walked to the edge of the grassy ledge and looked at the water below. I almost jumped and ended it all right there. Everything I'd let myself believe was wrong. I hated Bishop for decades for something Faith convinced him to do. All those years I spent psychoanalyzing myself were a waste, and she knew and said nothing. But she was talking now, and I let her keep talking and get it all out because I wasn't sure I'd give her the chance to talk to me again—deathbed or not.

She told me that, for years, under the guise of a work meeting, she saw a therapist at the hospital where they both worked. That's how she coped with what she had done. And that all those times I had asked her if she was okay because I sensed a sadness in her voice, there was. There always was.

She'd lived in a personal hell and stewed in a vat of ruthless guilt for decades. She'd spent a lifetime in agony over letting Bishop take the fall and blamed herself for the horrible things that happened to him at the psychiatric hospital. She saw not only her own family ripped apart by her actions, but Jack's as well. She had the blood of two men on her hands and had spent every second of every day in agony for it.

She asked if I wanted to know what she was praying for at the church. I didn't by that point and didn't answer her, but she told me anyway. She said she understood our Lord's punishment for her was leukemia and that she quit fighting it to take her penance. Admitting her guilt to me was the only way to repent. She couldn't go back and fix what happened, but she could fill in the blanks that caused me so much confusion for so many years, and she hoped her confession would bring me closure. Then she told me she loved me and that she wished we could go back to that day on the carousel, the day we moved to Riverton, and just start over.

She was right. Not about Jesus giving her leukemia as punishment, but that she'd served a life sentence of guilt over what she'd done.

I wished she hadn't confessed. Not knowing the truth meant I had no other person to blame but Bishop, and I had made peace with that a long time ago. With Faith's death looming, the pressure to forgive her wasn't something I had prepared myself for. Plus, I wasn't entirely convinced her confession was true. The Faith I knew could never have done something so heinous.

When I finally spoke, I asked if she'd told the therapist, or anyone else, what she did, and she said no. Her therapy sessions focused on surviving a traumatic event, and the guilt that can sometimes accompany that. But treatment for survivor's guilt, not actual guilt, is not the same.

I rejoined Faith on the bench. An overwhelming sense of calm had replaced my ire. That last piece of the puzzle finally pushed into place, tying together all the images I had of that night. My confusion cleared, and for the first time, I saw what was in front of me that whole time. Faith standing just inside the kitchen door, behind the ripped screen flapping in the breeze, as Bishop lifted his arm and pulled the trigger.

I picked up Faith's hand. "Somehow, I will forgive you."

It took every ounce of my being to say those words to her, and I wasn't entirely sure I meant them. I needed time to decide if I genuinely wanted to forgive her or not. Time she didn't have.

Unknown Gift

SLOANE 1985
ALABAMA

THE NEXT MORNING, I WENT for a drive. The peaceful water of the big river soothed my tension as it wound me around the corners I used to walk. As a child, I had retreated to the tearoom by Miss Maybelle's house whenever I needed to be alone. It wasn't an actual tearoom with cucumber sandwiches and macaroons but a cabin overlooking Pickwick Lake. Anyone was welcome to use it, but ladies who needed some quiet reflection often sipped tea from the rockers on the open deck. That's exactly what I needed.

I blazed down the overgrown path to the tearoom, surrounded by naked sugar maple shoots that had already lost their leaves. But when I reached the clearing, my heart sank. The tearoom was gone. I'd hoped it would give me the solitude and inspiration I needed to process Faith's confession. No one had ever shared such a life-altering secret with me. Was

I supposed to reveal it after Faith passed away? Or did Faith intend me to take it to *my* grave?

I found myself parked in front of the church. I don't even remember driving there. A man was straightening the hymnals when he heard me come in. "You caught me," he said. "I'm the one who lines them up, evenly spaced."

"I think it makes the congregation sing better," I said.

He laughed and came over to introduce himself. He was on the younger side, maybe midtwenties, so I was surprised when he said he was the pastor. My face must have shown it too.

"I know. I look like I just graduated from high school. But don't let my baby face fool you. I'm thirty-four, and I've had plenty of time to learn from my mistakes. That's how I ended up here. My choices were church or jail, and I think I chose wisely," he said with a wink.

He asked where I was from and was excited to have someone from a big city in his church. He wanted to hear about mine in Texas, and if I'd met any of the popular televangelists he'd seen on TV. I told him what I thought of their megachurches and that I much preferred the one I was standing in.

I introduced myself as Grace's daughter. He'd been the pastor for eight years and knew her well.

"I'm home visiting Faith and stopped by to pray for her," I said.

"How's she doing?"

"Not well, I'm afraid. She's been making amends and preparing for heaven."

"I'm truly sorry. I've always enjoyed seeing Faith when she attended service with your mother and Bishop, here and there. How are you holding up?"

"Honestly, I'm struggling. Faith asked me to forgive her for something she did many years ago. A secret she hid from me. I told her I'd forgive her, but I'm not sure I meant it. And I'm not sure I have it within me to do."

He opened a Bible from a nearby pew and fanned through it, knowing exactly where he needed to go to help me. "'For if you forgive other people when they sin against you, your heavenly Father will also forgive you. But if you do not forgive others their sins, your Father will not forgive your sins.' It's from Matthew 6:14–15," he said.

I'm not sure there's a more fitting verse in the entire Bible. It gave me clarity that forgiveness was indeed the right path. And the perspective I needed to admit I also had not lived a sinless life. Even though there was no comparison to the enormity of the lies Faith lived with. And it supplied me with the strength to fulfill my word to my sister because I'd been taught to live my life as the Bible dictates. I had never lost my faith in that, no matter how many times I questioned why God let horrible things happen to my family.

As hard as it would be, I needed to cherish the last days I had with Faith. My decision to one day forgive her was my first step in doing so. The rest could come in time. That was all I could offer at the moment, and that was good enough.

I thanked the pastor and promised I'd go to his Sunday service before I left for Dallas.

"I sincerely hope you do. I have a feeling this church is as special to you as it is to me," he said.

I shook his hand and drove back to Faith's house with a fresh mindset and a glimpse of forgiveness in my heart. As I crawled up her long, gravel driveway, rotating lights shone through the barren tree limbs. I stopped and watched, hoping my sinking stomach was wrong. Shortly after, the coroner pulled in behind me. I parked by the shed away from the house, so I wouldn't block the drive, then sat in my car, weeping. I had not made it back in time to tell Faith about my conversation with the pastor. To tell her again that I would, in time, forgive her. But this time, mean it.

Her husband came out and sat in the car with me. He couldn't bear to watch them wheel Faith out. "I knew it was coming, but now that it's here, I'm not sure what to do anymore," he said.

"When did it happen?" I asked.

"About thirty minutes ago. She was resting in bed, and when I checked on her, she opened her eyes and said something that didn't make any sense. Then she smiled and slipped away."

"What did she say, if you don't mind me asking?"

"'This time, I'll ride the giraffe beside yours.' Do you know what that means?"

A release of laughter came pouring out with my tears. I do not, for a single second, think it's a coincidence that when she crossed over, I was at the church talking to the pastor. She believed me when I told her I'd forgive her in time, but she *felt* it when I truly began to, standing inside our church. Her husband will never know the gift he gave me that day, but I will forever be grateful to him for sharing with me her last words. They're the ones that allowed Faith and me to both be free of guilt and resentment. She was starting over, and so was I.

FAITH HAD PLANNED HER OWN funeral. A simple service with those whom she loved the most. A bundle of lilacs sat beside her photo, and since they weren't in bloom, I imagine they were the one extra expense she justified.

Her husband was the first to speak, and he painted a picture of a wonderful life together on their farm. Her best friend, also a nurse, spoke of a dedicated healer with a pleasant bedside manner. Momma tried to read from notes she'd scribbled on a sheet of stationery but immediately sat back down. I didn't even try. Osee told stories about how Faith was a rebel as a teen but mellowed with age and built a successful career, always taking care of her family first.

He also talked vaguely about something I had not known—Momma wasn't the only one who visited Bishop at the psychiatric hospital. Today, the nursing program at UA is in Birmingham. But back when Faith and I attended, the nursing program was at the Tuscaloosa campus. In the very same town as the Alabama State Psychiatric Hospital. I did my best to ignore its existence, but Faith, as it turned out, was very familiar with it and visited Bishop regularly.

I looked over at Bishop, sitting on the other side of Momma from me, like when we were kids in church. He was smiling at Osee as he described how Faith checked on him every month and brought him a new baseball card and a box of Cracker Jack.

After the funeral, I asked Osee if he knew anything more about her and Bishop's visits. He said she felt like she needed to protect him, because of all those years of him trying to protect her. She had a special arrangement with Dr. Matthews to visit every month. He allowed it as part of his theory for positive reinforcement therapy, which Faith used as the basis for her college research papers. She learned a great deal from Dr. Matthews about how hospitals for the mentally ill work and gained an inside perspective on Bishop's treatment and the effects he suffered from it. So, for years, Faith had a relationship with Bishop and his medical staff no one knew about except Osee. And the only reason he found out was he saw a paper she was writing while she was home for Thanksgiving.

My sister sure had secrets, some bad and some good. She was an intensely private person, and after everything she confessed to me, I can see why. She was trying to protect herself and those she loved from even more harm than she'd already caused.

Now I had to carry her secrets. No good could come from me telling them, and everyone had moved on and made their peace. And as I listened to Faith's friends speak so fondly of her, I knew their words conveyed how she was meant to be remembered. Because that's who she fought so many years to be remembered as. Not the selfish teenager who snapped the night Daddy died, but the selfless person she became.

She helped save countless children who came through her hospital. Every week, on her day off, she made sure Momma and Bishop had everything they needed. And if they didn't, she'd take them to get it. She was active in her church and was always the first to volunteer. She did right by her family and her community, and she was deserving of the forgiveness she'd earned.

IT DIDN'T FEEL RIGHT STAYING at Faith's house after she'd passed. Her husband and kids needed time alone to mourn, so I stayed with Momma. As I pulled into the dirt-rut driveway, Bishop was out front getting the mail from the mailbox. I supposed they couldn't fend off progress forever. He hurried inside, no doubt to tell Momma I had arrived.

She came out, with Bishop following closely behind, and had him take my bags. I hadn't been in the house since the day before Ray and I moved to Dallas. It's a strange feeling to walk back into your childhood bedroom after being gone for so many years. Your head floods with memories, and the little things you loved about the room as a child stand out even more.

My favorite place in my room was the loose floorboard where I hid my diary. I rummaged in my purse for my metal nail file, then jabbed it into the well-worn gap between the boards and pried it up. There it was. I almost pulled it out to read it, but stopped midreach. Whatever I wrote in that diary was in there because I didn't want to share it with others. And while it was technically mine, it felt like I was about to invade someone else's privacy. I had become a different person than the one who grew up in that house. So, I gently laid the board down and decided I'd uncovered enough secrets that day and was happy keeping my own hidden underneath that floorboard.

I went right to work, helping Momma roll the dough for biscuits. "You know, Bishop's out in the garden. He might like your help," she said.

I knew what she was trying to do, so I played along.

The garden was twice the size I remembered and had an entire section designated for fall squash, which was what we were having for supper that night. And probably every night because that's how it worked; you ate what was in season.

I watched him rotate each squash a quarter turn to provide even sun exposure. For all the aspects of his life that were forever altered by the ECT, his gardening intuition did not fall victim. I stayed with him for an hour or so, turning the soil for the beet and carrot seeds that needed to be planted soon. We didn't speak much, but that was always how we gardened together. It was like we picked up right where we'd left off.

Supper was amazing. Nothing compares to a meal prepared from scratch, and even more so when the ingredients are the fruits of your labor. I tried to cook that way as much as possible in Dallas, but my fast-paced life allowed for it only on Sundays. After supper, Bishop sat outside by the fire, and

Momma retreated for her nightly bath, so I sat in the front room and read the trashy novel I never started on the airplane.

I was about halfway through the first chapter when the main character started making love to a strange man she'd met in a bar, on top of a baby grand piano. Well, that's stupid, I thought. The keys would all be randomly playing as her feet tapped on them, with her back suctioned to the frigid, lacquered wood. I glanced over at Momma's upright piano sitting across the room and confirmed my suspicions—that would not be romantic at all.

Momma's angels were still lining the top of the piano, and I remembered what Faith confessed. How she said she retrieved the hidden key taped to the underside of the hinged top and unlocked the gun cabinet, then put the key back.

I tried to ignore my curiosity and continue reading, but the memories of that night wouldn't let me. I peeked out the window to make sure Bishop was still by the fire and down the hall to check that the bathroom door was still closed. I tiptoed over to the piano, careful not to hit any creaky floorboards I remembered. I removed Momma's collection of angels, set them on the floor next to the piano, and slowly lifted the lid.

As it rose, I peeked under. And there it was. Still taped in the middle. The paper had turned to a faded cream, and decades of gravity created an indentation of the key inside it. I couldn't believe it. All this time, the key was still there, and the cedar cabinet was still sitting next to it. No doubt, filled with all of Papa T's guns.

With my curiosity satiated, I lowered the hinged top, but a flash of light purple caught my eye. The envelope had a three-cent liberty stamp in the upper right corner. It was not the same envelope I watched Papa T tape to the underside but rather the first envelope I had grabbed when he instructed me to get one off his desk. I had doubted Faith's story and her ability to do something so unspeakable, but that stamp confirmed it. When she said she grabbed a new envelope off Papa T's desk, she must have been going so fast that she grabbed the same envelope Papa T told me to put back, the one with the stamp already on it.

Respect

RYNN, 2020
WASHINGTON

I PRESSED STOP ON MY phone's voice recorder. Minus the break to mix a second scotch and soda, 02:01:47 was all the time my mother needed to expose the truth I so desperately wanted to know. A story she'd told no one in its entirety until today.

I wiped my cheek with my sleeve and searched for the perfect first word, in awe of the woman sitting across from me. She'd always been the pinnacle of perseverance in my eyes. Now I know where it came from. The only way out of her pain was straight through it, and she'd used her intelligence to survive.

As I opened my mouth to speak, a tissue box flew across the room, hitting me on the shoulder. My father giggled as I plucked a few tissues and wiped my face. It was the snap of the fingers we all needed to bring us back to the present. Back to November 7, 2020. To a day I have never loved my mother more.

My father reached his hand across the side table between their recliners, and as my mother took it, his voice quivered. "You did good. I wish I'd known. I could have helped you more."

She gently squeezed his hand. "Your patience was all I needed, and you have always given me that."

"Rynn, you okay over there?" she asked.

"Just trying to take it all in. The truth was so different from anything I'd imagined. Honestly, I regret asking you to relive it. But I also have a new level of respect for you too. I sincerely hope this hasn't caused you pain, Mom, because you've suffered so much already."

She swirled the melting ice in her glass, buying herself time to answer. "It's sad, but it's not upsetting to me anymore. It's surreal hearing myself say it out loud, though. Sixty-six years is a long time to hold the truth inside, and perhaps it shouldn't have come out. Apart from me, everyone there that night has since died. So, why tarnish the few memories you had of them?"

She continued, "I used to wonder if my life would be different had it not happened. But then I might not have become a psych nurse and Faith a pediatric nurse. The world can never have enough good ones. So, I guess things happen for a reason and lead you down the path you're meant to go. But I hope you don't view Faith and Bishop any differently because the people you met were the people they became, and that's who mattered. Not the selfish, manipulative teen Faith was, but the demure and selfless person she evolved into. And even though

Bishop carried out an unthinkable act, I hope you take less time than I did to realize it wasn't in his true nature."

"Everyone makes mistakes," I said. "Maybe not as egregious as what Faith did, but it's what you do *after* you make a mistake that reveals who you truly are. And she changed for the better. I wish I could have met my grandfather Hardy, though. At least I know more about him now. Even if he did have secrets of his own. I can't imagine what Faith must have felt when she saw him flirting with that hairdresser. It seemed so out in left field."

My mother shook her head. "I never saw Daddy look at another woman, let alone flirt with one. And I'd like to think Momma would have told me if she suspected he was a philanderer. But I suppose because of his train schedule, he could have easily hidden a double life. And if I had seen what Faith described, I may have snapped too. Just not in the same way she did."

"Maybe she didn't understand what she was seeing," I said.

My mother nodded in agreement. "That's what I tell myself."

"Faith seemed blind to a lot of things, really. I think because she was so consumed by Royce, she missed learning some perspective you gained early on. Perspective, you passed on to me through your stories."

"Oh? How do you mean?" she asked.

"J. B., paddling out to the top of that old lock, pretending to be Jesus. He taught you that seeing is believing, and you shouldn't ignore the little signs life throws at you. They could be a loved one guiding you along or an affirmation that you'd made the right choice, like the man who stopped to ask if you were okay, driving a car exactly like Hardy's. Signs are everywhere. You just have to pay attention and let them guide you.

"Miss Maybelle taught you anything is possible and a small-town girl can make a difference if she sets her mind to it. She was your greatest mentor and showed you how trust and encouragement can do wonders to uplift a person at their lowest. I also like to think your opening Cokes on her front porch contributed to the moon landing.

"The hidden ledger showed you generational stories are only part of a family's history and yours didn't need to be defined by one tragic event. There's always more to a story only a select few know, and sometimes those secrets need to be kept to protect others. And yourself.

"Junior became a glowing example of karma and irony banding together to right the wrongs in the world, intended or not. No one is immune. Not even someone who devotes their life to fighting for our country. Imprisoned by his wheelchair, his misfortune more than made up for the life-altering punch he blew Bishop, and it's those kinds of outcomes that make people both believe—and question—the work of our Lord.

"And my grandmother Grace showed you what true forgiveness looks like. To turn around after the grief and horror she'd been through and take care of the brother who caused it proves how Christian she was. Not only did she take care of Bishop after his fall, but she vowed to take care of him until his dying day, and she fulfilled that oath. I think Hardy would have been proud of her for following her heart."

My mother blushed. "I suppose I did learn all that. And you're right. Momma was a true Christian and put her pain and hurt aside to help Bishop through his."

"Rynn, before I told you the story, you asked me if I forgave Bishop. My answer is that I didn't for a very long time. But when I returned to Riverton to see Faith before she died and I saw Bishop at Osee's for the first time in three decades, hands shaking and with diminished mental capacity, I realized he'd lived a horrible life. He paid a price much worse than any prison sentence and suffered a torturous fate at the mercy of a misguided doctor, hell-bent on proving a dangerous theory. And it had a lobotomizing outcome.

"I knew psychiatric hospitals could be unpleasant, but I stuck my head in the sand because Bishop had to be locked up somewhere, and jail was no place for him. I didn't know how awful his doctor was, though, until I read Faith's notes and college papers from when she visited Bishop. She still had them, and before I returned to Dallas, I asked her husband if I could have them.

"It took me a while to read them, but that's how I know all the horrors Bishop faced. Faith took detailed interview notes with his doctors and nurses that described their appearances and what the inside of the hospital looked like. Notes about what happened on family visiting day, and Bishop's interactions with the other patients. Transcripts of Bishop himself, telling her pieces of conversations he remembered and how lost he felt. And logs describing the ECT sessions, including the one that nearly ended his life. I can honestly see why Faith told no one. The realities he faced in that place were too much to stomach.

"The hardest to read was Faith's paper that described the day Junior visited Bishop all those years after being away in the army. Bishop's memory of Junior was still alive somewhere inside his head and had manifested itself as the door-window man. A man he had talked about during therapy, but that everyone thought was Jerry the Waver because he'd said the man lived three doors down from his room, and three doors down was Jerry's room. But when Bishop told Dr. Holcomb that the man looked after him—comforted him when Momma couldn't—Dr. Holcomb realized Bishop *wasn't* talking about Jerry. He hated Jerry. No. The man Bishop saw wasn't even real. He was still hallucinating after months of the treatment Dr. Holcomb insisted was working, and his ego got the better of him. He was going to cure Bishop of his schizophrenia and end his hallucinations once and for all.

"For years, Faith's notes sat in a box under my bed. In fact, I think you found them once when you were a kid, Rynn. But they were an anchor I needed to break free from, so I threw them into the fireplace before we moved from Texas to Washington. They'd served their purpose, and I didn't want lingering reminders of pain amid a fresh start.

"That day on the Rose Trail Park bench, I told my sister I'd forgive her so she could leave this earth in peace, and I held her hand as her guilt left her heart. I was her bird, carrying away her pain. And when I left for Dallas at the end of that visit, I looked back at Momma's house one last time through the rearview mirror and saw Bishop sitting on the front porch rocking, watching through the screen, just like he was the day we moved to Riverton in 1948. He had lived a life of pain and suffered more than any person I have ever known, and it all traced back to a single moment in time out in the Ginhouse Hollow, when a boyhood tiff forever changed his life's course. And as I drove away, and Bishop disappeared from view, I forgave him too."

Epilogue

RYNN, 2022
ALABAMA

I'D PROMISED MY TEENAGE SELF that if I ever learned the secrets my mother held, it would likely make a good book, and I'd try my hand at writing it. Normally, I wouldn't have time to devote to such a feat. But like so many others, I suddenly found myself with more time than I knew what to do with.

When COVID shut down the world, some turned their home confinement into an opportunity to renovate their bathrooms. Others built a gym in their garage and focused on getting in shape. I did both, although the shape I got into was rounder than I intended. Writing a novel took much longer than I expected, and there was a lot of sitting involved. But it filled the time once occupied by my social calendar and kept me sane in an otherwise insane existence.

I bought a few books on how to write a book. I read novels by authors new to me and across genres I didn't typically read. I did everything the experts said to do, and I created the story

I'd dreamed of one day writing. But as I typed the last words inspired by my mother's story, something was still missing.

If you hail from Riverton, Alabama, you know I took liberties. I drew inspiration from my own memories and wove the truth into the imagined world I created. But I needed to see the *real* Riverton again. See the house my mother grew up in and walk the steps she ran. Her story had an ending, but I still needed to write mine.

COVID delayed many social events, one of which was my mother's high school reunion. She hadn't been back to Riverton in years and with each passing classmate, knew she needed to make the cross-country trek while she still could. But with her failing heart and caned walk, she needed help to make the journey. My father desperately wanted to go with her but feared his bum knee would only burden her travel. What she needed was an airport pack mule and chauffeur who could withstand the stickiness of the Alabama June heat, and I happily offered my services.

When we crossed the Colbert County line and I saw a billboard for Slim Chickens, I knew we'd arrived. If you've never been to the South, you're missing out on the literary genius of their restaurant names. And when my mother told me the name of the one where the reunion luncheon was being held, I knew the food would be amazing.

Too Fat Sisters is an unassuming place, with a parking lot rumored to overfill in the minutes preceding its opening. As you walk inside, the smell of country-fried steak slathered in thick gravy welcomes you. A packed dining area sat to the left, and Roll Tide stickers adorned a half-open barn door to the right.

When my mother stepped through that barn door and into the kitschy party room, a roar of excitement surrounded more hugs than I can count. As we mingled our way around the room, I was eager to meet the people I'd written about. See their faces and hear their voices. And as I listened to the words that made up their own life stories, I thought each one could fill a book all by itself. They were the most accomplished, intelligent, and authentic group of people I have ever met.

Their reunion emcee spoke fondly of classmates no longer sitting at the tables they once filled and gave updates on those in need of prayers. He teared up at the announcement of relapses and rejoiced at the miracles of remissions. And it saddened me when he spoke of the low attendance numbers threatening to close their alma mater. Their little town, which had once thrived with families, could not keep pace with the job opportunities of the larger city nearby.

Most people at the reunion had gone to school together from kindergarten to graduation. It was the place that held their memories of football games and spring dances and finally winning one of Miss Maybelle's Friday Freebies. They had a tough choice to make: donate their annual charity fund to a school that lacked a future or donate it to another place special to them.

The little library was an obvious choice, but the majority of votes went to the Lions' Den; a small red-brick building owned by the local Lions Club chapter. It's a community staple for gatherings and a place that, as kids, they'd spent as much time at as the library next door. The class secretary earmarked their charity donation for a projector so they, and others, could display slideshows.

As I finished the last of my okra and purple-hull peas, I listened to the reminiscing around me. The lifelong connections my mother's graduating class had with one another and their community were enviable. Her friends held a bond as solid today as the day they received their diplomas, and they are the people who helped uplift my mother when she was at her lowest, whether they knew it or not. My adoration for them is immeasurable.

THE NEXT DAY WAS ALL about sightseeing. Progress blurred the edges of town, but had not yet engulfed the isolated nook of Riverton. Once we crossed the railroad tracks that welcome you in, we were firmly in my mother's world. We wandered the grounds of her school, and she showed me where she ate lunch, watching the erection of the new building after the original one burned down the year before she graduated.

We drove past the plantation where Elsie Jo once lived and under the two trees that hid my mother and Mary Ruth, with their rope of scarves strung across the road. We wandered through the Rose Trail Park, bursting with runnin' roses of every color, and looked for the old locks. But they were still hiding below the waterline. And when I pulled off the road, in front of the house my mother grew up in, love filled both our hearts.

A bittersweet stop at the house tucked into the bend, with a history no one could guess if they tried. I wanted so badly to walk through its front door. To hear the dainty chime of the bell as I opened it, and rock on the porch as I listened to the soothing river branch. Sing back to the whip-poor-wills and drink from the spring behind the house. And sit on the back porch step where my mother had sat next to Faith, who was telling Sheriff Hayes the lie she almost carried to her grave.

But Dark Hollow had swallowed the house whole. Reclaimed by the descendants of the trees that built it, the house that once stood tall was nothing more than a dilapidated shack. With its walls caved in, and the roof consumed by moss, there was nothing to see but the snakes that slithered under its fallen boards.

We had one last stop before we left Riverton that day. A stop my mother always made when she was home for a visit. The Riverton church and cemetery are as picturesque as the big river they overlook. The grounds were immaculate, with perfectly pruned bushes and a weed-free flower bed that dressed up the entrance sign.

Down the short driveway, you come to a fork. To the left is my mother's childhood church. Plain white, with a simple belfry and steeple, it was picture-perfect for an intimate wedding.

To the right is the cemetery, and as usual, my mother had a fresh story to tell me the second we set foot on the hallowed ground. The cemetery has been around a lot longer than its burial records. And even though there's a list of who most of the occupants are, it's not always clear *where* they are. When a loved one dies, you simply show the caretaker your family's section, and they start digging. If they hit a coffin—or bones—they refill the hole and dig a few feet over, until they find an unoccupied bed of earth.

Then there are the famous Riverton graves. Maggie Williams, for one. Her stately marker stands in the foreground of another family's plot. Surrounded by a black wrought-iron fence, a massive evergreen stands centered with the graves inside. And that fence just happens to reveal the truth behind Maggie's mysterious light and ghost story that gave my mother such an entertaining fright. If you were to transport back to the night when the three hunters followed the light into the woods and peek behind Maggie's tombstone, you would have seen those hunters were chasing the lantern of iron thieves. And as far as Mrs. Newsom's account of seeing Maggie's face in the cold marble of her tombstone? Well, I'm sure if you miss someone enough, you will.

The Devil's Tombstone, as it's called, greets you as you enter through the cemetery gate and is the second most famous grave in Riverton. It's said the man buried beneath it isn't really dead, that he's stuck in purgatory and his grave is a portal to hell. It all started back in 1917, when his date of death disappeared from his marker a few months after his burial. The cemetery had the date re-etched, but it vanished again within the year. Again and again, the date would fade, and the only logical explanation—otherworldly. And even more mysterious, the finish on his tall spire tombstone would occasionally slough off and crumble to the ground, as if burned away by an inner heat. My mother almost had me going when she revealed the marble stone I was looking at wasn't the original. Sandstone, as it turns out, isn't a good match for Alabama elements. The man's family grew tired of refinishing it year after year, so they replaced the whole thing with one that was immune to the devilish weather.

Although I found the stories amusing, we weren't there to visit the devil or Maggie Williams. My mother wanted to ensure our family's graves didn't need maintenance and that their flowers were fresh. And by fresh, I mean dusted and secured. Most graves had silk flowers spiked into their grassy blankets. It's simply too hot for real flowers to survive more than a day.

I let my mother have some space. She wandered over to Grace's and Hardy's graves, next to Lila's and Osee's. Faith was laid to rest in her husband's family plot across the river, so she wasn't there to visit. But Bishop was.

I found his tombstone in the shade of a magnolia tree. It was more impressive than I'd expected, and his grave had more flowers on it than anyone else's in our family. It gave me comfort that someone so forgotten about in life hadn't been in death. As I reached down and cleared leaves from the base of this marker, a tiny fire ant bit my thumb. The bite was as hot as the midday sun, and I'd forgotten the sting and itch that accompanies them. I pressed my thumb against my water bottle to ease the welt. Then I wondered. Was that a sign? Did Bishop know I was there? Was he trying to tell me something? Or was my dumb luck just telling me to look out for ant hills?

I decided to listen. To my heart, that is. And it needed me to finish my story. It had guided me this whole time and led me down the path I was meant to go. From the day I found Faith's college notes in 1989 to thirty-one years later when my mother revealed the truth behind them, my heart knew the reason for it all. It wasn't just my mother's story I needed to write. Or mine. It was Bishop's story. Not to shame Faith or tarnish the good name of my own family, but to be the voice he never had. He was just a man who loved and depended on his sister so deeply, he couldn't bear the thought of her leaving. A man, who by no fault of his own, was unable to stand up for himself. And through my streaming tears and burning thumb, I placed my hand on top of his stone and promised him the world would know the only thing he was guilty of was innocence.

Please consider donating to your local Mental Health Organization.

Acknowledgments

FIRST AND FOREMOST, THANK YOU to my mother for allowing me to write an inspired version of your real-life experience, for your trust and guidance, and for showing me what true courage looks like.

To my family, whom I ignored for countless hours while fulfilling my lifelong dream of writing and publishing this story; thank you. I could not have done it without your support and willingness to forage for your own food.

To my father and sister: Thank you for believing in me. This story is just as much yours as it is mine, and while it may not be 100% *how* things happened, it is *what* happened. So this is my gift to you—clarity—for we all now know the *why*.

To my cousin and cousin-in-law: Thank you for going on this journey with me. I cherish the time we spent collaborating and every minute of our adventure through the faux pony-filled hollows of Riverton.

To the ladies of the Books & Brews book club: Thank you for being my beta readers, my cheerleaders, for dragging me out of my house so I didn't turn into a complete hermit, and for the laughs over many, many pints.

To my mother's high school graduating class: Thank you for helping my mother when she was at her lowest, and for your lifelong friendship. You are part of the few who know what's real inside The Ginhouse Hollow, and I hope you enjoyed the imagined world I created based on the real one you lived in. It's a world I now love as much as you do, and writing an inspired version of it was my way of protecting what you hold true.

To the real Miss Maudie and Miss Maybelle: You may no longer be with us, but your impact on my mother will live on forever in the pages of this book.

Finally, thank you to my amazing editor Alison Imbriaco for your encouragement and thorough fact-checking, to Kali Sakai for your manuscript review, and to Danna Mathias Steele for your beautiful cover and interior design. You helped my debut novel shine in all the right places and helped me understand what's needed to create an enjoyable story.

About the Author

KOREN FREEL LIVES WITH HER family in Camas, Washington. She enjoys tropical escapes from the soggy Pacific Northwest winters and hiking the waterfall trails of the Columbia River Gorge when the sun finally emerges. Koren's debut novel, The Ginhouse Hollow, is inspired by real events tangled within her family's roots and weaves together an imaginative tale of humor and heartbreak that shows how the secrets we keep shape who we become.

You can find Koren at
www.korenfreel.com

www.ingramcontent.com/pod-product-compliance
Lightning Source LLC
Chambersburg PA
CBHW030606310726
48979CB00003B/594

* 9 7 9 8 9 8 8 6 9 3 8 2 6 *